DISCARD

THE
DESERT
TRAIL

Center Point
Large Print

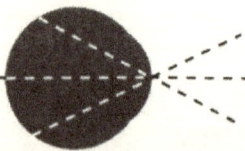

**This Large Print Book carries the
Seal of Approval of N.A.V.H.**

THE DESERT TRAIL

DANE COOLIDGE

CENTER POINT LARGE PRINT
THORNDIKE, MAINE

This Center Point Large Print edition
is published in the year 2023 by arrangement with
Golden West Inc.

Originally published in the UK by W. J. Watt & Company.

The text of this Large Print edition is unabridged.
In other aspects, this book may vary
from the original edition.
Printed in the United States of America
on permanent paper sourced using
environmentally responsible foresting methods.
Set in 16-point Times New Roman type.

ISBN 978-1-63808-766-3 (hardcover)
ISBN 978-1-63808-770-0 (paperback)

The Library of Congress has cataloged this record
under Library of Congress Control Number: 2023932293

I

The slow-rolling winter's sun rose coldly, far to the south, riding up from behind the saw-toothed Sierras of Mexico to throw a silvery halo on Gadsden, the border city. A hundred miles of desert lay in its path—a waste of broken ridges, dry arroyos, and sandy plains—and then suddenly, as if by magic, the city rose gleaming in the sun.

It was a big city, for the West, and swarming with traffic and men. Its broad main street, lined with brick buildings and throbbing with automobiles, ran from the railroad straight to the south until, at a line, it stopped short and was lost in the desert.

That line which marked the sudden end of growth and progress was the border of the United States; the desert was Mexico. And the difference was not in the land, but in the government.

As the morning air grew warm and the hoar frost dripped down from the roofs the idlers of the town crept forth, leaving chill lodgings and stale saloons for the street corners and the sun.

Against the dead wall of a big store the Mexicans gathered in shivering groups, their blankets wrapped around their necks and their brown ankles bare to the wind. On another corner a bunch of cowboys stood clannishly aloof, eying the passing crowd for others of their kind.

In this dun stream which flowed under the morning sun there were mining men, with high-laced boots and bulging pockets; graybeards, with the gossip of the town in their cheeks; hoboes, still wearing their Eastern caps and still rustling for a quarter to eat on; somber-eyed refugees and soldiers of fortune from Mexico—but idlers all, and each seeking his class and kind.

If any women passed that way they walked fast, looking neither to the right nor to the left; for they, too, being so few, missed their class and kind.

Gadsden had become a city of men, huge-limbed and powerful and with a questing look in their eyes; a city of adventurers gathered from the ends of the world. A common calamity had driven them from their mines and ranches and glutted the town with men; for the war was on in Mexico and from the farthermost corners of Sonora they still came, hot from some new scene of murder and pillage, to add their modicum to the general discontent.

As the day wore on the crowd on the bank corner, where the refugees made their stand, changed its complexion, grew big, and stretched far up the street. Men stood in shifting groups, talking, arguing, gazing moodily at those who passed.

Here were hawk-eyed Texas cattlemen, thinking of their scattered herds at Mababi or El Tigre; mining men, with idle prospects and deserted mines as far south as the Rio Yaqui; millmen, ranchers, and men of trades—all driven in from below the line and all chafing at the leash. While a hundred petty chiefs stood out against Madero and lived by ransom and loot, they must cool their heels in Gadsden and wait for the end to come.

Into this seething mass of the dispossessed, many of whom had lost a fortune by the war, there came two more, with their faces still drawn and red from hard riding through the cold. They stepped forth from the marble entrance of the big hotel and swung off down the street to see the town.

They walked slowly, gazing into the strange faces in the vague hope of finding some friend; and Gadsden, not to be outdone, looked them over curiously and wondered whence they had come.

The bunch of cowboys, still loitering on the corner, glanced scornfully at the smaller man, who sported a pair of puttees—and then at the big man's feet. Finding them encased in prospector's shoes they stared dumbly at his wind-burned face and muttered among themselves.

He was tall, and broad across the shoulders, with far-seeing blue eyes and a mop of light hair;

and he walked on his toes, stiff-legged, swaying from the hips like a man on horseback. The rumble of comment rose up again as he racked past and then a cowboy voice observed:

"I bet ye he's a cowpunch!"

The big man looked back at them mockingly out of the corner of his eye and went on without a word.

It is the boast of cowboys that they can tell another puncher at a glance; but they are not alone in this—there are other crafts that leave their mark and other men as shrewd. A group of mining men took one look at the smaller man, noting the candle-grease on his corduroys and the intelligence in his eyes; and to them the big man was no more than a laborer—or a shift-boss at most—and the little man was one of their kind. Every line in his mobile face spoke of intellect and decision, and as they walked it was he who did the talking, while the big man only nodded and smiled.

They took a turn or two up the street, now drifting into some clamorous saloon, now standing at gaze on the sidewalk; and as the drinks began to work, the little man became more and more animated, the big man more and more amiable in his assent and silence.

Then as they passed the crowd of refugees they stopped and listened, commenting on the various opinions by an exchange of knowing smiles.

An old prospector, white-haired and tanned to a tropic brown, finally turned upon a presumptuous optimist and the little man nodded approvingly as he heard him express his views.

"You can say what you please," the prospector ended, "but I'm going to keep out of that country. I've knowed them Mexicans for thirty years now and I'm telling you they're gitting treacherous. It don't do no good to have your gun with you— they'll shoot you from behind a rock—and if they can't git you that way, they'll knife you in your sleep.

"I've noticed a big change in them *paisanos* since this war come on. Before Madero made his break they used to be scared of Americans— thought if they killed one of us the rest would cross the border and eat 'em up. What few times they did tackle a white man he generally give a good account of himself, too, and I've traveled them trails for years without hardly knowing what it was to be afraid of anybody; but I tell you it's entirely different over there now."

"Sure! That's right!" spoke up the little man, with spirit. "You're talking more sense than any man on the street. I guess I ought to know— I've been down there and through it all—and it's got so now that you can't trust *any* of 'em. My pardner and I came clear from the Sierra Madres, riding nights, and we come pretty near knowing—hey, Bud?"

9

"That's right," observed Bud, the big man, with a reminiscent grin. "I begin to think them fellers would get us, for a while!"

"Mining men?" inquired the old prospector politely.

"Working on a lease," said the little man briefly. "Owner got scared out and let us in on shares. But no more for muh—this will hold me for quite a while, I can tell you!"

"Here, too," agreed the big man, turning to go. "Arizona is good enough for me—come on, Phil!"

"Where to?" The little man drew back half resentfully, and then he changed his mind. "All right," he said, falling into step, "a gin fizz for mine!"

"Not on an empty stomach," admonished his pardner; "you might get lit up and tell somebody all you know. How about something to eat?"

"Good! But where 're you going?"

The big man was leading off down a side street, and once more they came to a halt.

"Jim's place—it's a lunch-counter," he explained laconically. "The hotel's all right, and maybe that was a breakfast we got, but I get hungry waiting that way. Gimme a lunch-counter, where I can wrap my legs around a stool and watch the cook turn 'em over. Come on—I been there before."

An expression of pitying tolerance came

over the little man's face as he listened to this rhapsody on the quick lunch, but he drew away reluctantly.

"Aw, come on, Bud," he pleaded. "Have a little class! What's the use of winning a stake if you've got to eat at a dog-joint? And besides—say, that was a peach of a girl that waited on us this morning! Did you notice her hair? She was a pippin! I left four-bits under my plate!"

The big man waggled his hand resignedly and started on his way.

"All right, pardner," he observed; "if that's the deal she's probably looking for you. I'll meet you in the room."

"Aw, come on!" urged the other, but his heart was not in it, and he turned gaily away up the main street.

Left to himself, the big man went on to his lunch-counter, where he ordered oysters, "a dozen in the milk." Then he ordered a beefsteak, to make up for several he had missed, and asked the cook to fry it rare. He was just negotiating for a can of pears that had caught his eye when an old man came in and took the stool beside him, picking up the menu with a trembling hand.

"Give me a cup of coffee," he said to the waiter, "and"—he gazed at the bill of fare carefully—"and a roast-beef sandwich. No, just the coffee!" he corrected, and at that Bud gave him a look. He was a small man, shabbily dressed and with scraggly whiskers, and his nose was very red.

"Here," called Bud, coming to an instant conclusion, "give 'im his sandwich; I'll pay for it!"

"All right," answered the waiter, who was no other than Sunny Jim, the proprietor, and, whisking up a sandwich from the sideboard, he set it before the old man, who glanced at him in silence. For a fraction of a second he regarded the sandwich apathetically; then, with the aid of his coffee, he made way with it and slipped down off his stool.

"Say," observed the proprietor, as Bud was paying his bill, "do you know who that oldtimer was?"

"What oldtimer?" inquired Bud, who had forgotten his brusk benefaction.

"Why, that old feller that you treated to the sandwich."

"Oh—him! Some old drunk around town?" hazarded Bud.

"Well, he's that, too," conceded Sunny Jim, with a smile. "But lemme tell you, pardner, if you had half the rocks that old boy's got you wouldn't need to punch any more cows. That's Henry Kruger, the man that just sold the Cross-Cut Mine for fifty thousand cash, and he's got more besides."

"Huh!" grunted Bud, "he sure don't look it! Say, why didn't you put me wise? Now I've got to hunt him up and apologize."

"Oh, that's all right," assured the proprietor; "he won't take any offense. That's just like Old Henry—he's kinder queer that way."

"Well, I'll go and see him, anyway," said Bud. "He might think I was butting in."

And then, going about his duty with philosophical calm, he ambled off, stiff-legged, down the street.

II

It was not difficult to find Henry Kruger in Gadsden. The barkeepers, those efficient purveyors of information and drinks, knew him as they knew their thumbs, and a casual round of the saloons soon located him in the back room of the Waldorf.

"Say," began Bud, walking bluffly up to him, "the proprietor of that restaurant back there tells me I made a mistake when I insisted on paying for your meal. I just wanted to let you know—"

"Oh, that's all right, young man," returned Old Henry, looking up with a humorous smile; "we all of us make our mistakes. I knowed you didn't mean no offense and so I never took none. Fact is, I liked you all the better for it. This country is getting settled up with a class of people that never give a nickel to nobody. You paid for that meal like it was nothing, and never so much as looked at me. Sit down, sit down—I want to talk to you!"

They sat down by the stove and fell into a friendly conversation in which nothing more was said of the late inadvertence, but when Bud rose to go the old man beckoned him back.

"Hold on," he protested; "don't go off mad. I want to have a talk with you on business. You

14

seem to be a pretty good young fellow—maybe we can make some dicker. What are you looking for in these parts?"

"Well," responded Bud, "some kind of a leasing proposition, I reckon. Me and my pardner jest come in from Mexico, over near the Chihuahua line, and we don't hardly know what we do want yet."

"Yes, I've noticed that pardner of yours," remarked Henry Kruger dryly. "He's a great talker. I was listening to you boys out on the street there, having nothing else to do much, and being kinder on the lookout for a man, anyway, and it struck me I liked your line of talk best."

"You're easy satisfied, then," observed Bud, with a grin. "I never said a word hardly."

"That's it," returned Kruger significantly; "this job I've got *calls* for a man like that."

"Well, Phil's all right," spoke up Bud, with sudden warmth. "We been pardners for two years now and he never give nothing away yet! He talks, but he don't forget himself. And the way he can palaver them Mexicans is a wonder."

"Very likely, very likely," agreed Kruger, and then he sat a while in silence.

"We got a few thousand dollars with us, too," volunteered Bud at last. "I'm a good worker, if that's what you want—and Phil, he's a mining engineer."

"Um-m," grunted Kruger, tugging at his beard,

15

but he did not come out with his proposal.

"I tell you," he said at last. "I'm not doing much talking about this proposition of mine. It's a big thing, and somebody might beat me to it. You know who I am, I guess. I've pulled off some of the biggest deals in this country for a poor man, and I don't make many mistakes— not about mineral, anyway. And when I tell you that this is rich—you're talking with a man that knows."

He fixed his shrewd, blue eyes on the young man's open countenance and waited for him to speak.

"That's right," he continued, as Bud finally nodded non-committally; "she's sure rich. I've had an eye on this proposition for years—just waiting for the right time to come. And now it's come! All I need is the man. It ain't a dangerous undertaking—leastwise I don't think it is—but I got to have somebody I can trust. I'm willing to pay you good wages, or I'll let you in on the deal—but you'll have to go down into Mexico."

"Nothin' doing!" responded Bud with instant decision. "If it's in Arizona I'll talk to you, but no more Mexico for me. I've got something pretty good down there myself, as far as that goes."

"What's the matter?" inquired Kruger, set back by the abrupt refusal. "Scared?"

"Yes, I'm scared," admitted Bud, and he challenged the old man with his eyes.

16

"Must have had a little trouble, then?"

"Well, you might call it that," agreed Bud. "We been on the dodge for a month. A bunch of *revoltosos* tried to get our treasure, and when we skipped out on 'em they tried to get *us*."

"Well," continued Kruger, "this proposition of mine is different. You was over in the Sierra Madres, where the natives are bad. These Sonora Mexicans ain't like them Chihuahua fellers—they're Americanized. I'll tell you, if it wasn't that the people would know me I'd go down after this mine myself. The country's perfectly quiet. There's lots of Americans down there yet, and they don't even know there *is* a revolution. It ain't far from the railroad, you see, and that makes a lot of difference."

He lowered his voice to a confidential whisper as he revealed the approximate locality of his bonanza, but Bud remained unimpressed.

"Yes," he said, "*we* was near a railroad—the Northwestern—and seemed like them red-flaggers did nothing else but burn bridges and ditch supply trains. When they finally whipped 'em off the whole bunch took to the hills. That's where we got it again."

"Well," argued Kruger, "this railroad of ours is all right, and they run a train over it every day. The concentrator at Fortuna"—he lowered his voice again—"hasn't been shut down a day, and you'll be within fifteen miles of that town.

17

No," he whispered; "I could get a hundred Americans to go in on this to-morrow, as far's the revolution's concerned. It ain't dangerous, but I want somebody I can trust."

"Nope," pronounced Bud, rising ponderously to his feet; "if it was this side the line I'd stay with you till the hair slipped, on anything, but—"

"Well, let's talk it over again some time," urged Kruger, following him along out. "It ain't often I git took with a young feller the way I was with you, and I believe we can make it yet. Where are you staying in town?"

"Up at the Cochise," said Bud. "Come on with me—I told my pardner I'd meet him there."

They turned up the broad main street and passed in through the polished stone portals of the Cochise, a hotel so spacious in its interior and so richly appointed in its furnishings that a New Yorker, waking up there, might easily imagine himself on Fifth Avenue.

It was hardly a place to be looked for in the West, and as Bud led the way across the echoing lobby to a pair of stuffed chairs he had a vague feeling of being in church. Stained-glass windows above the winding stairways let in a soft light, and on the towering pillars of marble were emblazoned prickly-pears as an emblem of the West. From the darkened balconies above half-seen women looked down curiously as they entered, and in the broad lobby below were

18

gathered the prosperous citizens of the land.

There were cattlemen, still wearing their boots and overalls, the better to attend to their shipping; mining men, just as they had come from the hills; and others more elegantly dressed—but they all had a nod for Henry Kruger. He was a man of mark, as Bud could see in a minute; but if he had other business with those who hailed him he let it pass and took out a rank brier pipe, which he puffed while Bud smoked a cigarette.

They were sitting together in a friendly silence when Phil came out of the dining-room, but as he drew near the old man nodded to Bud and went over to speak to the clerk.

"Who was that oldtimer you were talking to?" inquired Phil, as he sank down in the vacant chair. "Looks like the-morning-after with him, don't it?"

"Um," grunted Bud; "reckon it is. Name's Kruger."

"What—the mining man?"

"That's right."

"Well," exclaimed Phil, "what in the world was he talking to you about?"

"Oh, some kind of a mining deal," grumbled Bud. "Wanted me to go down into Mexico!"

"What'd you tell him?" challenged the little man, sitting up suddenly in his chair. "Say, that old boy's got rocks!"

"He can keep 'em for all of me," observed

Bud comfortably. "You know what I think about Mexico."

"Sure; but what was his proposition? What did he want you to do?"

"Search me! He was mighty mysterious about it. Said he wanted a man he could trust."

"Well, holy Moses, Bud!" cried Phil, "wake up! Didn't you get his proposition?"

"No, he wasn't talking about it. Said it was a good thing and he'd pay me well, or let me in on the deal; but when he hollered Mexico I quit. I've got a plenty."

"Yes, but—" the little man choked and could say no more. "Well, you're one jim dandy business man, Bud Hooker!" he burst out at last. "You'd let—"

"Well, what's the matter?" demanded Hooker defiantly. "Do *you* want to go back into Mexico? Nor me, neither! What you kicking about?"

"You might have led him on and got the scheme, anyway. Maybe there's a million in it. Come on, let's go over and talk to him. I'd take a chance, if it was good enough."

"Aw, don't be a fool, Phil," urged the cowboy plaintively. "We've got no call to hear his scheme unless we want to go in on it. Leave him alone and he'll do something for us on this side. Oh, cripes! what's the matter with you?"

He heaved himself reluctantly up out of his chair and moved over to where Kruger was sitting.

"Mr. Kruger," he said, as the old man turned to meet him, "I'll make you acquainted with Mr. De Lancey, my pardner. My name's Hooker."

"Glad to know you, Hooker," responded Kruger, shaking him by the hand. "How'do, Mr. De Lancey."

He gave Phil a rather crusty nod as he spoke, but De Lancey was dragging up another chair and failed to notice.

"Mr. Hooker was telling me about some proposition you had, to go down into Mexico," he began, drawing up closer while the old man watched him from under his eyebrows. "That's one tough country to do business in right now, but at the same time—"

"The country's perfectly quiet," put in Kruger—"perfectly quiet."

"Well, maybe so," qualified De Lancey; "but when it comes to getting in supplies—"

"Not a bit of trouble in the world," said the old man crabbedly. "Not a bit."

"Well," came back De Lancey, "what's the matter, then? What is the proposition, anyway?"

Henry Kruger blinked and eyed him intently.

"I've stated the proposition to Hooker," he said, "and he refused it. That's enough, ain't it?"

De Lancey laughed and turned away.

"Well, yes, I guess it is." Then, in passing, he said to Bud: "Go ahead and talk to him."

He walked away, lighting a cigarette and

smiling good-naturedly, and the oldtimer turned to Bud.

"That's a smart man you've got for a pardner," he remarked. "A smart man. You want to look out," he added, "or he'll get away with you."

"Nope," said Bud. "You don't know him like I do. He's straight as a die."

"A man can be straight and still get away with you," observed the veteran shrewdly. "Yes, indeed." He paused to let this bit of wisdom sink in, and then he spoke again.

"You better quit—while you're lucky," he suggested. "You quit and come with me," he urged, "and if we strike it, I'll make you a rich man. I don't need your pardner on this deal. I need just one man that can keep his head shut. Listen now; I'll tell you what it is.

"I know where there's a lost mine down in Mexico. If I'd tell you the name you'd know it in a minute, and it's free gold, too. Now there's a fellow that had that land located for ten years, but he couldn't find the lead. D'ye see? And when this second revolution came on he let it go—he neglected to pay his mining taxes and let it go back to the government. And now all I want is a quiet man to slip in and denounce that land and open up the lead. Here, look at this!"

He went down into his pocket and brought out a buckskin sack, from which he handed over a piece of well-worn quartz.

"That's the rock," he said. "She runs four hundred dollars to the ton, and the ledge is eight inches wide between the walls. Nice ore, eh? And she lays between shale and porphyry."

His eyes sparkled as he carefully replaced the specimen, and then he looked up at Bud.

"I'll let you in on that," he said, "half and half—or I'll pay two hundred dollars a month and a bonus. You alone. Now how about it?"

For a moment Hooker looked at him as if to read his thoughts, then he shook his head and exhaled his smoke regretfully.

"Nope," he said. "Me and Phil are pardners. We work together."

"I'll give you three hundred!" cried Kruger, half rising in his chair.

"Nope," grunted Bud, "we're pardners."

"Huh!" snorted the mining man, and flung away in disgust. But as he neared the door a new thought struck him and he came as quickly back.

"You can do what you please about your pardner," he said. "I'm talking to *you*. Now—will you think about it?"

"Sure!" returned Hooker.

"Well, then," snapped Kruger, "meet me at the Waldorf in an hour!"

III

On the untrammeled frontier, where most men are willing to pass for what they are without keeping up any "front," much of the private business, as well as the general devilment, is transacted in the back rooms of saloons. The Waldorf was nicely furnished in this regard.

After a drink at the bar, in which De Lancey and Hooker joined, Henry Kruger led the way casually to the rear, and in a few moments they were safely closeted.

"Now," began Kruger, as he took a seat by the table and faced them with snapping eyes, "the first thing I want to make plain to you gentlemen is, if I make any deal to-day it's to be with Mr. Hooker. If you boys are pardners you can talk it over together, but I deal with one man, and that's Hooker.

"All right?" he inquired, glancing at De Lancey, and that young man nodded indulgently.

"Very well, then," resumed Kruger, "now to get down to business. This mine that I'm talking about is located down here in Sonora within three hours' ride of a big American camp. It isn't any old Spanish mine, or lost *padre* layout; it's a well-defined ledge running three or four hundred dollars to the ton—and I know right where it is, too.

24

"What I want to do is to establish the title to it now, while this revolution is going on, and make a bonanza out of it afterward. Of course, if you boys don't want to go back into Mexico, that settles it; but if you do go, and I let you in on the deal, you've got to see it through or I'll lose the whole thing. So make up your minds, and if you say you'll go, I want you to stick to it!"

"We'll go, all right," spoke up De Lancey, "if it's rich enough."

"How about you?" inquired Kruger, turning impatiently on Bud. "Will you go?"

"Yes, I'll go," answered Bud sullenly. "But I ain't stuck on the job," he added. "Jest about get it opened up when a bunch of rebels will jump in and take everything we've got."

"Well, you get a title to it and pay your taxes and you can come out then," conceded Henry Kruger.

"No," grumbled Hooker, "if I go I'll stay with it." He glanced at his pardner at this, but he, for one, did not seem to be worried.

"I'll try anything—once!" he observed with a sprightly air, and Bud grinned sardonically at the well-worn phrase.

"Well," said Kruger, gazing inquiringly from one to the other, "is it a go? Will you shake hands on it?"

"What's the proposition?" broke in De Lancey eagerly.

"The deal is between me and Hooker," corrected Kruger. "I'll give him three hundred a month, or an equal share in the mine, expenses to be shared between us."

"Make it equal shares," said Hooker, holding out his hand, "and I'll give half of mine to Phil."

"All right, my boy!" cried the old man, suddenly clapping him on the shoulder, "I'll go you—and you'll never regret it," he added significantly. Then, throwing off the air of guarded secrecy which had characterized his actions so far, he sat down and began to talk.

"Boys," he said, "I'm feeling lucky to-day or I'd never have closed this deal. I'm letting you in on one of the biggest things that's ever been found in Sonora. Just to show you how good it is, here's my smelter receipts for eight hundred pounds of picked ore—one thousand and twenty-two dollars! That's the first and last ore that's ever been shipped from the old Eagle Tail. I dug it out myself, and sacked it and shipped it; and then some of them crooked Mexican officials tried to beat me out of my title and I blowed up the whole works with dynamite!

"Yes, sir, clean as a whistle! I had my powder stored away in the drift, and the minute I found out I was euchred I laid a fuse to it and brought the whole mountain down. That was ten years ago, and old Aragon and the *agente mineral* have had the land located ever since.

"I bet they've spent five thousand pesos trying to find that lead, but being nothing but a bunch of ignorant Mexicans, of course they never found nothing. Then Francisco Madero comes in and fires the *agente mineral* off his job and old Aragon lets the land revert for taxes. I've got a Mexican that keeps me posted, and ever since he sent me word that the title had lapsed I've been crazy to relocate that claim.

"Well, now, that don't look so bad, does it?" he asked, beaming paternally at Bud. "There ain't a man in town that wouldn't have jumped at the chance, if I was where I could talk about it, but that's just what I couldn't do. I had to find some stranger that wouldn't sense what mine I was talking about and then git him to go in on it blind.

"Now here's the way I'm fixed, boys," he explained, brushing out his unkempt beard and smiling craftily. "When I dynamited the Eagle Tail it was mine by rights, but Cipriano Aragon— he's the big Mexican down at old Fortuna—and Morales, the mineral agent, had buncoed me out of the title.

"So, according to law, I blowed up their mine, and if I ever showed up down there I reckon they'd throw me into jail. And if at any time they find out that you're working for me, why, we're ditched—that's all! They'll put you out of business. So, after we've made our agreement and I've told you what to do, I don't want to hear a word out of you—I don't want you to come near me, nor even write me a letter—just go ahead the best you can until you win out or go broke.

"It ain't a hard proposition," he continued, "if you keep your mouth shut, but if they tumble, it'll be a fight to a finish. I'm not saying this for you, Hooker, because I know you're safe; I'm saying it for your pardner here. You talk too much, Mr. De Lancey," he chided, eying him with sudden severity. "I'm afraid of ye!"

"All right," broke in Hooker good-naturedly, "I reckon we understand. Now go ahead and tell us where this mine is and who there is down there to look out for."

"The man to look out for," answered Kruger with venom, "is Cipriano Aragon. He's the man that bilked me out of the mine once, and he'll do it again if he can. When I went down there—it was ten years and more ago—I wasn't onto those Spanish ways of his, and he was so dog-goned polite and friendly I thought I could trust him anywhere.

"He owns a big ranch and mescal still, runs cattle, works a few placers, sends out pack-trains, and has every Mexican and Indian in the country in debt to him through his store, so if he happens to want any rough work done there's always somebody to do it.

"Well, just to show you how he did me, I got

to nosing round those old Spanish workings east of Fortuna and finally I run across the ledge that I'm telling you about, not far from an abandoned shaft. But the Mexican mining laws are different from ours, and an American has lots of trouble anyway, so I made a trade with old Aragon that he should locate the claim for me under a power of attorney. Didn't know him then like I do now. The papers had to be sent to Moctesuma and Hermosillo, and to the City of Mexico and back, and while I was waiting around I dug in on this lead and opened up the prettiest vein of quartz you ever saw in your life. Here's a sample of it, and it's sure rich."

He handed De Lancey the familiar piece of quartz and proceeded with his story.

"That ore looked so good to me that I couldn't wait—I shipped it before I got my title. And right there I made my mistake. When Aragon saw the gold in that rock he just quietly recorded the concession in his own name and told me to go to blazes. That's the greaser of it! So I blew the whole mine up and hit for the border. That's the Dutch of it, I reckon," he added grimly. "Anyway, my old man was Dutch."

He paused, smiling over the memory of his misplaced credulity, and Hooker and De Lancey joined in a hearty laugh. From the town bum that he had first seemed this shabbly little man had changed in their eyes until now he was a border

Croesus, the mere recital of whose adventures conjured up in their minds visions of gold and hidden treasure.

The rugged face of Bud Hooker, which had been set in grim lines from the first, relaxed as the tale proceeded and his honest eyes glowed with admiration as he heard the well-planned scheme. As for De Lancey, he could hardly restrain his enthusiasm, and, drawn on by the contagion, Henry Kruger made maps and answered questions until every detail was settled.

After the location had been marked, and the lost tunnel charted from the corner monuments, he bade them remember it well—and destroyed every vestige of paper. Then, as a final admonition, he said:

"Now go in there quietly, boys—don't hurry. Prospect around a little and the Mexicans will all come to you and try to sell you lost mines. Cruz Mendez is the man you're looking for— he's honest, and he'll take you to the Eagle Tail. After that you can use your own judgment. So good-by"—he took them by the hands—"and don't talk!"

He held up a warning finger as they parted, and Bud nodded briefly in reply. Silence was a habit with him, desert-bred, and he nodded his head for two.

IV

From the times of David and Jonathan down to the present day the world has been full of young men sworn to friendship and seeking adventure in pairs. "Pardners," they call them in the West, and though the word has not crept into the dictionary yet, it is as different from "partner" as a friend is from a business associate.

They travel together, these pardners of the West, and whether they be cowboys or "Cousin Jacks," the boss who fires one of them fires both of them, and they go share and share in everything.

Bud Hooker and Philip De Lancey had met by chance in El Paso when the revolution was just beginning to boil and the city was swarming with adventurers. The agents of the rebels were everywhere, urging Americans to join their cause. Military preferment, cash payments, and grants of land were the baits they used, but Hooker stood out from the first and took De Lancey with him. A Mexican promise did not pass current where he was born and they went to the mines instead.

Then the war broke out and, while fugitives streamed out of stricken Chihuahua, they finally struck out against the tide, fighting their way to a certain mine far back in the Sierra Madres, where they could dig the gold on shares.

Behind them the battle waged; Casas Grandes was taken and retaken; Juarez, Agua Negra, and Chihuahua fell; Don Porfirio, the Old Man of Mexico, went out and Madero took his place; and still they worked for their stake.

Then new arms and ammunition flowed in from across the border; Orozco and his rebel chiefs went out, and the breath of war fanned higher against the hills. At last the first broken band of rebels came straggling by, and, reading hate and envy in their lawless eyes, the Americans dug up their gold at sundown and rode all the night for their lives.

And now, welded together by all that toil and danger, they were pardners, cherishing no delusions as to each other's strength or weaknesses, but joined together for better or worse.

It was the last thing that either of them expected, but three days after they fled out of Mexico, and with all their money unspent, the hand of fate seized upon them and sent them back on another adventure.

It was early morning again, with crowds along the street, and as they ambled slowly along toward the line, the men on the corners stared at them. The bunch of cowboys gazed at Bud, who sported a new pair of high-heeled boots, and knew him by the way he rode; and the mining men looked searchingly at De Lancey, as if to guess the secret of his quest.

A squad of mounted troopers, riding out on border patrol, gazed after them questioningly, but Bud and Phil rode on soberly, leading their pack, and headed for Agua Negra across the line.

It was a grim place to look at, this border town of Agua Negra, for the war had swept it twice. A broad waste of level land lay between it and the prosperous American city, and across this swath, where the Mausers and machine guns had twice mowed, lay the huddle of low houses which marked the domain of Mexico.

Fussy little customs officials, lurking like spiders in their cooped-up guard-houses, rushed out as they crossed the deep trench and demanded their permit to bear arms. The moment they crossed the line the air seemed to be pervaded with Latin excitability and Indian jealousy, but De Lancey replied in florid Spanish, and before his polite assurances and fulsome compliments it was dissipated in a moment.

"Good! Pass on, *amigos*," cried the beady-eyed little *jefe*, pasting a label on their pack. "*Adios, señor*," he added, returning Phil's salute with a military flourish, and with a scornful glance at Bud he observed that the *gentleman* was *muy caballero*.

"Huh!" remarked Bud, as they rode on through

the town, "we're in Mexico all right, all right. Talk with both hands and get busy with your eyebrows—and holy Joe, look at them *pelónes*!"

The *pelónes* referred to were a squad of Mexican Federal soldiers, so-called from their heads being shaved, and they were marching doggedly to and fro through the thorny mesquit-bushes in response to shouted orders from an officer. Being from Zacatecas, where the breed is short, they stood about as high as their guns; and their crumpled linen suits and flapping sandals detracted sadly from the soldierly effect.

Big and hulking, and swelling with the pride of his kind, Hooker looked them over slowly, and spoke his hidden thought.

"I wonder," he said, turning to Phil, "how many of them I could lick with one hand?"

"Well, they're nothing but a lot of petty convicts, anyway," answered De Lancey, "but here's some boys ahead that I'll bet could hold you, man for man, husky as you are, old fellow."

They were riding past a store, now serving as an improvised barracks, and romping about in the street were a pair of tall Yaqui Indians, each decorated with a cartridge-belt about his hips in token of his military service. Laughing and grabbing for holds, they frolicked like a couple of boys until finally they closed in a grapple that revealed a sudden and pantherlike strength.

And a group of others, sunning themselves against the wall, looked up at the Americans with eyes as fearless as mountain eagles.

"Yes, that's right," admitted Bud, returning their friendly greeting, "but we'll never have no trouble with them."

"Well, these *Nacionales* are not so bad," defended Phil, as they passed the State soldiers of Sonora on the street, "but they're just as friendly as the Yaquis."

"Sure," jeered Bud, "when they're sober! But you get a bunch of 'em drunk and ask 'em what they think of the Gringos! No, you got to show me—I've seen too much of 'em."

"You haven't seen as much of 'em as *I* have, yet," retorted De Lancey, quickly. "I've been all over the republic, except right here in Sonora, and I swear these Sonorans here look good to me. There's no use holding a grouch against them, Bud—they haven't done us any dirt."

"No, they never had no chance," grumbled Bud, gazing grimly to the south. "But wait till the hot weather comes and the *revoltosos* come out of their holes; wait till them Chihuahua greasers thaw out up in the Sierras and come down to get some fresh mounts. Well, I'll tell 'em one thing," he ended, reaching down to pat his horse, "they'll never get old Copper Bottom here—not unless they steal him at night. It's all right to be cheerful about this, Phil, and you keep right on being glad, but I got a low-down hunch that we're going to get in bad."

"Well, I've got just as good a hunch," came back De Lancey, "that we're going to make a killing."

"Yes, and speaking of killings," said Bud, "you don't want to overlook *that.*"

He pointed at a group of dismantled adobe buildings standing out on the edge of the town and flanked by a segment of whitewashed wall all spattered and breached with bullet-holes.

"There's where these prize Mexicans of yourn pulled off the biggest killing in Sonora. I was over here yesterday with that old prospector and he told me that that wall is the bull-ring. After the first big fight they gathered up three hundred and fifty men, more or less, and throwed 'em in a trench along by the wall—then they blowed it over on 'em with a few sticks of dynamite and let 'em pass for buried. No crosses or nothing. Excuse *me,* if they ever break loose like that—we might get planted with the rest!"

"By Jove, old top!" exclaimed De Lancey, laughing teasingly, "you've certainly got the blues to-day. Here, take something out of this bottle and see if it won't help."

He brought out a quart bottle from his saddle-bags and Bud drank, and shuddered at the bite of it.

"All right," he said, as he passed it back, "and

while we're talking, what's the matter with cutting it out on booze for this trip?"

"What are we going to drink, then?" cried De Lancey in feigned alarm. "Water?"

"Well, something like that," admitted Bud. "Come on—what do you say? We might get lit up and tell something."

"Now lookee here, Bud," clamored Phil, who had had a few drinks already, "you don't mean to insinuate, do you? Next thing I know you'll be asking me to cut it out on the hay—might talk in my sleep, you know, and give the whole snap away!"

"No, you're a good boy when you're asleep, Phil," responded Bud, "but when you get about half shot it's different. Come on, now—I'll quit if you will. That's fair, ain't it?"

"What? No little toots around town? No serenading the *señoritas* and giving the *rurales* the hotfoot? Well, what's the use of living, Bud, if you can't have a little fun? Drinking don't make any difference, as long as we stick together. What's the use of swearing off—going on record in advance? We may find some fellow that we can't work any other way—we may have to go on a drunk with him in order to get his goat. But will you stick? That's the point!"

Bud glanced at him and grunted, and for a long time he rode on in silence. Before them lay a rolling plain, dipping by broad gulches and dwindling ridges to the lower levels of Old Mexico, and on the skyline, thin and blue, stood the knifelike edges of the Fortunas miles away.

With desert-trained eyes he noted the landmarks, San Juan Mountain to the right, Old Niggerhead to the left, and the feather-edge of mountains far below; and as he looked he stored it away in his mind in case he should come back on the run some night.

It was not a foreboding, but the training of his kind, to note the lay of the ground, and he planned just where he would ride to keep under cover if he ever made a dash for the line. But all the time his pardner was talking of friendship and of the necessity of their sticking together.

"I'll tell you, Bud," he said at last, his voice trembling with sentiment, "whether we win or lose, I won't have a single regret as long as I know we've been true to one another. You may know Texas and Arizona, Bud, but I know Old Mexico, the land of *mañana* and broken promises. I know the country, Bud—and the climate—and the women!

"They play the devil with the best of us, Bud, these dark-eyed *señoritas*! That's what makes all the trouble down here between man and man, it's these women and their ways. They're not satisfied to win a man's heart—they want him to kill somebody to show that he really loves them. By Jove! they're a fickle lot, and nothing pleases 'em more than setting man against man, one pardner against another."

"We never had no trouble yet," observed Bud sententiously.

"No, but we're likely to," protested De Lancey. "Those Indian women up in the Sierras wouldn't turn anybody's head, but we're going down into the hot country now, where the girls are pretty, ta-ra, ta-ra, and we talk through the windows at midnight."

"Well, if you'll cut out the booze," said Hooker shortly, "you can have 'em all, for all of me."

"Sure, that's what you say, but wait till you see them! Oh, la, la, la!"—he kissed his fingers ecstatically—"I'll be glad to see 'em myself! But listen, Bud, here's the proposition: Let's take an oath right now, while we're starting out, that whatever comes up we'll always be true to each other. If one of us is wounded, the other stays with him; if he's in prison, he gets him out; if he's killed, he avenges his—"

"Say," broke in Bud, jostling him rudely as he reached into the saddle-bags, "let me carry that bottle for a while."

He took a big drink out of it to prevent De Lancey from getting it all and shoved it inside his overalls.

"All right, pardner," he continued, with a mocking smile, "anything you say. I never use oaths myself much, but anything to oblige."

39

"No, but I mean it, Bud!" cried De Lancey. "Here's the proposition now: Whatever happens, we stay with each other till this deal is finished; on all scratch cases we match money to see who's it; and if we tangle over some girl the best man wins and the other one stays away. We leave it to the girl which one wins. Will you shake hands on that?"

"Don't need to," responded Bud; "I'll do it anyway."

"Well, shake on it, then!" insisted De Lancey, holding out his hand.

"Oh, Sally!" burst out Bud, hanging his head in embarrassment, "what's the use of getting mushy?"

But a moment later he leaned over in his saddle and locked hands with a viselike grip.

"My old man told me not to make no such promises," he muttered, "but I'll do it, being's it's you."

V

The journey to Fortuna is a scant fifty miles by measure, but within those eighty kilometers there is a lapse of centuries in standards. As Bud and De Lancey rod out of battle-scarred Agua Negra they traveled a good road, well worn by the Mexican wood-wagons that hauled in mesquit from the hills. Then, as they left the town and the wood roads scattered, the highway changed by degrees to a broad trail, dug deep by the feet of pack-animals and marked but lightly with wheels. It followed along the railroad, cutting over hills and down through gulches, and by evening they were in the heart of Old Mexico.

Here were men in sandals and women barefooted; chickens tied up by the legs outside of brush *jacales*; long-nosed hogs, grunting fiercely as they skirmished for food; and half-naked children, staring like startled rabbits at the strangers.

The smell of garlic and fresh-roasting coffee was in the air as they drew into town for the night, and their room was an adobe chamber with tile floor and iron bars across the windows. Riding south the next day they met *vaqueros*, mounted on wiry mustangs, who saluted them gravely, taking no shame for their primitive wooden saddle-trees and pommels as broad as soup-plates.

As they left the broad plain and clambered up over the back of a mountain they passed Indian houses, brush-built and thatched with long, coarse grasses, and by the fires the women ground corn on stone *metates* as their ancestors had done before the fall. For in Mexico there are two peoples, the Spaniards and the natives, and the Indians still remember the days when they were free.

It was through such a land that Phil and Hooker rode on their gallant ponies, leading a pack-animal well loaded with supplies from the north, and as the people gazed from their miserable hovels and saw their outfit they wondered at their wealth.

But if they were moved to envy, the bulk of a heavy pistol, showing through the swell of each coat, discouraged them from going further; and the cold, searching look of the tall cowboy as he ambled past stayed in their memory long after the pleasant "*Adios!*" of De Lancey had been forgotten.

Americans were scarce in those days, and what few came by were riding to the north. How bold, then, must this big man be who rode in front— and certainly he had some great reward before him to risk such a horse among the *revoltosos*! So reasoned the simple-minded natives of the mountains, gazing in admiration at Copper Bottom, and for that look in their eyes Bud returned his forbidding stare.

There is something about a good horse that fascinates the average Mexican—perhaps because they breed the finest themselves and are in a position to judge—but Hooker had developed a romantic attachment for his trim little chestnut mount and he resented their wide-eyed gapings as a lover resents glances at his lady. This, and a frontier education, rendered him short-spoken and gruff with the *paisanos* and it was left to the cavalier De Lancey to do the courtesies of the road.

As the second day wore on they dipped down into a rocky cañon, with huge cliffs of red and yellow sandstone glowing in the slanting sun, and soon they broke out into a narrow valley, well wooded with sycamores and mesquits and giant hackberry-trees.

The shrill toots of a dummy engine came suddenly from down below and a mantle of black smoke rose majestically against the sky—then, at a turn of the trail, they topped the last hill and Fortuna lay before them.

In that one moment they were set back again fifty miles—clear back across the line—for Fortuna was American, from the power-house on the creek-bank to the mammoth concentrator on the hill.

All the buildings were of stone, square and uniform. First a central plaza, flanked with offices and warehouses; then behind them barracks and lodging-houses and trim cottages in orderly rows; and over across the cañon loomed the huge bulk of the mill and the concentrator with its aerial tramway and endless row of gliding buckets.

Only on the lower hills, where the rough country rock cropped up and nature was at its worst, only there did the real Mexico creep in and assert itself in a crude huddle of half-Indian huts; the dwellings of the care-free natives.

"Well, by Jove!" exclaimed De Lancey, surveying the scene with an appraising eye, "this doesn't look very much like Mexico—or a revolution, either!"

"No, it don't," admitted Bud; "everything running full blast, too. Look at that ore-train coming around the hill!"

"Gee, what a burg!" raved Phil. "Say, there's some class to this—what? If I mistake not, we'll be able to find a few congenial spirits here to help us spend our money. Talk about a company town! I'll bet you their barroom is full of Americans. There's the corral down below—let's ride by and leave our horses and see what's the price of drinks. They can't faze me, whatever it is—we doubled our money at the line."

Financially considered, they had done just that—for, for every American dollar in their pockets they could get two that were just as good, except for the picture on the side. This in itself was a great inducement for a ready spender and, finding good company at the Fortuna hotel bar, Phil bought five dollars' worth of drinks, threw down a five-dollar bill, and got back five dollars—Mex.

The proprietor, a large and jovial boniface, pulled off this fiscal miracle with the greatest good humor and then, having invited them to partake of a very exquisite mixture of his own invention, propped himself upon his elbows across the bar and inquired with an ingenuous smile:

"Well, which away are you boys traveling, if I may ask?"

"Oh, down below a ways," answered De Lancey, who always constituted himself the board of strategy. "Just rambling around a little—how's the country around here now?"

"Oh, quiet, quiet!" assured their host. "These Mexicans don't like the cold weather much—they would freeze, you know, if it was not for that *zarape* which they wind about them so!"

He made a motion as of a native wrapping his entire wardrobe about his neck and smiled, and De Lancey knew that he was no Mexican. And yet that soft "which away" of his betrayed a Spanish tongue.

"Ah, excuse me," he said, taking quick

45

advantage of his guess, "but from the way you pronounce that word '*zarape*' I take it that you speak Spanish."

"No one better," replied the host, smiling pleasurably at being taken at his true worth, "since I was born in the city of Burgos, where they speak the true Castilian. It is a different language, believe me, from this bastard Mexican tongue. And do you speak Spanish also?" he inquired, falling back into the staccato of Castile.

"No, indeed!" protested De Lancey in a very creditable imitation; "nothing but a little Mexican, to get along with the natives. My friend and I are mining men, passing through the country, and we speak the best we can. How is this district here for work along our line?"

"None better!" cried the Spaniard, shaking his finger emphatically. "It is of the best, and, believe me, my friend, we should be glad to have you stop with us. The country down below is a little dangerous—not now, perhaps, but later, when the warm weather comes on.

"But in Fortuna—no! Here we are on the railroad; the camp is controlled by Americans; and because so many have left the country the Mexicans will sell their prospects cheap.

"Then again, if you develop a mine nearby, it will be very easy to sell it—and if you wish to work it, that is easy, too. I am only the proprietor of the hotel, but if you can use my poor services in any way I shall be very happy to please you. A room? One of the best! And if you stay a week or more I will give you the lowest rate."

They passed up the winding stairs and down a long corridor, at the end of which the proprietor showed them into a room, throwing open the outer doors and shutters to let them see the view from the window.

"Here is a little balcony," he said, stepping outside, "where you can sit and look down on the plaza. We have the band and music when the weather is fine, and you can watch the pretty girls from here. But you have been in Mexico— you know all that!" And he gave Phil a roguish dig.

"*Bien*, my frien', I am glad to meet you—" He held out his hand in welcome and De Lancey gave his in return. "My name," he continued, "is Juan de Dios Brachamonte y Escalon; but with these Americans that does not go, as you say, so in general they call me Don Juan.

"There is something about that name—I do not know—that makes the college boys laugh. Perhaps it is that poet, Byron, who wrote so scandalously about us Spaniards, but certainly he knew nothing of our language, for he rimes Don Juan with 'new one' and 'true one'! Still, I read part of that poem and it is, in places, very interesting—yes, *very* interesting—but 'Don Joo-an'! Hah!"

47

He threw up his hand in despair and De Lancey broke into a jollying laugh.

"Well, Don Juan," he cried, "I'm glad to meet you. My name is Philip De Lancey, and my pardner here is Mr. Hooker. Shake hands with him, Don Juan de Dios! But certainly a man so devoutly named could never descend to reading *much* of Don Joo-an!"

"Ah, no," protested Don Juan, rolling his dark eyes and smiling rakishly, "not moch—only the most in-teresting passages!"

He saluted and disappeared in a roar of laughter, and De Lancey turned triumphantly on his companion, a self-satisfied smile upon his lips.

"Aha!" he said; "you see? That's what five dollars' worth of booze will do in opening up the way. Here's our old friend Don Juan willing, nay, anxious, to help us all he can—he sees I'm a live wire and wants to keep me around. Pretty soon we'll get him feeling good and he'll tell us all he knows. Don't you never try to make me sign the pledge again, brother—a few shots just gets my intellect to working right and I'm crafty as a fox.

"Did you notice that *coup* I made—asking him if he was a Spaniard? There's nothing in the world makes a Spaniard so mad as to take him for a Mexican—on the other hand, nothing makes him your friend for life like recognizing him for a blue-blooded Castilian. Now maybe our old friend Don Juan has got a few drops of Moorish blood in his veins—to put it politely, but—" he raised his tenor voice and improvised—

"Jest because my hair is curly
Dat's no reason to call me 'Shine'!"

"No," agreed Bud, feeling cautiously of the walls, "and jest because you're happy is no reason for singing so loud, neither. These here partitions are made of inch boards, covered with paper—do you get that? Well, then, considering who's probably listening, it strikes me that Mr. Brachamonte is the real thing in Spanish gentlemen; and I've heard that all genuwine Spaniards have their hair curly, jest like a—huh?"

But De Lancey, made suddenly aware of his indiscretion, was making all kinds of exaggerated signs for silence, and Bud stopped with a slow, good-natured smile.

"S-s-st!" hissed De Lancey, touching his finger to his lips. "Don't say it—somebody might hear you!"

"All right," agreed Bud; "and don't you say it, either. I hate to knock, Phil," he added, "but sometimes I think the old man was right when he said you talk too much."

"Psst!" chided De Lancey, shaking his finger like a Mexican. Tiptoeing softly over to Bud, he

49

whispered in his ear: "S-s-st, I can hear the feller in the next room—shaving himself!"

Laughing heartily at this joke, they went downstairs for supper.

VI

If the Eagle Tail mine had been located in Arizona—or even farther down in Old Mexico—the method of jumping the claim would have been delightfully simple.

The title had lapsed, and the land had reverted to the government. All it needed in Arizona was a new set of monuments, a location notice at the discovery shaft, a pick and shovel thrown into the hole, and a few legal formalities.

But in Mexico it is different. Not that the legal formalities are lacking—far from it—but the whole theory of mines and mining is different. In Mexico a mining title is, in a way, a lease, a concession from the general government giving the *concessionaire* the right to work a certain piece of ground and to hold it as long as he pays a mining tax of three dollars an acre per year.

But no final papers or patents are ever issued, the possession of the surface of the ground does not go with the right to mine beneath it, and in certain parts of Mexico no foreigner can hold title to either mines or land.

A prohibited or frontier zone, eighty kilometers in width, lies along the international boundary line, and in that neutral zone no foreigner can denounce a mining claim and no foreign corporation can acquire a title to one. The Eagle Tail was just inside the zone.

But—there is always a "but" when you go to a good lawyer—while for purposes of war and national safety foreigners are not allowed to hold land along the line, they are at perfect liberty to hold stock in Mexican corporations owning property within the prohibited zone; and—here is where the graft comes in—they may even hold title in their own name if they first obtain express permission from the chief executive of the republic.

Not having any drag with the chief executive, and not caring to risk their title to the whims of succeeding administrations, Hooker and De Lancey, upon the advice of a mining lawyer in Gadsden, had organized themselves into the Eagle Tail Mining Company, under the laws of the republic of Mexico, with headquarters at Agua Negra. It was their plan to get some Mexican to locate the mine for them and then, for a consideration, transfer it to the company.

The one weak spot in this scheme was the Mexican. By trusting Aragon, Henry Kruger had not only lost title to his mine, but he had been outlawed from the republic. And now he had bestowed upon Hooker and De Lancey the task of finding an honest Mexican, and keeping him honest until he made the transfer.

While the papers were being made out there

might be a great many temptations placed before that Mexican—either to keep the property for himself or to hold out for a bigger reward than had been specified. After his experience with the aristocratic Don Cipriano Aragon y Tres Palacios, Kruger was in favor of taking a chance on the lower classes. He had therefore recommended to them one Cruz Mendez, a wood vender whom he had known and befriended, as the man to play the part.

Cruz Mendez, according to Kruger, was hard-working, sober, and honest—for a Mexican. He was also simple-minded and easy to handle, and was the particular man who had sent word that the Eagle Tail had at last been abandoned. And also he was easy to pick out, being a little, one-eyed man and going by the name of "El Tuerto."

So, in pursuance of their policy of playing a waiting game, Hooker and De Lancey hung around the hotel for several days, listening to the gossip of Don Juan de Dios and watching for one-eyed men with prospects to sell.

In Sonora he is a poor and unimaginative man indeed who has not at least one lost mine or "prospecto" to sell; and prosperous-looking strangers, riding through the country, are often beckoned aside by half-naked *paisanos* eager to show them the gold mines of the Spanish *padres* for a hundred dollars Mex.

It was only a matter of time, they thought,

until Cruz Mendez would hunt them up and try to sell them the Eagle Tail; and it was their intention reluctantly to close the bargain with him, for a specified sum, and then stake him to the denouncement fees and gain possession of the mine.

As this was a commonplace in the district—no Mexican having capital enough to work a claim and no American having the right to locate one—it was a very natural and inconspicuous way of jumping Señor Aragon y Tres Palacios's abandoned claim. If they discovered the lead immediately afterward it would pass for a case of fool's luck, or at least so they hoped, and, riding out a little each day and sitting on the hotel porch with Don Juan the rest of the time, they waited until patience seemed no longer a virtue.

"Don Juan," said De Lancey, taking up the probe at last, "I had a Mexican working for me when we were over in the Sierras—one of your real, old-time workers that had never been spoiled by an education—and he was always talking about 'La Fortuna,' I guess this was the place he meant, but it doesn't look like it—according to him it was a Mexican town. Maybe he's around here now—his name was Mendez."

"José Maria Mendez?" inquired Don Juan, who was a living directory of the place. "Ricardo? Pancho? Cruz?"

"Cruz!" cried De Lancey. "That was it!"

"He lives down the river a couple of miles," said Don Juan, "down at Old Fortuna."

"Old Fortuna!" repeated Phil. "I didn't know there was such a place."

"Why, my gracious!" exclaimed Don Juan de Dios, scandalized by such ignorance. "Do you mean to say you have been here three days and never heard about Fortuna Vieja? Why, *this* isn't Fortuna! This is an American mining camp—the old town is down below.

"That's where this man Aragon, the big Mexican of the country, has his ranch and store. Spanish? Him? No, indeed—*mitad*! He is half Spanish and half Yaqui Indian, but his wife is a pure Spaniard—one of the few in the country. Her father was from Madrid and she is a Villanueva—a very beautiful woman in her day, with golden hair and the presence of a queen!

"No, *not* Irish! My goodness, you Americans think that everybody with red hair is Irish! Why, the most beautiful women in Madrid have chestnut hair as soft as the fur of a dormouse. It is the old Castilian hair, and they are proud of it. The Señora Aragon married beneath her station—it was in the City of Mexico, and she did not know that he was an Indian—but she is a very nice lady for all that and never omits to bow to me when she comes up to take the train. I remember one time—"

"Does Cruz Mendez work for him?" interjected De Lancey desperately.

"No, indeed!" answered Don Juan patiently. "He packs in wood from the hills—but as I was saying—" and from that he went on to tell of the unfailing courtesy of the Señora Aragon to a gentleman whom, whatever his present station might be, she recognized as a member of one of the oldest families in Castile.

De Lancey did not press his inquiries any further, but the next morning, instead of riding back into the hills, he and Bud turned their faces down the cañon to seek out the elusive Mendez. They had, of course, been acting a part for Don Juan, since Kruger had described Old Fortuna and the Señor Aragon with great minuteness.

And now, in the guise of innocent strangers, they rode on down the river, past the concentrator with its multiple tanks, its gliding tramway and mountains of tailings, through the village of Indian houses stuck like dugouts against the barren hill—then along a river-bed that oozed with slickings until they came in sight of the town.

La Fortuna was an old town, yet not so old as its name, since two Fortunas before it had been washed away by cloudbursts and replaced by newer dwellings. The settlement itself was some four hundred years old, dating back to the days of the Spanish *conquistadores*, when it yielded up many mule-loads of gold.

The present town was built a little up from the river in the lee of a great ridge of rocks thrust down from the hill and well calculated to turn aside a glut of waters. It was a comfortable huddle of whitewashed adobe buildings set on both sides of a narrow and irregular road—the great trail that led down to the hot country—and was worn deep by the pack-trains of centuries.

On the lower side was the ample store and *cantina* of Don Cipriano, where the thirsty *arrieros* could get a drink and buy a *panoche* of sugar without getting down from their mounts. Behind the store were the pole corrals and adobe warehouses and the quarters for the peons, and across the road was the *mescal* still where, in huge copper retort and worm, the fiery liquor was distilled from the sugar-laden heads of Yuccas.

This was the town, but the most important building—set back in the shade of mighty cottonwoods and pleasantly aloof from the road—was the residence of Señor Aragon. It was this, in fact, which held the undivided attention of De Lancey as they rode quietly through the village, for he had become accustomed from a long experience in the tropics to look for something elusive, graceful, and feminine in houses set back in a garden. Nothing stirred, however, and, having good reason to avoid Don Cipriano, they jogged steadily on their way.

"Some house!" observed Phil, with a last, hopeful look over his shoulder.

"Uh," assented Bud, as they came to a fork in the road. "Say," he continued, "let's turn off on this trail. Lot of burro tracks going out—expect it's our friend, Mr. Mendez."

"All right," said De Lancey absently. "Wonder where old Aragon keeps that bee-utiful daughter of his—the one Don Joo-an was telling about. Have to stop on the way back and sample the old man's *mescal*."

"Nothing doing!" countered Hooker instantly. "Now you heard what I told you—there's two things you leave alone for sixty days—booze and women. After we cinch our title you can get as gay as you please."

"Oo-ee!" piped Phil, "hear the boy talk!" But he said no more of wine and women, for he knew how they do complicate life.

They rode to the east now, following the long, flat footprints of the burros, and by all the landmarks Bud saw that they were heading straight for the old Eagle Tail mine. At Old Fortuna the river turns west and at the same time four cañons come in from the east and south. Of these they had taken the first to the north and it was leading them past all the old workings that Kruger had spoken about. In fact, they were almost at the mine when Hooker swung down suddenly from his horse and motioned Phil to follow.

"There's some burros coming," he said, glancing back significantly; and when the pack-train came by, each animal piled high with broken wood, the two Americans were busily tapping away at a section of country rock. A man and a boy followed behind the animals, gazing with wonder at the strangers, and as Phil bade them a pleasant *"Buenos días!"* they came to a halt and stared at their industry in silence. In the interval Phil was pleased to note that the old man had only one eye.

"Que busca?" the one-eyed one finally inquired. "What are you looking for?"

And when Phil oracularly answered, "Gold!" the old man made a motion to the boy to go on and sat down on a neighboring rock.

"Do you want to buy a prospect?" he asked, and Bud glanced up at him grimly.

"We find our own prospects," answered Phil.

"But I know of a very rich prospect," protested Mendez; *"very rich!"* He shrilled his voice to express how rich it was.

"Yes?" observed Phil. "Then why don't you dig the gold out? But as for us, we find our own mines. That is our business."

"Seguro!" nodded Mendez, glancing at their outfit approvingly. "But I am a poor man—very poor—I cannot denounce the mine. So I wait for some rich American to come and buy it. I have a friend—a very rich man—in Gadsden,

but he will not come; so I will sell it to you."

"Did you get that, Bud?" jested Phil in English. "The old man here thinks we're rich Americans and he wants to sell us a mine."

Bud laughed silently at this, and Mr. Mendez, his hopes somewhat blasted by their levity, began to boast of his find, giving the history of the Eagle Tail with much circumstantiality and explaining that it was a lost *padre* mine.

"Sure," observed Phil, going back to his horse and picking up the bridle, "that's what they all say. They're *all* lost *padre* mines, and you can see them from the door of the church. Come on, Bud, let's go!"

"And so you could this," cried Mendez, running along after them as they rode slowly up the cañon, "from the old church that was washed away by the flood! This is the very mine where the *padres* dug out all their gold! Are you going up this way? Come, then, and I will show you— the very place, except that the *Americano* ruined it with a blast!"

He tagged along after them, wheedling and protesting while they bantered him about his mine, until they finally came to the place—the ruins of the old Eagle Tail.

It lay spraddled out along the hillside, a series of gopher-holes, dumps, and abandoned workings, looking more like a badly managed stone-quarry than a relic of *padre* days. Kruger's magazine of giant powder exploded in one big blast, had destroyed all traces of his mine, besides starting an avalanche of loose shale that had poured down and filled the pocket.

Added to this, Aragon and his men had rooted around in the debris in search of the vein, and the story of their inefficient work was told by great piles of loose rock stacked up beside caved-in trenches and a series of timid tunnels driven into the neighboring ridges.

Under the circumstances it would certainly call for a mining engineer to locate the lost lead, and De Lancey looked it over thoughtfully as he began to figure on the work to be done. Undoubtedly there was a mine there—and the remains of an old Spanish smelter down the creek showed that the ground had once been very rich—but if Kruger had not told him in advance he would have passed up the job in a minute.

"Well," he said, turning coldly upon the fawning Mendez, who was all curves in his desire to please, "where is your *prospecto*?"

"*Aqui, señor!*" replied the Mexican, pointing to the disrupted rockslide. "Here it was that the *Americano* Crooka had his mine—rich with gold—*much* gold!"

He shrilled his voice emphatically, and De Lancey shrilled his in reply.

"Here?" he exclaimed, gazing blankly at the hillside, and then he broke into a laugh. "All

61

right, my friend," he said, giving Bud a facetious wink; "how much do you want for this prospect?"

"Four hundred dollars," answered Mendez in a tone at once hopeful and apologetic. "It is very rich. Señor Crooka shipped some ore that was full of gold. I packed it out for him on my burros; but, I am sorry, I have no piece of it."

"Yes," responded De Lancey, "I am sorry, too. So, of course, we cannot buy the prospecto since you have no ore to show; but I am glad for this, Señor Mendez," he continued with a kindly smile; "it shows that you are an honest man, or you would have stolen a piece of ore from the sacks. So show us now where the gold was found, the nearest that you can remember, and perhaps, if we think we can find it, we will pay you to denounce the claim for us."

At this the one good eye of Cruz Mendez lighted up with a great hope and, skipping lightly over the rock-piles with his sandaled feet, he ran to a certain spot, locating it by looking across the cañon and up and down the creek.

"Here, *señores*," he pronounced, "is where the mouth of the old tunnel came out. Standing inside it I could see that tree over there, and looking down the river I could just see the smelter around the point. So, then, the gold must be in there." He pointed toward the hill.

"Surely," said De Lancey; "but where?"

The old Mexican shrugged his shoulders deprecatingly.

"I do not know, *señor*," he answered; "but if you wish to dig I will denounce the claim for you."

"For how much?" inquired De Lancey guardedly.

"For one hundred dollars," answered Mendez, and to his delight the American seemed to be considering it. He walked back and forth across the slide, picking up rocks and looking at them, dropping down into the futile trenches of Aragon, and frowning with studious thought. His pardner, however, sat listlessly on a boulder and tested the action of his six-shooter.

"Listen, my friend," said De Lancey, coming back and poising his finger impressively. "If I should find the ledge the one hundred dollars would be nothing to me, *sabe*? And if I should spend all my money for nothing it would be but one hundred dollars more. But listen! I have known some false Mexicans who, when an American paid them to denounce a mine, took advantage of his kindness and refused to give it over. Or, if it turned out to be rich, they pulled a long face and claimed that they ought to be paid more. Now if—"

"Ah, no, no, *señor*!" clamored Mendez, holding up his hand in protest. "I am a poor man, but I am honest. Only give me the hundred dollars—"

63

"Not a dollar do you get!" cried De Lancey sternly; "not a dollar—until you turn over the concession to the mine. And if you play us false—" he paused impressively—"*cuidado, hombre*—look out!"

Once more Cruz Mendez protested his honesty and his fidelity to any trust, but De Lancey silenced him impatiently.

"Enough, *hombre*!" he said. "Words are nothing to us. Do you see my friend over there?" He pointed to Bud who, huge and dominating against the sky-line, sat toying with his pistol. "*Buen'*! He is a cowboy, *sabe*? A Texan! You know the *Tejanos*, eh? They do not like Mexicans. But my friend there, he likes Mexicans—when they are honest. If not—no! Hey, Bud," he called in English, "what would you do to this fellow if he beat us out of the mine?"

Bud turned upon them with a slow, good-natured smile.

"Oh, nothing much," he answered, putting up his gun; and the deep rumble of his voice struck fear into the old man's heart.

Phil laughed and looked grimly at Mendez while he delivered his ultimatum.

"Very well, my friend," he said. "We will stay and look at this mine. If we think it is good we will take you to the mining agent and get a permit to dig. For sixty days we will dig, and if we find nothing we will pay you fifty dollars, anyway.

If we find the ledge we will give you a hundred dollars. All right?"

"*Sí, señor—sí, señor!*" cried Mendez, "one hundred dollars!"

"When you give us the papers!" warned Phil. "But remember—be careful! The Americans do not like men who talk. And come to the hotel at Fortuna to-morrow—then we will let you know."

"And you will buy the mine?" begged Mendez, backing off with his hat in his hand.

"Perhaps," answered De Lancey. "We will tell you to-morrow."

"*Buen*'!" bowed Mendez. "And many thanks!"

"It is nothing," replied De Lancey politely, and then with a crooked smile he gazed after the old man as he went hurrying off down the cañon.

"Well," he observed, "I guess we've got Mr. Mendez started just about right—what? Now if we can keep him without the price of a drink until we get our papers we stand a chance to win."

"That's right," said Bud; "but I wish he had two good eyes. I knowed a one-eyed Mex up in Arizona and he was sure a thieving son of a goat!"

VII

There are doubtless many philanthropists in the Back Bay regions of Boston who would consider the whipsawing of Cruz Mendez a very reprehensible act. And one hundred dollars Mex was certainly a very small reward for the service that he was to perform.

But Bud and Phil were not traveling for any particular uplift society, and one hundred pesos was a lot of money to Cruz Mendez. More than that, if they had offered him a thousand dollars for the same service he would have got avaricious and demanded ten thousand.

He came to the hotel very early the next morning and lingered around an hour or so, waiting for the American gentlemen to arise and tell him his fate. A hundred dollars would buy everything that he could think of, including a quantity of *mescal*. His throat dried at the thought of it.

Then the gentlemen appeared and asked him many questions—whether he was married according to law, whether his wife would sign the papers with him, and if he believed in a here-after for those who played false with Americans. Having answered all these in the affirmative, he was taken to the *agente mineral*, and, after signing his name—his one feat in penmanship—

to several imposing documents, he was given the precious permit.

Then there was another trip to the grounds with a surveyor, to make report that the claim was actually vacant, and Mendez went back to his normal duties as a packer.

In return for this service as a dummy locator, and to keep him under their eye, the Americans engaged El Tuerto, the one-eyed, to pack out a few tools and supplies for them; and then, to keep him busy, they employed him further to build a stone house.

All these activities were, of course, not lost on Don Cipriano Aragon y Tres Palacios, since, by a crafty arrangement of fences, he had made it impossible for anyone to reach the lower country without passing through the crooked street of Old Fortuna.

During the first and the second trip of the strange Americans he kept within his dignity, hoping perhaps that they would stop at his store, where they could be engaged in conversation; but upon their return from a third trip, after Cruz Mendez had gone through with their supplies, he cast his proud Spanish reserve to the winds and waylaid them on the street.

"*Buenas tardes, señores,*" he saluted, as they rode past his store, and then, seeing that they did not break their gait, he held up his hand for them to stop.

"Excuse me, gentlemen," he said, speaking genially but with an affected Spanish lisp. "I have seen you ride past several times—are you working for the big company up at New Fortuna?"

"No, *señor*," answered De Lancey courteously, "we are working for ourselves."

"Good!" responded Aragon with fatherly approval. "It is better so. And are you looking at mines?"

"Yes," said De Lancey non-committally; "we are looking at mines."

"That is good, too," observed Aragon; "and I wish you well, but since you are strangers to this country and perhaps do not know the people as well as some, I desire to warn you against that one-eyed man, Cruz Mendez, with whom I have seen you riding. He is a worthless fellow—a very *pelado* Mexican, one who has nothing—and yet he is always seeking to impose upon strangers by selling them old mines which have no value.

"I have no desire to speak ill of my neighbors, but since he has moved into the brush house up the river I have lost several fine little pigs; and his eye, as I know, was torn from his head as he was chasing another man's cow. I have not suffered him on my ranch for years, he is such a thief, and yet he has the effrontery to represent himself to strangers as a poor but honest man. I hope that he has not imposed upon you in any way?"

"No; not at all, thank you," responded De Lancey, as Bud raised his bridle-reins to go. "We hired him to pack out our tools and supplies and he has done it very reasonably. But many thanks, sir, for your warning. *Adios*!"

He touched his hat and waved his hand in parting, and Bud grinned as he settled down to a trot.

"You can't help palavering 'em, can you, Phil?" he said. "No matter what you think about 'em, you got to be polite, haven't you? Well, that's the way you get drawn in—next time you go by now the old man will pump you dry—you see. No, sir, the only way to get along with these Mexicans is not to have a thing to do with 'em. 'No savvy'—that's my motto."

"Well, '*muchas gracias*' is mine," observed De Lancey. "It doesn't cost anything, and it buys a whole lot."

"Sure," agreed Bud; "but we ain't buying nothing from him—he's the one particular *hombre* we want to steer clear of, and keep him guessing as long as we can. That's my view of it, pardner."

"Oh, that's all right," laughed De Lancey, "he won't get anything out of me—that is, nothing but a bunch of hot air. Say, he's a shrewd-looking old guinea, isn't he? Did you notice that game eye? He kept it kind of drooped, almost shut, until he came to the point—and then he opened it up real fierce. Reminds me of a big fighting owl waking up in the day-time. But you just watch me handle him, and if I don't fool the old boy at every turn it'll be because I run out of bull."

"Well, you can hand him the bull if you want to," grumbled Bud, "but the first time you give anything away I'm going to pick such a row with the old cuss that we'll have to make a new trail to get by. So leave 'im alone, if you ever expect to see that girl!"

A close association with Phil De Lancey had left Bud not unaware of his special weaknesses, and Phil was undoubtedly romantic. Given a barred and silent house, shut off from the street by whitened walls and a veranda screened with flowers, and the questing eyes of Mr. De Lancey would turn to those barred windows as certainly as the needle seeks the pole.

On every trip, coming and going, he had conned the Aragon house from the vine-covered *corredor* in front to the walled-in summer-garden behind, hoping to surprise a view of the beautiful daughter of the house. And unless rumor and Don Juan were at fault, she was indeed worthy of his solicitude—a gay and sprightly creature, brown-eyed like her mother and with the same glorious chestnut hair.

Already those dark, mischievous eyes had been busy and, at the last big dance at Fortuna, she had set many heads awhirl. Twice within two years her father, in a rage, had sent her away to school in order to break off some ill-considered love-affair; and now a battle royal was being waged between Manuel del Rey, the dashing captain of the *rurales* stationed at Fortuna, and Feliz Luna, son of a rich *haciendado* down in the hot country, for the honor of her hand.

What more romantic, then, than that a handsome American, stepping gracefully into the breach, should keep the haughty lovers from slaying each other by bearing off the prize himself?

So reasoned Philip De Lancey, musing upon the ease with which he could act the part; but for prudential purposes he said nothing of his vaunting ambitions, knowing full well that they would receive an active veto from Bud.

For, while De Lancey did most of the talking, and a great deal of the thinking for the partnership, Hooker was not lacking in positive opinions; and upon sufficient occasion he would express himself, though often with more force than delicacy. Therefore, upon this unexpected sally about the girl, Phil changed the subject abruptly and said no more of Aragon or the hopes within his heart.

It was not so easy, however, to avoid Aragon, for that gentleman had apparently taken the pains to inform himself as to the place where they were at work, and he was waiting for them in the morning with a frown as black as a thunder-cloud.

"He's on!" muttered Phil, as they drew near enough to see his face. "What shall we do?"

"Do nothing," growled Bud through his teeth; "you jest let me do the talking!"

He maneuvered his horse adroitly and, with a skillful turn, cut in between his pardner and Aragon.

" 'S días," he greeted, gazing down in burly defiance at the militant Aragon; and at the same moment he gave De Lancey's horse a furtive touch with his spur.

"*Buenos días, señores!*" returned Aragon, striding forward to intercept them; but as neither of the Americans looked back, he was left standing in the middle of the street.

"That's the way to handle 'im," observed Hooker, as they trotted briskly down the lane. "Leave 'im to me."

"It'll only make him mad," objected De Lancey crossly. "What do you want to do that for?"

"He's mad already," answered Bud. "I *want* to quarrel with him, so he can't ask us any questions. Get him so mad he won't talk—then it'll be a fair fight and none of this snake-in-the-grass business."

"Yes, but don't put it on him," protested De Lancey. "Let him be friendly for a while, if he wants to."

"Can't be friends," said Bud laconically; "we jumped his claim."

"Maybe he doesn't want it," suggested Phil hopefully. "He's dropped a lot of money on it."

"You bet he wants it," returned Hooker, with conviction. "I'm going to camp out there—the old boy is liable to jump us."

"Aw, you're crazy, Bud!" cried Phil; but Hooker only smiled.

"You know what happened to Kruger," he answered. "I'll tell you what, we got to keep our eye open around here."

They rode on to their mine, which was only about five miles from Fortuna, without discussing the matter further; for, while Phil had generally been the leader, in this particular case Kruger had put Bud in charge, and he seemed determined to have his way so far as Aragon was concerned. In the ordering of supplies and the laying out of development work he deferred to Phil in everything, but for tactics he preferred his own judgment.

It was by instinct rather than reason that he chose to fight, and people who follow their instincts are hard to change. So they put in the day in making careful measurements, according to the memoranda that Kruger had given them; and, having satisfied themselves as to the approximate locality of the lost vein, they turned back again toward town with their heads full of cunning schemes.

Since it was the pleasure of the Señor Aragon to make war on all who entered his preserves, they checkmated any attempt on his part to locate the lead by driving stakes to the north of their ledge; and, still further to throw him off, they decided to mark time for a while by doing dead work on a cut. Such an approach would be needed to reach the mouth of their tunnel.

At the same time it would give steady employment to Mendez and keep him under their eye, and as soon as Aragon showed his hand they could make out their final papers in peace and send them to the City of Mexico.

And not until those final papers were recorded and the transfer duly made would they so much as stick a pick into the hill-side or show a lump of quartz.

But for a Spanish gentleman, supposed to be all supple curves and sinuous advance, Don Cipriano turned out somewhat of a surprise, for when they rode back through his narrow street again he met them squarely in the road and called them to a halt.

"By what right, gentlemen—" he demanded in a voice tremulous with rage,—"by what right do you take possession of my mine, upon which I have paid the taxes all these years, and conspire with that rogue, Cruz Mendez, to cheat me out of it? It is mine, I tell you, no matter what the *agente mineral* may say, and—"

"Your mine, nothing!" broke in Hooker scornfully, speaking in the ungrammatical border-Mexican of the cowboys. "We meet one Mexican—he shows us the mine—that is all. The expert of the mining agent says it is vacant—we take it. *Stawano!*"*

He waved the matter aside with masterful indifference, and Aragon burst into a torrent of excited Spanish.

"Very likely, very likely," commented Bud dryly, without listening to a word; "*sí, señor, yo pienso!*"

A wave of fury swept over the Spaniard's face at this gibe and he turned suddenly to De Lancey.

"*Señor*," he said, "you seem to be a gentleman. Perhaps you will listen to me. This mine upon which you are working is mine. I have held it for years, seeking for the lost vein of the old *padres*. Then the rebels came sweeping through the land. They stole my horses, they drove off my cattle, they frightened my workmen from the mine. I was compelled to flee—myself and my family— to keep from being held for ransom. Now you do me the great injustice to seize my mine!"

"Ah, no, *señor*," protested De Lancey, waving

---

* A shortening of *está bueno*—it is good—a common expression in cowboy Spanish.

his finger politely for silence, "you are mistaken. We have inquired about this mine and it has been vacant for some time. There is no vein—no gold. Anyone who wished could take it. While we were prospecting we met this poor one-eyed man and he has taken out a permit to explore it. So we are going to dig—that is all."

"But, *señor!*" burst out Aragon—and he voiced his rabid protests again, while sudden faces appeared in the windows and wide-eyed peons stood gawking in a crowd. But De Lancey was equally firm, though he glimpsed for the first time the adorable face of La Gracia as she stared at him from behind the bars.

"No, *señor*," he said, "you are mistaken. The land was declared forfeit for non-payment of taxes by the minister of Fomento and thrown open for location. We have located it—that is all."

For a minute Don Cipriano stood looking at him, his black eyes heavy with rage; then his anger seemed to fall away from him and he wiped the sweat from his brow.

"Very well," he said at last, "I perceive that you are a gentleman and have acted in good faith—it is only that that fellow Mendez has deceived you. Let it pass, then—I will not quarrel with you, my friend—it is the fortune of war. But stop at my store when you go by and come and see me. It is indeed lonely here at times, and perhaps I can pass a pleasant hour with you. My name, *señor*, is Don Cipriano Aragon y Tres Palacios—and yours?"

He held out his hand with a little gesture.

"Philip De Lancey," replied that gentleman, clasping the proffered hand; and with many expressions of good-will and esteem, with a touching of hats and a wriggling of fingers from the distance, they parted, in spite of Bud, apparently the best of friends.

VIII

There are some people in this world with whom it seems impossible to quarrel, notably the parents of attractive daughters.

Perhaps, if Gracia Aragon had not been watching him from the window, Philip De Lancey would not have been quite so cordial with her father—at least, that was what Hooker thought, and he was so badly peeved at the way things had gone that he said it, too.

Then, of course, they quarreled, and one thing leading to another, Phil told Bud he had a very low way of speaking. Bud replied, that whatever his deficiencies of speech might be, he was not fool enough to be drawn in by a skirt, and Phil rebuked him again. Then, with a scornful grunt, Bud Hooker rode on in silence and they said no more about it.

It was a gay life that they led at night, for the Fortuna Hotel was filled with men of their kind, since all the staid married men had either moved across the line with their families or were under orders to come straight home.

In the daytime the hotel was nearly deserted, for every man in town was working for the company; but in the evening, when they gathered around the massive stove, it was a merry company indeed.

There were college men, full of good stories and stories not so good, world-wanderers and adventurers with such tales of the East and West as never have been written in books. But not a college boy could match stories with Phil De Lancey, and few wanderers there were who could tell him anything new about Mexico. Also, when it came to popular songs, he knew both the words and the tune. So he was much in demand, and Don Juan passed many drinks across the bar because of him.

In all such festivities the two pardners stayed together; Bud, with a broad, indulgent grin, listening to the end, and Phil, his eyes alight with liquor and good cheer, talking and laughing far into the night.

Outside the winter winds were still cold and the Mexicans went wrapped to the eyebrows; but within the merry company was slow to quit, and Phil, making up for the lonely months when he had entirely lacked an audience, sat long in the seat of honor and was always the last to go.

But on the evening after their spat Bud sat off to one side, and even Phil's sprightly and ventriloquistic conversation with the-little-girl-behind-the-door called forth only a fleeting smile.

Bud was thinking, and when engaged in that arduous occupation even the saucy little girl behind the door could not beguile him.

But, after he had studied it all out and come to a definite conclusion, he did not deliver an ultimatum. The old, good-natured smile simply came back to his rugged face; he rolled a cigarette; and then for the rest of the evening he lay back and enjoyed the show. Only in the morning, when they went out to the corral to get their horses, he carried his war-bag with him and, after throwing the saddle on Copper Bottom, he did the same for their spare mount.

"What are you going to pack out, Bud?" inquired Phil, and Bud slapped his canvas-covered bed for an answer. Then, with a heave, he snaked it out of the harness-room where it had been stored and slung it deftly across the pack-saddle.

"Why, what's the matter?" said De Lancey, when they were on their way. "Don't you like the hotel?"

"Hotel's fine," conceded Bud, "but I reckon I'd better camp out at the mine. Want to keep my eye on that Mexican of ours."

"Aw, he's all right," protested Phil.

"Sure," said Bud; "I ain't afraid he'll steal something—but he might take a notion to quit the country."

"Why, what for?" challenged De Lancey. "He's got his wife and family here."

"That's nothing—to a Mexican!" countered Bud. "But I ain't figuring on the excuse he'd give—that won't buy me nothing—what I want to do is to keep him from going. Because if we lose that Mex now, we lose our mine."

"And—"

"No 'and' to it," said Bud doggedly. "We ain't going to lose him."

"But if we did," persisted De Lancey, "why, then you think—"

"Your friend would get it," finished Hooker grimly.

"Ah, I see," nodded De Lancey, noting the accent on "friend." "You don't approve of my making friends with Aragon."

"Oh, that's all right," shrugged the big cowboy. "It won't make no difference now. Go ahead, if you want to."

"You mean you can get along without me?"

"No," answered Bud. "I don't mean nothing—except what I say. If you want to palaver around with Aragon, go to it. I'll round up Mendez and his family and keep 'em right there at the mine until we get them papers signed—after that I don't care what happens."

"Oh, all right," murmured De Lancey in a subdued tone; but if his conscience smote him for the moment it did not lead to the making of any sentimental New Year's resolutions, for he stopped when he came to the store and exchanged salutations with Aragon, who was lounging expectantly before his door.

"*Buenos días*, Don Cipriano!" he hailed. "How are you this morning?"

"Ah, good morning, Don Felipe," responded Aragon, stepping forth from the shadow of the door. "I am very well, thank you—and you?"

"The same!" answered Phil, as if it were a great piece of news. "It is fine weather—no?"

"Yes, but a little dry," said Aragon, and so they passed it back and forth in the accepted Spanish manner, while Bud hooked one leg over the horn of his saddle and regarded the *hacienda* with languid eyes.

But as his gaze swept the length of the vine-covered *corredor* it halted for a moment and a slow smile came over his face. In the green depths of a passion-flower vine he had detected a quick, birdlike motion; and then suddenly, like a transformation scene, he beheld a merry face, framed and illuminated by soft, golden locks, peering out at him from among the blossoms. Except for that brief smile he made no sign that he saw her, and when he looked up again the face had disappeared.

Don Cipriano showed them about his *mescal* plant, where his men kept a continual stream of liquid fire running from the copper worm, and gave each a raw drink; but though De Lancey gazed admiringly at the house and praised the orange-trees that hung over the garden wall, Spanish hospitality could go no farther, and the visit ended in a series of *adioses* and *muchas graciases.*

"Quick work!" commented Phil, as they rode toward the mine. "The old man has got over his grouch."

"Um," mused Bud, with a quiet, brooding smile; and the next time he rode into town he looked for the masked face among the flowers and smiled again. That was the way Gracia Aragon affected them all.

He did not point out the place to Phil, nor betray her by any sign. All he did was to glance at her once and then ride on his way, but somehow his heart stood still when he met her eyes, and his days became filled with a pensive, brooding melancholy.

"What's the matter, Bud?" rallied Phil, after he had jollied him for a week. "You're getting mighty quiet lately. Got another hunch—like that one you had up at Agua Negra?"

"Nope," grinned Bud; "but I'll tell you one thing—if old Aragon don't spring something pretty soon I'm going to get uneasy. He's too dog-goned good-natured about this."

"Maybe he thinks we're stuck," suggested De Lancey.

"Well, he's awful happy about something," said Bud. "I can see by the way he droops that game eye of his—and smiles that way—that he knows we're working for him. If we don't get a title to this mine, every tap of work we do on it is all to the good for him, that's a cinch. So sit down now and think it out—where's the joker?"

"Well," mused Phil, "the gold is here somewhere. He knows we're not fooled there. And he knows we're right after it, the way we're driving this cut in. Our permit is good—he hasn't tried to buffalo Mendez—and it's a cinch he can't denounce the claim himself."

"Maybe he figures on letting us do all the work and pay all the denouncement fees and then spring something big on old One-Eye," propounded Bud. "Scare 'im up or buy 'im off, and have him transfer the title to *him*. That's the way he worked Kruger."

"Well, say," urged Phil, "let's go ahead with our denouncement before he starts something. Besides, the warm weather is coming on now, and if we don't get a move on we're likely to get run out by the *revoltosos*."

"Nope," said Bud; "I don't put this into Mendez's hands until I know he's our man—and if I ever do go ahead I'll keep him under my six-shooter until the last paper is signed, believe me. I know we're in bad somewhere, but hurrying up won't help none.

"Now I tell you what we'll do—you go to the mining agent and get copies of all our papers and send them up to that Gadsden lawyer. I'm going to go down and board with Mendez and see if I can read his heart."

So they separated, and while Phil stayed in town to look over the records Bud ate his beans and *tortillas* with the Mendez family.

They were a happy little family, comfortably installed in the stone house that Mendez had built, and rapidly getting fat on three full meals a day. From his tent farther up the cañon Bud could look down and watch the children at play and see the comely Indian wife as she cooked by the open fire.

Certainly no one could be more innocent and contented than she was, and El Tuerto was all bows and protestations of gratitude. And yet, you never can tell.

Bud had moved out of the new house to furnish quarters for El Tuerto and had favored him in every way; but this same consideration might easily be misinterpreted, for the Mexicans are slow to understand kindness.

So, while on the one hand he had treated them generously, he had always kept his distance, lest they be tempted to presume. But now, with Phil in town for a few days, he took his meals with Maria, who was too awed to say a word, and made friends with the dogs and the children.

The way to the dog's heart was easy, almost direct, and he finally won the attention of little Pancho and Josefa with a well-worn Sunday supplement. This gaudy institution, with its spicy stories and startling illustrations, had penetrated even to the wilds of Sonora, and every Sunday as regularly as the paper came Bud sat down and had his laugh over the funny page.

But to Pancho, who was six years old and curious, this same highly colored sheet was a mystery of mysteries, and when he saw the big American laughing he crept up and looked at it wistfully.

"*Mira*," said Bud, laying his finger upon the smirking visage of one of the comic characters, "look, and I will tell you the story."

And so, with laborious care, he translated the colored fun, while the little Mendezes squirmed with excitement and leaped with joy. Even the simple souls of El Tuerto and Maria were moved by the *comicas*, and Mendez became so interested that he learned the words by heart, the better to explain them to others.

But as for Mexican treachery, Bud could find none of it. In fact, finding them so simple-hearted and good-natured, he became half ashamed of his early suspicions and waited for the return of Phil to explain Don Cipriano's complacency.

But the next Sunday, as Bud lay reading in his tent, the mystery solved itself. Cruz Mendez came up from the house, hat in hand and an apologetic smile on his face, and after the customary roundabout remarks he asked the boss as a favor if he would lend him the page of comic pictures.

"*Seguro!*" assented Bud, rolling over and fumbling for the funny sheet; then, failing to find it instantly, he inquired: "What do you want it for?"

"Ah, to show to my boy!" explained El Tuerto, his one eye lighting up with pride.

"Who—Pancho?"

"Ah, no, *señor*," answered Mendez simply, "my boy in La Fortuna, the one you have not seen."

Bud stopped fumbling for the paper and sat up suddenly. Here was a new light on their faithful servitor, and one that might easily take away from his value as a dummy locator.

"Oh!" he said, and then: "How many children have you, Cruz?"

Cruz smiled deprecatingly, as parents will, and turned away.

"By which woman?" he inquired, and Bud became suddenly very calm, fearing the worst. For if Cruz was not legally married to Maria, he could not transfer the mining claim.

"By all of them," he said quietly.

"Five in all," returned Cruz—"three by Maria, as you know—two by my first woman—and one other. I do not count him."

"Well, you one-eyed old reprobate!" muttered Bud in his throat, but he passed it off and returned smiling to the charge.

"Where does your boy live now?" he asked

87

with flattering solicitude, the better to make him talk, "and is he old enough to understand the pictures?"

"Ah, yes!" beamed Mendez, "he is twelve years old. He lives with his mother now—and my little daughter, too. Their *mama* is the woman of the *mayordomo* of the Señor Aragon—a bad man, very ugly—she is not married to *him*."

"But with you—" suggested Bud, regarding him with a steely stare.

"Only by the judge!" explained Mendez virtuously. "It was a love-match and the priest did not come—so we were married by the judge. Then this bad *mayordomo* stole her away from me—the pig—and I married Maria instead. Maria is a good woman and I married her before the priest—but I love my other children too, even though they are not lawful."

"So you married your first wife before the judge," observed Bud cynically, "and this one before the priest. But how could you do that, unless you had been divorced?"

"Ah, *señor*," protested Mendez, holding out his hands, "you do not understand. It is only the church that can really marry—the judge does it only for the money. Maria is my true wife—and we have three nice children—but as I am going through La Fortuna I should like to show the picture paper to my boy."

Bud regarded him in meditative silence, then

he rose up and began a determined search for the funny sheet.

"All right," he said, handing it over, "and here is a *panoche* of sugar for your little girl—the one in La Fortuna. It is nothing," he added, as Mendez began his thanks.

"But oh, you marrying Mexican," he continued, relapsing into his mother tongue as El Tuerto disappeared; "you certainly have dished us right!"

IX

Not the least of the causes which have brought Mexico to the brink of the abyss is the endless quarrel between church and state, which has almost destroyed the sanctity of marriage and left, besides, a pitiful heritage of deserted women and fatherless children as its toll.

Many an honest laborer has peoned himself to pay the priest for his marriage, only to be told that it is not legal in the eyes of the law; and many another, married by the judge, has been gravely informed by the *padre* that the woman is only his mistress, and the children born out of wedlock.

So that now, to be sure that she is wedded, a woman must be married twice, and many a couple, on account of the prohibitive fees, are never married at all.

Cruz Mendez was no different from the men of his class, and he believed honestly that he was married to the comely Maria; but Hooker could have enlightened him on that point if he had cared to do it.

Bud was playing a game, with the Eagle Tail mine for a stake; and, being experienced at poker, he stood pat and studied his hand. Without doubt Mendez had lost his usefulness as a locator of the mine, since Maria was not his legal wife and could not sign the transfer papers as such. According to the law of the land, the woman now living with Aragon's *mayordomo* was the "legitimate" wife of the contract, and she alone could release the title to the mine once Mendez denounced the claim.

But Mendez had not yet denounced the claim—though for a period of some thirty days yet he had the exclusive privilege of doing so—and Bud did not intend that he should.

Meanwhile they must walk softly, leaving Aragon still to hug the delusion that he would soon, through his *mayordomo*, have them in his power—and when the full sixty days of Cruz Mendez's mining permit had expired they could locate the mine again.

But how—and through whom? That was the question that Bud was studying upon when Phil rode up the trail, and in his abstraction he barely returned his gay greeting.

"Well, cheer up, old top!" cried De Lancey, throwing his bridle-reins to the ground and striding up to the tent. "What ho, let down the portcullis, me lord seneschal! And cease your vain repining, Algernon—our papers are all O. K. and the lawyer says to go ahead. But that isn't half the news! Say, we had a dance up at the hotel last night and I met—"

"Yes—sure you did," broke in Bud; "but

listen to this!" And he told him of El Tuerto's matrimonial entanglements.

"Why, the crooked devil!" exclaimed De Lancey, leaping up at the finish. "*Oyez!* Mendez!"

"Don't say a word," warned Bud, springing to the tent door to intercept him, "or you'll put us out of business! It is nothing," he continued in Spanish as Mendez came out of his house, "but put Don Felipe's horse in the corral when he is cool."

"*Sí, señor*—with great pleasure!" smirked Mendez, running to get the horse, and after he had departed Bud turned back and shook his head.

"We can't afford to quarrel with Mr. Mendez," he said; "because if Aragon ever gets hold of him we're ditched. Jest let everything run on like we'd overlooked something until the sixty days are up—then, if we get away with it, we'll locate the mine ourselves."

"Yes; but how?"

"Well, the's two ways," returned Bud; "either hunt up another Mexican citizen or turn Mexican ourselves."

"Turn Mexican!" shrilled Phil, and then he broke down and laughed. "Well, you're a great one, Bud," he chortled; "you sure are!"

"I come down here to get this mine," said Bud laconically.

"Yes, but you're a Texan—or was one!"

"That makes no difference," answered Bud stoutly. "The hot weather is coming on—revolution is likely to begin any time—and there ain't a single Mexican we can trust. Jest one more break now and we lose out—now how about it?"

"Who's going to turn Mexican," questioned De Lancey, "you or me?"

"Well—*I* will, then!"

"No, you won't, either!" cried Phil, forgetting his canny shrewdness. "I'll do it myself! I'm half Mexican already, I've been eating chili so long!"

"Now here," began Bud, "listen to me. I've been thinking this over all day and you jest heard about it. The man that turns Mexican is likely to get mixed up with the authorities and have to skip the country, but the other feller is in the other way—he's got to stay with the works till hell freezes over.

"Now you're an engineer and you know how to open up a mine—I don't. So, if you say so, I'll take out the papers and you hold the mine—or if you want to *you* can turn Mex."

"Well," said De Lancey, his voice suddenly becoming soft and pensive, "I might as well tell you, Bud, that I'm thinking of settling in this country, anyway. Of course, I don't look at Aragon the way you do—I think you are prejudiced and misjudge him—but ever since I've known Gracia I've—"

"Gracia!" repeated Bud; and then, stirred by

some great and unreasoning anger, he rose up and threw down his hat pettishly. "I'd think, Phil," he muttered, "you'd be satisfied with all the other girls in the world without—"

"Now here!" shouted Phil, rising as unreasoningly to his feet, "don't you say another word against that girl, or I'll—"

"Shut your mouth, you little shrimp!" bellowed Bud, wheeling upon him menacingly. "You seem to think you're the only man in the world that—"

"Oh, slush, Bud!" cried Phil in disgust. "You don't mean to tell me you're in love with Gracia too!"

"Who—me?" demanded Hooker, his face suddenly becoming fixed and mask-like; and then he laughed hoarsely in derision and sank down on the bed.

Certainly, of the two of them, he was the more surprised at his sudden outbreak of passion; and yet when the words were spoken he was quick to know that they were true.

Undoubtedly, in his own way, he was in love— but he would never admit it, that he knew, too. So he sank down on the blankets and swore harshly, while De Lancey stared at him in unfeigned surprise.

"Well, then," he went on, taking Bud's answer for granted, "what 're you making such a row about? Can't I go to a dance with a girl without you jumping down my throat?"

"W'y, sure you can!" rumbled Bud, now hot with a new indignation. "But after getting me to go into this deal against my will and swearing me to some damn-fool pledge, the first thing you do is to make friends with Aragon and then make love to his daughter. Is that your idea of helping things along? D'ye think that's the way a pardner ought to act? No, I tell you, it is not!"

"Aw, Bud," protested De Lancey plaintively, "what's the matter with you? Be reasonable, old man; I never meant to hurt your feelings!"

"Hurt my feelings!" echoed Hooker scornfully. "Huh, what are we down here for, anyway—a Sunday-school picnic? My feelings are nothing, and they can wait; but we're sitting on a mine that's worth a million dollars mebbe—and it ain't ours, either—and when you throw in with old Aragon and go to making love to his daughter you know you're not doing right! That's all there is to it—you're doing me and Kruger dirt!"

"Well, Bud," said De Lancey with mock gravity, "if that's the way you feel about it I won't do it any more!"

"I wish you wouldn't," breathed Bud, raising his head from his hands; "it sure wears me out, Phil, worrying about it."

"Well, then, I won't do it," protested Phil sincerely. "So that's settled—now who's going to turn Mexican citizen?"

"Suit yourself," said Bud listlessly.

"I'll match you for it!" proposed De Lancey, diving into his pocket for money.

"Don't need to," responded Bud; "you can do what you please."

"No; I'll match you!" persisted Phil. "That was the agreement—whenever it was an even break we'd let the money talk. Here's your quarter—and if I match you I'll become the Mexican citizen. All set? Let 'er go!"

He flipped the coin into the air and caught it in his hand.

"Heads!" he called, without looking at it. "What you got?"

"Heads!" answered Bud, and Phil chucked his money into the air again and laughed as it dropped into his palm.

"Heads she is again!" he cried, showing the Mexican eagle. "I never did see the time when I couldn't match you, anyway. So now, old socks, you can keep right on being a Texan and hating Mexicans like horny toads, and I'll denounce the Eagle Tail the minute the time is up. And I won't go near the Aragon outfit unless you're with me—is that a go? All right, shake hands on it, pard! I wouldn't quarrel with you for anything!"

"Aw, that's all right," mumbled Bud, rising and holding out his hand. "I knowed you didn't mean nothing." He sat down again after that and gazed drearily out the door.

"Say, Bud," began Phil, his eyes sparkling with

amusement, "I've got something to tell you about that dance last night. If I didn't put the crusher on Mr. Feliz Luna and Manuel del Rey! Wow! I sure wished you were there to see me do it.

"This Feliz Luna is the son of an old sugar-planter down in the hot country somewhere. He got run out by the *revoltosos* and now he's up here trying to make a winning with Gracia Aragon—uniting two noble families, and all that junk. Well, sir, of all the conceited, swelled-up little squirts you ever saw in your life he's the limit, and yet the old man kind of favors him.

"But this Manuel del Rey is the captain of the *rurales* around here and a genuine Mexican fire-eater—all buckskin and fierce *mustachios*, and smells like chili peppers and garlic—and the two of 'em were having it back and forth as to who got the next dance with Gracia.

"Well, you know how it is at a Mexican dance—everybody is supposed to be introduced to everybody else—and when I saw those two young turkey-cocks talking with their hands and eyebrows and everybody else backing off, I stepped in close and looked at the girl.

"And she's some girl, too, believe me! The biggest brown eyes you ever saw in your life, a complexion like cream, and hair—well, there never was such hair! She was fanning herself real slow, and in the language of the fan that means: 'This don't interest me a bit!' So, just to show

97

her I was wise, I pulled out my handkerchief and dropped it on the floor, and when she saw me she stopped and began to count the ribs in her fan. That was my cue—it meant she wanted to speak with me—so I stepped up and said:

" 'Excuse me, *señorita*, but while the gentlemen talk—and if the *señora*, your mother, will permit—perhaps we can enjoy a dance?'

"And say, Bud, you should have seen the way she rose to it. That girl is a sport, believe me, and the idea of those two *novios* chewing the rag while she sat out the dance didn't appeal to her at all. So she gave me her hand and away we went, with all the old ladies talking behind their fans and Manuel del Rey blowing up like a volcano in a bunch of *carambas* or worse. Gee, it was great, and she could dance like a queen.

"But here's the interesting part of it—what do you think she asked me, after we'd had our little laugh? Well, you don't need to get so grouchy about it—she asked about *you!*"

"Aw!"

"Yes, she did! So you see what you get for throwing her down!"

"What did she ask?"

"Well, she asked—" here he stopped and laughed—"she asked if you were a cowboy!"

"No!" cried Bud, pleased in spite of himself. "What does she know about cowboys?"

"Oh, she's wise!" declared Phil. "She's been

98

to school twice in Los Angeles and seen the wild West show. Yes, sir, she's just like an American girl and speaks English perfectly. She told me she didn't like the Mexican men—they were too stuck on themselves—and say, Bud, when I told her you were a genuine Texas cowboy, what do you think she said?"

"W'y, I don't know," answered Bud, smiling broadly in anticipation; "what did she say?"

"She said she'd like to know you!"

"She did not!" came back Bud with sudden spirit.

Though he laughed the thought away, a great burden seemed to be lifted from his heart, and he found himself happy again.

X

To an American, accustomed to getting things done first and talking about it afterward, there is nothing so subtly irritating as the Old World formalism, the polite evasiveness of the Mexicans; and yet, at times, they can speak to the point with the best of us.

For sixty days Don Cipriano Aragon had smiled and smiled and then, suddenly, as the last day of their mining permit passed by and there was no record of a denouncement by Cruz Mendez, he appeared at the Eagle Tail mine with a pistol in his belt and a triumphant sneer on his lips.

Behind him rode four Mexicans, fully armed, and they made no reply to De Lancey's polite *"Buenos días!"*

"Take your poor things," burst out Aragon, pointing contemptuously at their tent and beds, "and your low, *pelado* Mexican—and go! This mine no longer stands in the name of Cruz Mendez, and I want it for myself! No, not a word!" he cried, as De Lancey opened his mouth to explain. "Nothing! Only go!"

"No, *señor*," said Hooker, dropping his hand to his six-shooter which hung low by his leg and stepping forward, "we will not go!"

"What?" stormed Aragon. "You—"

"Be careful there!" warned Bud, suddenly fixing his eyes on one of the four retainers. "If you touch that gun I'll kill you!"

There was a pause, in which the Mexicans sat frozen to their saddles, and then De Lancey broke the silence.

"You must not think, Señor Aragon," he began, speaking with a certain bitterness, "that you can carry your point like this. My friend here is a Texan, and if your men stir he will kill them. But there is a law in this country for every man—what is it that you want?"

"I want this mining claim," shouted Aragon, "that you have so unjustly taken from me through that scoundrel Mendez! And I want you to step aside, so that I can set up my monuments and take possession of it."

"The Señor Aragon has not been to the *agente mineral* to-day," suggested De Lancey suavely. "If he had taken the trouble he would not—"

"Enough!" cried Aragon, still trying to carry it off cavalierly. "I sent my servant to the mining agent yesterday and he reported that the permit had lapsed."

"If he had taken the pains to inquire for new permits, however," returned De Lancey, "he would have found that one has been issued to me. I am now a Mexican citizen, like yourself."

"*You!*" screamed Aragon, his eyes bulging with astonishment; and then, finding himself tricked, he turned suddenly upon one of his retainers and struck him with his whip.

"Son of a goat!" he stormed. "Pig! Is this the way you obey my orders?"

But though he raved and scolded, he had gone too far, and there was no putting the blame on his servant. In his desire to humiliate the hated gringos he had thrown down all his guards, and even De Lancey saw all too clearly what his intentions in the matter had been.

"Spare your cursing, Señor Aragon," he said, "and after this," he added, "you can save your pretty words, too—for somebody else. We shall remain here and hold our property."

"Ha! You *Americanos*!" exclaimed Aragon, as he chewed bitterly on his defeat. "You will rob us of everything—even our government. So you are a Mexican citizen, eh? You must value this barren mine very highly to give up the protection of your government. But perhaps you are acquainted with a man named Kruger?" he sneered.

"*He* would sell his honor any time to defraud a Mexican of his rights, and I doubt not it was he who sent you here. Yes, I have known it from the first—but I will fool him yet!

"So you are a Mexican citizen, Señor De Lancey? *Bien*, then you shall pay the full price of your citizenship. Before our law you are now no more than that poor *pelado*, Mendez. You cannot appeal now to your consul at

Gadsden—you are only a Mexican! Very well!"

He shrugged his shoulders and smiled significantly.

"No," retorted De Lancey angrily; "you are right—I cannot appeal to my government! But let me tell you something, Señor Mexicano! An American needs no government to protect him—he has his gun, and that is enough!"

"Yes," added Bud, who had caught the drift of the last, "and he has his friends, too; don't forget that!" He strode over toward Aragon and menaced him with a threatening finger.

"If anything happens to my friend," he hissed, "you will have *me* to whip! And now, *señor*," he added, speaking in the idiom of the country, "go with God—and do not come back!"

"Pah!" spat back Aragon, his hate for the pushing foreigner showing in every glance; "I will beat you yet! And I pray God the *revoltosos* come this way, if they take the full half of my cattle—so long as they get you two!"

"Very well," nodded Bud as Aragon and his men turned away, "but be careful you do not send any!

"Good!" he continued, smiling grimly at the pallid Phil; "now we got him where we want him—out in the open. And I'll just remember them four *paisanos* he had with him—they're his handy men, the boys with nerve—and don't never let one of 'em catch you out after dark."

De Lancey sat down on a rock and wiped his face.

"Heavens, Bud," he groaned, "I never would have believed it of him—I thought he was on the square. But it just goes to prove the old saying— every Mexican has got a streak of yellow in him somewhere. All you've got to do is to trust him long enough and you'll find it out. Well, we're hep to Mr. Aragon, all right!"

"I have never seen one of these polite, palavering Mexicans yet," observed Bud sagely, "that wasn't crooked. And this feller Aragon is mean, to boot. But that's a game," he added, "that two can play at. I don't know how you feel, Phil, but we been kinder creeping and slipping around so long that I'm all cramped up inside. Never suffered more in my life than the last sixty days—being polite to that damn' Mexican. Now it's our turn. Are you game?"

"Count me in!" cried De Lancey, rising from his rock. "What's the play?"

"Well, we'll go into town pretty soon," grinned Bud, "and if I run across old Aragon, or any one of them four bad Mexicans, I'm going to make a show. And as for that big brindle dog of his— well, he's sure going to get roped and drugged if he don't mend his ways. Come on, let's ketch up our horses and go in for a little time."

"I'll go you!" agreed Phil with enthusiasm, and half an hour later, each on his favorite horse, they were clattering down the cañon. At the turn of the trail, where it swung into the Aragon lane, Bud took down his rope and smiled in anticipation.

"You go on ahead," he said, shaking out his loop, "and I'll try to put the catgut on Brindle."

"Off like a flash!" answered De Lancey, and, putting the spurs to his fiery bay, he went dashing down the street, scattering chickens and hogs in all directions. Behind came Bud, rolling jovially in his saddle, and as the dogs rushed out after his pardner he twirled his loop once and laid it skillfully across the big brindle's back. But roping dogs is a difficult task at best, and Bud was out of practise. The sudden blow struck Brindle to the ground and the loop came away unfilled. The Texan laughed, shifting in his saddle.

"Come again!" commented Bud, leaning side-wise as he coiled his rope, and as the womenfolk and idlers came rushing to see what had happened he turned Copper Bottom in his tracks and came back like a streak of light.

"Look out, you ugly man's dog!" he shouted, whirling his rope as he rode; and then, amid a chorus of indignant protests, he chased the yelping Brindle down the lane and through a hole in the fence. Then, with no harm done, he rode back up the street, smiling amiably and looking for more dogs to rope.

In the door of the store stood Aragon, pale with fury, but Bud appeared not to see him. His eyes were turned rather toward the house where, on the edge of the veranda, Gracia Aragon and her mother stood staring at his antics.

"Good morning to you, ladies!" he saluted, taking off his sombrero with a flourish. "Lovely weather, ain't it?" And with his tongue in his cheek and a roguish glance at Aragon, who was stricken dumb by this last effrontery, he went rollicking after his pardner, sending back a series of joyous yips.

"Now that sure does me good," he confided to Phil, as they rode down between cottonwoods and struck into the muddy creek. "No sense in it, but it gets something out of my system that has kept me from feeling glad. Did you see me bowing to the ladies? Some class to that bow— no? You want to look out—I got my eye on that gal, and I'm sure a hard one to head. Only thing is, I wouldn't like the old man for a father-in-law the way matters stand between us now."

He laughed boisterously at this witticism, and the little Mexican children, playing among the willows, crouched and lay quiet like rabbits. Along the sides of the rocky hills, where the peons had their mud-and-rock houses, mothers came anxiously to open doors; and as they jogged along up the river the Chinese gardeners, working in each separate nook and eddy of the storm-washed creek-bed, stopped grubbing to gaze at them inquiringly.

"Wonder what's the matter with them chinks?" observed Bud, when his happiness had ceased to effervesce. "They sit up like a village of prairie-dogs. Whole country seems to be on the rubberneck. Must be something doing."

"That's right," agreed Phil. "Did you notice how those peons scattered when I rode down the street? Maybe there's been some *insurrectos* through. But say—listen!"

He stopped his horse, and in the silence a bugle-call came down the wind from the direction of Fortuna.

"Soldiers!" he said. "Now where did they come from? I was in Fortuna day before yesterday, and—well, look at that!"

From the point of the hill just ahead of them a line of soldiers came into view, marching two abreast, with a mounted officer in the lead.

"Aha!" exclaimed Bud with conviction; "they've started something down below. This is that bunch of Federals that we saw drilling up at Agua Negra."

"Yep," admitted De Lancey regretfully; "I guess you're right for once—the open season for rebels has begun."

They drew out of the road and let them pass—a long, double line of shabby infantrymen, still wearing their last-year's straw hats and summer uniforms and trudging along in flapping sandals.

In front were two men bearing lanterns, to

search out the way by night; slatternly women, the inevitable camp-followers, trotted along at the sides with their bundles and babies; and as the little brown men from Zacatecas, each burdened with his heavy gun and a job lot of belts and packs, shuffled patiently past the Americans, they flashed the whites of their eyes and rumbled a chorus of "Adios!"

"*Adios, Americanos!*" they called, gazing enviously at their fine horses, and Phil in his turn touched his hat and wished them all God-speed.

"Poor devils!" he murmured, as the last tottering camp-followers, laden with their burdens, brought up the rear and a white-skinned Spanish officer saluted from his horse. "What do those little *pelónes* know about liberty and justice, or the game that is being played? Wearing the same uniforms that they had when they fought for Diaz, and now they are fighting for Madero. Next year they may be working for Orozco or Huerta or Salazar."

"Sure," muttered Bud; "but that ain't the question. If the's rebels in the hills, where do *we* get off?"

XI

The plaza at Fortuna, ordinarily so peaceful and sleepy, was alive with hurrying men when Bud and Phil reached town. Over at the station a special engine was wheezing and blowing after its heavy run and, from the train of commandeered ore-cars behind, a swarm of soldiers were leaping to the ground. On the porch of the hotel Don Juan de Dios Brachamonte was making violent signals with his hands, and as they rode up he hurried out to meet them.

"My gracious, boys," he cried, "it's a good thing you came into town! Bernardo Bravo has come over the mountains and he's marching to take Moctezuma!"

"Why, that doesn't make any difference to us!" answered Phil. "Moctezuma is eighty miles from here—and look at all the soldiers. How many men has Bernardo got?"

"Well, that I do not know," responded Don Juan; "some say more and some less, but if you boys hadn't come in I would have sent a man to fetch you. Just as soon as a revolution begins the back country becomes unsafe for Americans. Some of these low characters are likely to murder you if they think you have any money."

"Well, we haven't," put in Bud; "but we've

got a mine—and we're going to keep it, too."

"Aw, Bernardo Bravo hasn't got any men!" scoffed Phil. "I bet this is a false alarm. He got whipped out of his boots over in Chihauhua last fall, and he's been up in the Sierra Madres ever since. Probably come down to steal a little beef.

"Why, Don Juan, Bud and I lived right next to a trail all last year and if we'd listened to one-tenth of the *revoltoso* stories we heard we wouldn't have taken out an ounce of gold. I'm going to get my denouncement papers to-morrow, and I'll bet you we work that mine all summer and never know the difference. These rebels won't hurt you any, anyhow!"

"No! Only beg a little grub!" added Bud scornfully. "Come on, Phil; let's go over and look at the soldiers—it's that bunch of Yaquis we saw up at Agua Negra."

They tied their horses to the rack and, leaving the solicitous Don Juan to sputter, hurried over to the yard. From the heavy metal ore-cars, each a rolling fortress in itself, the last of the active Yaquis were helping out their women and pet dogs, while the rest, talking and laughing in high spirits, were strung out along the track in a perfunctory line.

If the few officers in command had ever attempted to teach them military discipline, the result was not apparent in the line they formed; but any man who looked at their swarthy faces,

110

the hawklike profiles, and deep-set, steady eyes, would know that they were fighters.

After all, a straight line on parade has very little to do with actual warfare, and these men had proved their worth under fire.

To be sure, it was the fire of Mexican guns, and perhaps that was why the officers were so quiet and unassertive; for every one of these big, upstanding Indians had been captured in the Yaqui wars and deported to the henequen fields of Yucatan to die in the miasma and heat.

But they had come from a hardy breed and the whirligig of fortune was flying fast—Madero defeated Porfirio Diaz; fresh revolutions broke out against the victor, and, looking about in desperation for soldiers to fill his ranks, Madero fell upon the Yaquis.

Trained warriors for generations, of a race so fierce that the ancient Aztecs had been turned aside by them in their empire-founding migration, they were the very men to whip back the rebels, if he could but win them to his side.

So Madero had approached Chief Bule, whom Diaz had taken under a flag of truce, and soon the agreement was made. In return for faithful service, Mexico would give back to the Indians the one thing they had been fighting a hundred and sixty years to attain, their land along the Rio Yaqui; and there they should be permitted to live in peace as their ancestors had done before them.

And so, with a thousand or more of his men, the crafty old war-chief had taken service in the Federal army, though his mind, poisoned perhaps by the treachery he had suffered, was not entirely free from guile.

"It is the desire of the Yaquis," he had said, when rebuked for serving under the hated flag of Mexico, "to kill Mexicans, And," he added grimly, "the Federals at this time seem best able to give us guns for that purpose."

But it had been a year now since Bule had passed his word and, though they had battled valiantly, their land had not been given back to them. The wild Yaquis, the irreconcilables who never came down from the hills, had gone on the war-path again, but Bule and his men still served.

Only in two things did they disobey their officers—they would not stack their arms, and they would not retreat while there were still more Mexicans to be killed. Otherwise they were very good soldiers.

But now, after the long campaign in Chihuahua and a winter of idleness at Agua Negra, they were marching south toward their native land and, in spite of the stern glances of their leaders, they burst forth in weird Yaqui songs which, if their words had been known, might easily have caused their Mexican officers some slight uneasiness.

It was, in fact, only a question of days, months, or years until the entire Yaqui contingent would desert, taking their arms and ammunition with them.

"Gee! what a bunch of men!" exclaimed Bud, as he stood off and admired their stark forms.

"There's some genuine fighters for you," he observed to Phil; and a giant Yaqui, standing near, returned his praise with a smile.

"W'y, hello there, Amigo!" hailed Bud, jerking his head in a friendly salute. "That's a feller I was making signs to up in Agua Negra," he explained. "Dogged if I ain't stuck on these Yaquis—they're all men, believe me!"

"Good workers, all right," conceded De Lancey, "but I'd hate to have 'em get after me with those guns. They say they've killed a lot of Americans, one time and another."

"Well, if they did it was for being caught in bad company," said Hooker. "I'd take a chance with 'em any time—but if you go into their country with a Mexican escort they'll kill you on general principles. Say," he cried impulsively, "I'm going over to talk with Amigo!"

With a broad grin on his honest face he advanced toward the giant Yaqui and shook hands ceremoniously.

"Where you go?" he inquired in Spanish, at the same time rolling a cigarette and asking by a sign for a match.

"Moctezuma," answered the Indian gravely. Then, as Bud offered him the makings, he, too, rolled a cigarette and they smoked for a minute in silence.

"You live here?" inquired the Yaqui at last.

"Come here," corrected Bud. "I have a mine—ten miles—over there."

He pointed with the flat of his hand, Indian fashion, and Amigo nodded understandingly.

He was a fine figure of a man, standing six feet or better in his well-cut sandals and handling his heavy Mauser as a child would swing a stick. Across his broad chest he wore a full cartridge-belt, and around his waist he had two more, filled to the last hole with cartridges and loaded clips. At his feet lay his blanket, bound into a tight roll, and a canteen and coffee-cup completed his outfit, which, so far as impedimenta were concerned, was simplicity itself.

But instead of the cheap linen uniform of the Federals he was dressed in good American clothes—a striped shirt, overalls, and a sombrero banded with a bright ribbon—and in place of the beaten, hunted look of those poor conscripts he had the steady gaze of a free man.

They stood and smoked for a few moments, talking briefly, and then, as the Yaquis closed up their ranks and marched off to make camp for the night, Bud presented his strange friend with the sack of tobacco and went back to join his pardner.

That evening the plaza was filled with the wildest rumors, and another train arrived

114

during the night, but through it all Bud and Phil remained unimpressed. In the morning the soldiers went marching off down the trail, leaving a great silence where all had been bugle-calls and excitement, and then the first fugitive came in from down below.

He was an old Mexican, with trembling beard and staring eyes, and he told a tale of outrage that made their blood run cold. The red-flaggers had come to his house at night; they had killed his wife and son, left him upon the ground for dead, and carried off his daughter, a prisoner.

But later, when the *comisario* questioned him sharply, it developed that he lived not far away, had no daughter to lose, and was, in fact, only a crazed old man who told for truth that which he feared would happen.

Notwithstanding the dénouement, his story stirred the Mexican population to the depths, and when Bud and Phil tried to hire men to push the work on the mine, they realized that their troubles had begun. Not only was it impossible to engage laborers at any price, but on the following day Cruz Mendez, with his wife and children and all his earthy possessions on his burros, came hurrying in from the camp and told them he could serve them no more.

"It is my woman," he explained; "my Maria! Ah, if those *revoltosos* should see Maria they would steal her before my eyes!"

So he was given his pay and the fifty dollars he had earned and, after the customary *"Muchas gracias,"* and with the faithful Maria by his side, he went hurrying off to the store.

And now in crowded vehicles, with armed men riding in front and behind, the refugees from Moctezuma and the hot country began to pour into town, adding by their very haste to the panic of all who saw them.

They were the rich property-owners who, having been subjected to forced contribution before, were now fleeing at the first rumor of danger, bringing their families with them to escape any being held for ransom.

In half a day the big hotel presided over by Don Juan de Dios Brachamonte was swarming with staring-eyed country mothers and sternly subdued families of children; and finally, to add éclat to the occasion and compensate for the general confusion, Don Cipriano Aragon y Tres Palacios came driving up to the door with his wife and the smiling Gracia.

If she had been in any fear of capture by bold marauders, Gracia Aragon did not show it now, as she sprang lightly from the carriage and waited upon her lady mother. Perhaps, after a year or more of rumors and alarms, she had come to look upon impending revolutionary conflicts as convenient excuses for a trip to town, a long stop at the hotel, and even a dash to gay Gadsden in case the rebels pressed close.

However that may be, while Don Juan exerted himself to procure them a good room she endured the gaze of the American guests with becoming placidity and, as that took some time, she even ventured to look the Americans over and make some comments to her mother.

And then—or as it seemed to Bud—the mother glanced up quickly and fixed her eyes upon *him*. After that he was in less of a hurry to return to the mine, and Phil said they would stay inside for a week. But as for Don Cipriano, when he came across them it was with malignant insolence and he abruptly turned his back.

At La Fortuna he was the lord and master, with power to forbid them the place; but now once more the fortunes of war had turned against him, and he was forced to tolerate their presence.

The band played in the plaza that evening, it being Thursday of the week, and as the cornet led with "La Paloma," and the bass viol and guitars beat the measure, all feet seemed to turn in that direction, and the fear of the raiders was stilled.

Around and around the band-stand and in and out beneath the trees the pleasure-loving maidens from down below walked decorously with their mothers; and the little band of Fortuna Americans, to whom life for some months had been a trifle burdensome, awoke suddenly to the beauty of the evening.

And among the rest of the maidens, but far more ravishing and high-bred, walked Gracia Aragon, at whom Bud in particular stole many secret glances from beneath the broad brim of his hat, hoping that by some luck the *insurrectos* would come upon the town, and he could defend her—he alone. For he felt that he could do it against any hundred Mexicans that ever breathed.

XII

In its inception the Fortuna hotel had not been intended for the use of Mexicans—in fact, its rates were practically prohibitive for any one not being paid in gold—but, since most of the Americans had left, and seven dollars a day Mex was no deterrent to the rich refugee landowners, it became of a sudden international, with a fine mixture of purse-proud Spaniards and race-proud American adventurers.

Not a very pleasing combination for the parents of romantic damsels destined for some prearranged marriage of state, but very exciting for the damsels and most provocative to the Americans.

After the promenade in the plaza the mothers by common consent preempted the up-stairs reception-room, gathering their precious charges in close; while the Americans, after their custom, forgathered in the lobby, convenient to the bar. Hot arguments about the revolution, and predictions of events to come, served to pass the early evening, with many scornful glances at the Mexican dandies who went so insolently up the stairs. And then, as the refugees retired to their apartments and the spirit of adventure rose uppermost, Phil De Lancey made a dash out into the darkness and came back with a Mexican string band.

"A serenade, boys!" he announced, as the musicians filed sheepishly into the hotel. "Our guests, the fair *señoritas*, you know! We'll make those young Mexican dudes look like two-spots before the war is over. Who's game now for a song beneath the windows? You know the old stand-bys—'La Paloma' and 'Teresita Mia'— and you want to listen to me sing 'Me Gustan Todas' to Gracia, the fairest of the fair! Come on, fellows, out in the plaza, and then listen to the old folks cuss!"

They adjourned then, after a drink for courage, to the moonlight and the plaza; and there, beneath the shuttered windows and vacant balconies, the guitars and violins took up "La Paloma," while Phil and a few brave spirits sang.

A silence followed their first attempt, as well as their second and third, and the *comisario* of police, a mild creature owned and paid by the company, came around and made a few ineffectual protests.

But inside the company's concession, where by common consent the militant *rurales* kept their hands off, the Americans knew they were safe, and they soon jollied the *comisario* into taking a drink and departing. Then De Lancey took up the burden, and the string band, hired by the hour, strummed on as if for eternity.

One by one the windows opened; fretful fathers stepped out on the balcony and, bound by the custom and convention of the country, thanked them and bade them good night. But the two windows behind which the Señor Aragon and his family reposed did not open and, though the dwindling band stood directly under their balcony, and all knew that his daughter was the fairest of the fair, Don Cipriano did not wish them good night.

Perhaps he recognized the leading tenor—and the big voice of Bud Hooker, trying to still the riot—but, however it was, he would not speak to them, and De Lancey would not quit.

"Try 'em on American music," he cried, as everyone but Bud went away in disgust, "the latest rag from Broadwa-ay, New York. Here, gimme that guitar, *hombre*, and listen to this now!"

He picked out a clever bit of syncopation and pitched his voice to a heady twang:

"Down in the garden where the red roses grow,
Oh my, I long to go!
Pluck me like a flower, cuddle me an hour,
Lovie, let me learn the Rose Red Ra-ag!"

There was some swing to that, and it seemed to make an impression, for just as he was well started on the chorus the slats of one of the shutters parted and a patch of white shone through the spaces. It was the ladies, then, who were getting interested! Phil wailed on:

"Swee-eet honey-bee, be sweet to me!
My heart is free, but here's the key!"

And then, positively, he could see that patch of white beat time. He took heart of grace at that and sang on to the end, and at a suggestion of clapping in dumb-show he gave an encore and ragged it over again.

" 'Ev'rybody's doin' it, doin' it, doin' it!' " he began, as the shadow dance ceased.

" 'Honey, I declare, it's a bear, it's a bear, it's a bear!' " he continued temptingly, and was well on his way to further extravagancies when the figure in white swiftly vanished and a door slammed hard inside the house.

Several minutes later the form of Don Juan appeared at the lower door, and in no uncertain tones he requested them to cease.

"The Señor Aragon informs me," he said, "that your music annoys him."

"Well, let him come to the balcony and say his 'buenas noches,' " answered Phil resentfully.

"The gentleman refuses to do that," responded Don Juan briefly.

"Then let him go to bed!" replied De Lancey,

strumming a few syncopated chords. "I'm singing to his daughter."

At that Don Juan came down off the porch in his slippers and they engaged in a protracted argument.

"What, don't I get a word," demanded Phil grievously, "not a pleasant look from anybody? 'Swee-eet honey-bee, be sweet to me!' " he pleaded, turning pathetically to the lady's balcony; and then, with a sudden flourish, a white handkerchief appeared through the crack of the shutters and Gracia waved him good night.

"Enough, Don Juan!" he cried, laying down the guitar with a thump. "This ends our evening's entertainment!"

After paying and thanking the stolid musicians Phil joined Bud and the pair adjourned to their room where, in the intervals of undressing, Phil favored the occupants of the adjoining apartments with an aria from "Beautiful Doll."

But for all such nights of romance and music there is always a morning afterward; and a fine tenor voice set to rag-time never helped much in the development of a mine. Though Bud had remained loyally by his friend in his evening serenade he, for one, never forgot for a moment that they were in Fortuna to work the Eagle Tail and not to win the hearts of Spanish-Mexican *señoritas*, no matter how attractive they might be.

Bud was a practical man who, if he ever made love, would doubtless do it in a perfectly businesslike way, without hiring any string bands. But at the same time he was willing to make some concessions.

"Well, go ahead and get your sleep, then," he growled, after trying three times in the morning to get his pardner up; "I'm going out to the mine!"

Then, with a saddle-gun under his knee and his six-shooter hung at his hip, he rode rapidly down the road, turning out from time to time to let long cavalcades of mules string by. The dead-eyed *arrieros*, each with his combined mule-blind and whip-lash swinging free, seemed to have very little on their minds but their pack-lashings, and yet they must be three days out from Moctezuma.

Their mules, too, were well loaded with the products of the hot country—*fanegas* of corn in red leather sacks, oranges and fruits in hand-made crates, *panoches* of sugar in balanced frames, long joints of sugar-cane for the *dulce* pedlers, and nothing to indicate either haste or flight.

Three times he let long pack-trains go by without a word, and then at last, overcome by curiosity, he inquired about the *revoltosos*.

"What *revoltosos*?" queried the old man to whom he spoke.

"Why, the men of Bernardo Bravo," answered Bud; "the men who are marching to take Moctezuma."

"When I left Moctezuma," returned the old man politely, "all was quiet—there were no *revoltosos*. Since then, I cannot say."

"But the soldiers!" cried Bud. "Surely you saw them! They were marching to fight the rebels."

"Perhaps so," shrugged the *arriero*, laying the lash of his *topojo* across the rump of a mule; "but I know nothing about it."

"No," muttered Bud, as he continued on his way; "and I'll bet nobody else does."

Inquiry showed that in this, too, he was correct. From those who traveled fast and from those who traveled slow he received the same wondering answer—the country might be filled with *revoltosos*; but as for them, they knew nothing about it.

Not until he got back to Fortuna and the busy Federals' telegraph-wire did he hear any more news of rapine and bloodshed, and the light which dawned upon him then was gradually dawning upon the whole town.

It was a false alarm, given out for purposes of state and the "higher politics" with which Mexico is cursed, and the most that was ever seen of Bernardo Bravo and his lawless men was twenty miserable creatures, half-starved, but with guns in their hand, who had come down out of the mountains east of Moctezuma and killed a few cows for beef.

Thoroughly disgusted, and yet vaguely alarmed at this bit of opera-bouffe warfare, Bud set himself resolutely to work to hunt up men for their mine, and, as many poor people were out of employment because of the general stagnation of business, he soon had ten Mexicans at his call.

Then, as Phil had dropped out of sight, he ordered supplies at the store and engaged Cruz Mendez—who had spent his fortune in three days—to pack the goods out on his mules.

They were ready to start the next morning if De Lancey could be found to order the powder and tools, and as the afternoon wore on and no Phil appeared, Bud went on a long hunt which finally discovered him in the balcony of their window, making signs in the language of the bear.*

"Say, Phil," he hailed, disregarding his pardner's obvious preoccupation; "break away for a minute and tell me what kind of powder to get to break that schist—the store closes at five o'clock, and—"

He thrust his head out the door as he spoke and paused, abashed. Through the half-closed portal

---

*   In Mexico a man who flirts with a woman, or courts her surreptitiously through the bars of her window, is called a "bear."

of the next balcony but one he beheld the golden hair of Gracia Aragon, and she fixed her brown eyes upon him with a dazzling, mischievous smile.

"O-ho!" murmured Bud, laying a compelling hand on De Lancey and backing swiftly out of range; "so this is what you're up to—talking signs! But say, Phil," he continued, beckoning him peremptorily with a jerk of his head, "I got ten men hired and a lot of grub bought, and if you don't pick out that mining stuff we're going to lose a day. So get the lady to excuse you and come on now."

"In a minute," pleaded Phil, and he went at the end of his allotted time, and perhaps it was the imp of jealousy that put strength into Hooker's arm.

"Well, that's all right," said Bud, as Phil began his laughing excuses; "but you want to remember the Maine, pardner—we didn't come down here to play the bear. When the's any love-making to be done I want to be in on it. And you want to remember that promise you made me—you said you wouldn't have a thing to do with the Aragon outfit unless I was with you!"

"Why, you aren't—you aren't jealous, are you, Bud?"

"Yes, I'm jealous," answered Hooker harshly; "jealous as the devil! And I want you to keep that promise, see?"

"Aw, Bud—" began De Lancey incredulously; but Hooker silenced him with a look. Perhaps he was really jealous, or perhaps he only said so to have his way, but Phil saw that he was in earnest, and he went quietly by his side.

But love had set his brain in a whirl, and he thought no more of his promise—only of some subtler way of meeting his inamorata, some way which Bud would fail to see.

XIII

For sixty days and more, while the weather had been turning from cold to warm and they had been laboring feebly to clear way the great slide of loose rock that covered up the ledge, the Eagle Tail mine had remained a mystery.

Whether, like the old Eagle Tail of frontier fable, it was so rich that only the eagle's head was needed to turn the chunks into twenty-dollar gold pieces; or whether, like many other frontier mines, it was nothing but a hole in the ground, was a matter still to be settled. And Bud, for one, was determined to settle it quickly.

"Come on," he said, as Phil hesitated to open up the way to the lead; "we got a month, maybe less, to get to the bottom of this; and then the hills will be lousy with rebels. If the's nothing here, we want to find out about it quick and skip—and if we strike it, by grab! the' ain't enough red-flaggers in Sonora to pry me loose from it. So show these *hombres* where to work and we'll be up against rock by the end of the week."

The original Eagle Tail tunnel had been driven into the side of a steep hill; so steep, in fact, that the loose shale stretched in long shoots from the base of the frowning porphyry dikes that crowned the tops of the hills to the bottom of the cañon.

On each side of the discovery gulch sharp ridges, perforated by the gopher-holes of the Mexicans, and the ancient workings of the Spaniards, ran directly up the hill to meet the contact. But it was against the face of the big ridge itself that Kruger had driven his drift and exploded his giant blast of dynamite, and the whole slope had been altered and covered with a slide of rock.

Against this slide, in the days when they were marking time, Bud and his pardner had directed their energies, throwing the loose stones aside, building up walls against the slip, and clearing the way to the solid schist. There, somewhere beneath the jumble of powder-riven rock, lay the ledge which, if they found it, would make them rich; and now, with single-jack and drill, they attacked the last huge fragments, blasting them into pieces and groveling deeper until they could strike the contact, where the schist and porphyry met and the gold spray had spewed up between.

It was slow work; slower than they had thought, and the gang of Mexicans that they had hired for muckers were marvels of ineptitude. Left to themselves, they accomplished nothing, since each problem they encountered seemed to present to them some element of insuperable difficulty, to solve which they either went into caucus or waited for the boss. Meanwhile they kept themselves awake by smoking cigarettes and telling stories about Bernardo Bravo.

To the Mexicans of Sonora Bernardo Bravo was the personification of all the malevolent qualities—he being a bandit chief who had turned first general and then rebel under Madero—and the fact that he had at last been driven out of Chihuahua and therefore over into Sonora, made his malevolence all the more imminent.

Undoubtedly, somewhere over to the east, where the Sierras towered like a blue wall, Bernardo and his outlaw followers were gathering for a raid, and the raid would bring death to Sonora.

He was a bad man, this Bernardo Bravo, and if half of the current stories were true, he killed men whenever they failed to give him money, and was never too hurried to take a fair daughter of the country up behind him, provided she took his fancy.

Yes, surely he was a bad man—but that did not clear away the rock.

For the first week Phil took charge of the gang, urging, directing, and cajoling them, and the work went merrily on, though rather slowly. The Mexicans liked to work for Don Felipe, he was so polite and spoke such good Spanish; but at the end of the week it developed that Bud could get more results out of them.

Every time Phil started to explain anything to one Mexican all the others stopped to listen to him, and that took time. But Bud's favorite

131

way of directing a man was by grunts and signs and bending his own back to the task. Also, he refused to understand Spanish, and cut off all long-winded explanations and suggestions by an impatient motion to go to work, which the *trabajadores* obeyed with shrugs and grins.

So Don Felipe turned powder-man and blacksmith, sharpening up the drills at the little forge they had fashioned and loading the holes with dynamite when it became necessary to break a rock, while Bud bossed the unwilling Mexicans.

In an old tunnel behind their tent they set a heavy gate, and behind it they stored their precious powder. Then came the portable forge and the blacksmith-shop, just inside the mouth of the cave, and the tent backed up against it for protection. For if there is any one thing, next to horses, that the rebels are wont to steal, it is giant powder to blow up culverts with, or to lay on the counters of timorous country merchants and frighten them into making contributions.

As for their horses, Bud kept them belled and hobbled, close to the house, and no one ever saw him without his gun. In the morning, when he got up, he took it from under his pillow and hung it on his belt, and there it stayed until bedtime.

He also kept a sharp watch on the trail, above and below, and what few men did pass through were conscious of his eye. Therefore it was all the more surprising when, one day, looking up suddenly from heaving at a great rock, he saw the big Yaqui soldier, Amigo, gazing down at him from the cut bank.

Yes, it was the same man, yet with a difference—his rifle and cartridge-belts were absent and his clothes were torn by the brush. But the same good-natured, competent smile was there, and after a few words with Bud he leaped nimbly down the bank and laid hold upon the rock. They pulled together, and the boulder that had balked Bud's gang of Mexicans moved easily for the two of them.

Then Amigo seized a crowbar and slipped it into a cranny and showed them a few things about moving rocks. For half an hour or more he worked along, seemingly bent on displaying his skill, then he sat down on the bank and watched the Mexicans with tolerant, half-amused eyes.

If he was hungry he showed it only by the cigarettes he smoked, and Hooker, studying upon the chances he would take by hiring a deserter, let him wait until he came to a decision.

"*Oyez*, Amigo," he hailed at last and, rubbing his hand around on his stomach he smiled questioningly, whereat the Yaqui nodded his head avidly.

"*Stawano!*" said Hooker. "*Ven.*" And he left his Mexicans to dawdle as they would while he led the Indian to camp. There he showed him the coffeepot and the kettle of beans by the fire, set out a slab of Dutch-oven bread and a sack of jerked beef, some stewed fruit and a can of sirup, and left him to do his worst.

In the course of half an hour or so he came back and found the Yaqui sopping up sirup with the last of the bread and humming a little tune. So they sat down and smoked a cigarette and came to the business at hand.

"Where you go?" inquired Bud; but Amigo only shrugged enigmatically.

"You like to work?" continued Bud, and the Indian broke into a smile of assent.

"*Muy bien*," said Hooker with finality; "I give Mexicans two dollars a day—I give you four. Is that enough?"

"*Sí*," nodded the Yaqui, and without more words he followed Bud back to the cut. There, in half a day, he accomplished more than all the Mexicans put together, leaping boldly up the bank to dislodge hanging boulders, boosting them by main strength up onto the ramshackle tram they had constructed, and trundling them out to the dump with the shove of a mighty hand.

He was a willing worker, using his head every minute; but though he was such a hustler and made their puny efforts seem so ineffectual by comparison, he managed in some mysterious way to gain the immediate approval of the Mexicans. Perhaps it was his all-pervasive good nature, or the respect inspired by his hardihood; perhaps the

134

qualities of natural leadership which had made him a picked man among his brother Yaquis. But when, late in the afternoon, Bud came back from a trip to the tent he found Amigo in charge of the gang, heaving and struggling and making motions with his head.

"Good enough!" he muttered, after watching him for a minute in silence, and leaving the new boss in command, he went back and started supper.

That was the beginning of a new day at the Eagle Tail, and when De Lancey came back from town—whither he went whenever he could conjure up an errand—he found that, for once, he had not been missed.

Bud was doing the blacksmithing, Amigo was directing the gang, and a fresh mess of beans was on the fire, the first kettleful having gone to reenforce the Yaqui's backbone. But they were beans well spent, and Bud did not regret the raid on his grub-pile. If he could get half as much work for what he fed the Mexicans he could well rest content.

"But how did this Indian happen to find you?" demanded Phil, when his pardner had explained his acquisition. "Say, he must have deserted from his company when they brought them back from Moctezuma!"

"More'n likely," assented Bud. "He ain't talking much, but I notice he keeps his eye out—

they'd shoot him for a deserter if they could ketch him. I'd hate to see him go that way."

"Well, if he's as good as this, let's take care of him!" cried Phil with enthusiasm. "I'll tell you, Bud, there's something big coming off pretty soon and I'd like to stay around town a little more if I could. I want to keep track of things."

"F'r instance?" suggested Hooker dryly. It had struck him that Phil was spending a good deal of time in town already.

"Well, there's this revolution. Sure as shooting they're going to pull one soon. There's two thousand Mexican miners working at Fortuna, and they say every one of 'em has got a rifle buried. Now they're beginning to quit and drift out into the hills, and we're likely to hear from them any time."

"All the more reason for staying in camp, then," remarked Bud. "I'll tell you, Phil, I need you here. That dogged ledge is lost, good and plenty, and I need you to say where to dig. We ain't doing much better than old Aragon did—just rooting around in that rock-pile—let's do a little timbering, and sink."

"You can't timber that rock," answered De Lancey decidedly. "And besides, it's cheaper to make a cut twenty feet deep than it is to tunnel or sink a shaft. Wait till we get to that porphyry contact—then we'll know where we're at."

"All right," grumbled Bud; "but seems like

136

we're a long time getting there. What's the news downtown?"

"Well, the fireworks have begun again over in Chihuahua—Orozco and Salazar and that bunch—but it seems there was something to this Moctezuma scare, after all. I was talking to an American mining man from down that way and he told me that the Federals marched out to where the rebels were and then sat down and watched them cross the river without firing on them—some kind of an understanding between Bernardo Bravo and these blackleg Federals.

"The only fighting there was was when a bunch of twenty Yaquis got away from their officers in the rough country and went after Bernardo Bravo by their lonesome. That threw a big scare into him, too, but he managed to fight them off—and if I was making a guess I'd bet that your Yaqui friend was one of that fighting twenty."

"I reckon," assented Bud; "but don't you say nothing. I need that *hombre* in my business. Come on, let's go up and look at that cut—I come across an old board to-day, down in the muck, and I bet you it's a piece that Kruger left. Funny we don't come across some of his tools, though, or the hole where the powder went off."

"When we do that," observed Phil, "we'll be where we're going. Nothing to do then but lay off the men and wait till I get my papers. That's why I say don't hurry so hard—we haven't got our title to this claim, pardner, and we won't get it, either—not for some time yet. Suppose you'd hit this ledge—"

"Well, if I hit it," remarked Bud, "I'll stay with it—you can trust me for that. Hello, what's the Yaqui found?"

As they came up the cut Amigo quit work and, while the Mexicans followed suit and gathered expectantly behind him, he picked up three rusty drills and an iron drill-spoon and presented them to Bud.

Evidently he had learned the object of their search from the Mexicans, but if he looked for any demonstrations of delight at sight of these much-sought-for tools he was doomed to disappointment, for both Bud and Phil had schooled themselves to keep their faces straight.

"Um-m," said Bud, "old drills, eh? Where you find them?"

The Yaqui led the way to the face of the cut and showed the spot, a hole beneath the pile of riven rock; and a Mexican, not to be outdone, grabbed up a handful of powdered porphyry and indicated where the dynamite had pulverized it.

"*Bien*," said Phil, pawing solemnly around in the bottom of the hole; and then, filling his handkerchief with fine dirt, he carried it down to the creek. There, in a miner's pan, he washed it out carefully, slopping the waste over the edge and swirling the water around until at last only a little dirt was left in the bottom of the pan. Then, while all the Mexicans looked on, he tailed this toward the edge, scanning the last remnant for gold—and quit without a color.

"*Nada*!" he cried, throwing down the pan, and in some way the Mexicans sensed the fact that the mine had turned out a failure. Three times he went back to the cut and scooped up the barren dust, and then he told the men they could quit.

"No more work!" he said, affecting a dejected bitterness. "*No hay nada*—there is nothing!" And with this sad, but by no means unusual, ending to their labors, the Mexicans went away to their camp, speculating among themselves as to whether they could get their pay. But when the last of them had gone Phil beckoned Bud into the tent and showed him a piece of quartz.

"Just take a look at that!" he said, and a single glance told Hooker that it was full of fine particles of gold.

"I picked that up when they weren't looking," whispered De Lancey, his eyes dancing with triumph. "It's the same rock—the same as Kruger's!"

"Well, put 'er there, then, pardner!" cried Bud, grabbing at De Lancey's hand. "We've struck it!"

And with a broad grin on their deceitful faces they danced silently around the tent, after which they paid off the Mexicans and bade them "*Adios*!"

XIV

It is a great sensation—striking it rich—one of the greatest in the world.

Some men punch a burro over the desert all their lives in the hope of achieving it once; Bud and Phil had taken a chance, and the prize lay within their grasp. Only a little while now—a month, maybe, if the officials were slow—and the title would be theirs.

The Mexican miners, blinded by their ignorance, went their way, well contented to get their money. Nobody knew. There was nothing to do but to wait. But to wait, as some people know, is the hardest work in the world.

For the first few days they lingered about the mine, gloating over it in secret, laughing back and forth, singing gay songs—then, as the ecstasy passed and the weariness of waiting set in, they went two ways. Some fascination, unexplained to Bud, drew De Lancey to the town. He left in the morning and came back at night, but Hooker stayed at the mine.

Day and night, week-days and Sundays, he watched it jealously, lest someone should slip in and surprise their secret—and for company he had his pet horse, Copper Bottom, and the Yaqui Indian, Amigo.

Ignacio was the Indian's real name, for the Yaquis are all good Catholics and named uniformly after the saints; but Bud had started to call him Amigo, or friend, and Ignacio had conferred the same name on him.

Poor Ignacio! his four-dollar-a-day job had gone glimmering in half a day, but when the Mexican laborers departed he lingered around the camp, doing odd jobs, until he won a place for himself.

At night he slept up in the rocks, where no treachery could take him unaware, but at the first peep of dawn it was always Amigo who arose and lit the fire.

Then, if no one got up, he cooked a breakfast after his own ideas, boiling the coffee until it was as strong as lye, broiling meat on sticks, and went to turn out the horses.

With the memory of many envious glances cast at Copper Bottom, Hooker had built a stout corral, where he kept the horses up at night, allowing them to graze close-hobbled in the daytime.

A Mexican *insurrecto* on foot is a contradiction of terms, if there are any horses or mules in the country, and several bands of ex-miners from Fortuna had gone through their camp in that condition, with new rifles in their hands. But if they had any designs on the Eagle Tail livestock they speedily gave them up; for, while he would feed them and even listen to their false tales of patriotism, Bud had no respect for numbers when it came to admiring his horse.

Even with the Yaqui, much as he trusted him, he had reservations about Copper Bottom; and once, when he found him petting him and stroking his nose, he shook his head forbiddingly. And from that day on, though he watered Copper Bottom and cared for his wants, Amigo was careful never to caress him.

But in all other matters, even to lending him his gun, Bud trusted the Yaqui absolutely. It was about a week after he came to camp that Amigo sighted a deer, and when Bud lent him his rifle he killed it with a single shot.

Soon afterward he came loping back from a scouting trip and made signs for the gun again, and this time he brought in a young peccary, which he roasted in a pit, Indian style. After that, when the meat was low, Bud sent him out to hunt, and each time he brought back a wild hog or a deer for every cartridge.

The one cross under which the Yaqui suffered was the apparent failure of the mine and, after slipping up into the cut a few times, he finally came back radiant.

"*Mira!*" he said, holding out a piece of rock; and when Hooker gazed at the chunk of quartz he pointed to the specks of gold and grunted "*Oro!*"

"*Seguro!*" answered Bud, and going down into

his pocket, he produced another like it. At this the Yaqui cocked his head to one side and regarded him strangely.

"Why you no dig gold?" he asked at last, and then Bud told him his story.

"We have an enemy," he said, "who might steal it from us. So now we wait for papers. When we get them, we dig!"

"Ah!" breathed Amigo, his face suddenly clearing up. "And can I work for you then?"

"*Sí*," answered Bud, "for four dollars a day. But now you help me watch, so nobody comes."

"*Stawano!*" exclaimed the Indian, well satisfied, and after that he spent hours on the hilltop, his black head thrust out over the crest like a chucka-walla lizard as he conned the land below.

So the days went by until three weeks had passed and still no papers came. As his anxiety increased Phil fell into the habit of staying in town overnight, and finally he was gone for two days. The third day was drawing to a close, and Bud was getting restless, when suddenly he beheld the Yaqui bounding down the hill in great leaps and making signs down the cañon.

"Two men," he called, dashing up to the tent; "one of them a *rural*!"

"Why a *rural*?" asked Bud, mystified.

"To take me!" cried Amigo, striking himself vehemently on the breast. "Lend me your rifle!"

"No," answered Bud, after a pause; "you might get me into trouble. Run and hide in the rocks—I will signal you when to come back."

"*Muy bien*," said the Yaqui obediently and, turning, he went up over rocks like a mountain-sheep, bounding from boulder to boulder until he disappeared among the hilltops. Then, as Bud brought in his horse and shut him hastily inside the corral, the two riders came around the point—a *rural* and Aragon!

Now in Mexico a *rural*, as Bud well knew, means trouble—and Aragon meant more trouble, trouble for him. Certainly, so busy a man as Don Cipriano would not come clear to his camp to help capture a Yaqui deserter. Bud sensed it from the start that this was another attempt to get possession of their mine, and he awaited their coming grimly.

"*'S tardes*," he said in reply to the *rural*'s salute, and then he stood silent before his tent, looking them over shrewdly. The *rural* was a hard-looking citizen, as many of them are, but on this occasion he seemed a trifle embarrassed, glancing inquiringly at Aragon. As for Aragon, he was gazing at a long line of jerked meat which Amigo had hung out to dry, and his drooped eyes opened up suddenly as he turned his cold regard upon Hooker.

"*Señor*," he said, speaking with an accusing harshness, "we are looking for the men who are stealing my cattle, and I see we have not far to go. Where did you get that meat?"

"I got it from a deer," returned Bud. "There is his hide on the fence; you can see it if you'll look."

The *rural*, glad to create a diversion, rode over and examined the hide and came back satisfied, but Aragon was not so easily appeased.

"By what right," he demanded truculently, "do you, an American, kill deer in our country? Have you the special permit which is required?"

"No, *señor*," answered Hooker soberly; "the deer was killed by a Mexican I have working for me."

"Ha!" sneered Aragon, and then he paused, balked.

"Where is this Mexican?" inquired the *rural*, his professional instincts aroused, and while Bud was explaining that he was out in the hills somewhere, Aragon spurred his horse up closer and peered curiously into his tent.

"What are you looking for?" demanded Hooker sharply, and then Aragon showed his hand.

"I am looking for the drills and drillspoon," he said; "the ones you stole when you took my mine!"

"Then get back out of there," cried Bud, seizing his horse by the bit and throwing him back on his haunches; "and stay out!" he added, as he dropped his hand to his gun. "But if the

145

rural wishes to search," he said, turning to that astounded official, "he is welcome to do so."

"*Muchas gracias*, no!" returned the *rural*, shaking a finger in front of his face, and then he strode over to where Aragon was muttering and spoke in a low tone.

"No!" dissented Aragon, shaking his head violently. "No—no! I want this man arrested!" he cried, turning vindictively upon Bud. "He has stolen my tools—my mine—my land! He has no business here—no title! This land is mine, and I tell him to go! *Pronto*!" he shouted, menacing Hooker with his riding-whip, but Bud only shifted his feet and stopped listening to his excited Spanish.

"No, *señor*," he said, when it was all over, "this claim belongs to my pardner, De Lancey. You have no—"

"Ha! De Lancey!" jeered Aragon, suddenly indulging himself in a sardonic laugh. "De Lancey! Ha, ha!"

"What's the matter?" cried Hooker, as the *rural* joined in with a derisive smirk. "Say, speak up, *hombre*!" he threatened, stepping closer as his eyes took on a dangerous gleam. "And let me tell you now," he added, "that if any man touches a hair of his head I'll kill him like a dog!"

The *rural* backed his horse away, as if suddenly discovering that the American was dangerous, and then, saluting respectfully as he took his leave, he said:

"The Señor De Lancey is in jail!"

They whirled their horses at that and galloped off down the cañon, and as Bud gazed after them he burst into a frenzy of curses. Then, with the one thought of setting Phil free, he ran out to the corral and hurled the saddle on his horse.

It was through some chicanery, he knew— some low-down trick on the part of Aragon—that his pardner had been imprisoned, and he swore to have him out or know the reason why. Either that or he would go after Aragon and take it out of his hide.

It was outside Bud's simple code even to question his pardner's innocence; but, innocent or guilty, he would have him out if he had to tear down the jail.

So he slapped his saddle-gun into the sling, reached for his quirt, and went dashing down the cañon. At a turn in the road he came suddenly upon Aragon and the *rural*, split a way between them, and leaned forward as Copper Bottom burned up the trail.

It was long since the shiny sorrel had been given his head, and he needed neither whip not spurs—but a mile or two down the arroyo Bud suddenly reined him in and looked behind. Then he turned abruptly up the hillside and jumped

147

him out on a point, looked again, and rode slowly back up the trail.

Aragon and the *rural* were not in sight—the question was, were they following? For a short distance he rode warily, not to be surprised in his suspicion; then, as he found tracks turning back, he gave head to his horse and galloped swiftly to camp.

The horses of the men he sought stood at the edge of the mine-dump and, throwing his bridle-rein down beside them, Bud leaped off and ran up the cut. Then he stopped short and reached for his six-shooter. The two men were up at the end, down on their knees, and digging like dogs after a rabbit.

So eager were they in their search, so confident in their fancied security, that they never looked up from their work, and the tramp of Hooker's boots was drowned by their grubbing until he stood above them. There he paused, his pistol in hand, and waited grimly for developments.

"Ha!" cried Aragon, grabbing at a piece of quartz that came up. "*Aqui lo tengo!*" He drew a second piece from his pocket and placed them together. "It is the same!" he said.

Still half-buried in the excavation, he turned suddenly, as a shadow crossed him, to get the light, and his jaw dropped at the sight of Bud.

"I'll trouble you for that rock," observed Bud, holding out his hand, and as the *rural* jumped,

Aragon handed over the ore. There was a moment's silence as Bud stood over them—then he stepped back and motioned them out with his gun.

Down the jagged cut they hurried, awed into a guilty silence by his anger, and when he let them mount without a word the *rural* looked back, surprised. Even then Bud said nothing, but the swing of the Texan's gun spoke for him, and they rode quickly out of sight.

"You dad-burned greasers!" growled Bud, returning his pistol with a jab to its holster. Then he looked at the ore. There were two pieces, one fresh-dug and the other worn, and as he gazed at them the worn piece seemed strangely familiar. Aragon had been comparing them—but where had he got the worn piece?

Once more Bud looked it over, and then the rock fell from his hand. It was the first piece they had found—the piece that belonged to Phil!

XV

When the solid earth quakes, though it moves but a thousandth of an inch beneath our feet, the human brain reels and we become dizzy, sick, and afraid. So, too, at the thought that some trusted friend has played us false, the mind turns back upon itself and we doubt the stability of everything—for a moment. Then, as we find all the trees straight up, the world intact, and the hills in their proper places, we cast the treacherous doubts aside and listen to the voice of reason.

For one awful moment Hooker saw himself betrayed by his friend, either through weakness or through guile; and then his mind straightened itself and he remembered that Phil was in jail.

What more natural, then, than that the *rurales* should search his pockets and give the ore to Aragon? He stooped and picked up the chunk of rock—that precious, pocket-worn specimen that had brought them the first sure promise of success—and wiped it on his sleeve.

Mechanically he placed it beside the other piece which Aragon had gouged from the ledge, and while he gazed at them he wondered what to do—to leave their mine and go to his friend, or to let his friend wait and stand guard by their treasure—and his heart told him to go to his friend.

So he swung up on his horse and followed slowly, and as soon as it was dark he rode secretly through Old Fortuna and on till he came to the jail. It was a square stone structure, built across the street from the *cantina* in order to be convenient for the drunks, and as Bud rode up close and stared at it, someone hailed him through the bars.

"Hello there, pardner," called Hooker, swinging down and striding over to the black window, "how long have they had you in here?"

"Two days," answered Phil from the inner darkness; "but it seems like a lifetime to me. Say, Bud, there's a Mexican in here that's got the jim-jams—regular *tequila* jag—can't you get me out?"

"Well, I sure will!" answered Bud. "What have they got you in for? Where's our friend, Don Juan? Why didn't he let me know?"

"You can search me!" railed De Lancey. "Seems like everybody quits you down here the minute you get into trouble. I got arrested night before last by those damned *rurales*—Manuel del Rey was behind it, you can bet your life on that—and I've been here ever since!"

"Well, what are you pinched for? Who do I go and see?"

"Pinched for nothing!" cried De Lancey

bitterly. "Pinched because I'm a Mexican citizen and can't protect myself! I'm *incomunicado* for three days!"

"Well, I'll get you out, all right," said Hooker, leaning closer against the bars. "Here, have a smoke—did they frisk you of your makings?"

"No," snapped De Lancey crossly, "but I'm out of everything by this time. Bud, I tell you I've had a time of it! They threw me in here with this crazy, murdering Mexican and I haven't had a wink of sleep for two days. He's quiet now, but I don't want any more."

"Well, say," began Bud again, "what are you charged with? Maybe I can grease somebody's paw and get you out tonight!"

There was an awkward pause at this, and finally De Lancey dropped his white face against the bars and his voice became low and beseeching.

"I'll tell you, Bud," he said, "I haven't been quite on the square with you—I've been holding out a little. But you know how it is—when a fellow's in love. I've been going to see Gracia!"

"Oh!" commented Hooker, and stood very quiet while he waited.

"Yes, I've been going to see her," hurried on Phil. "I know I promised; but honest, Bud, I couldn't help it. It just seemed as if my whole being was wrapped up in her, and I had to do it. She'd be looking for me when I came and went—and then I fixed it with her maid to take her a

152

letter. And then I met her secretly, back by the garden gate. You know they've got some holes punched in the wall—loopholed during the fight last summer—and we'd—"

"Sure, I'll take your word for that," broke in Hooker harshly. "But get to the point! What are you pinched for?"

"Well," went on De Lancey, his voice quavering at the reproof, "I was going to tell you, if you'll listen to me. Somebody saw us there and told Aragon—he shut her up for a punishment and she slipped me out a note. She was lonely, she said. And that night—well, I couldn't stand it—I hired the string band and we went down there in a hack to give her a serenade. But this cad, Manuel del Rey, who has been acting like a jealous ass all along, swooped down on us with a detachment of his *rurales* and took us all to jail. He let the musicians out the next morning, but I've been here ever since."

"Yes, and what are you charged with?" demanded Bud bruskly.

"Drunk," confessed Phil, and Bud grunted.

"Huh!" he said, "and me out watching that mine night and day!"

"Oh, I know I've done you dirt, Bud," wailed De Lancey; "but I didn't mean to, and I'll never do it again."

"Never do what?" inquired Bud roughly.

"I won't touch another drop of booze as long

as I'm in Mexico!" cried Phil. "Not a drop!"

"And how about the girl?" continued Bud inexorably. "Her old man was out and tried to jump our mine to-day—how about her?"

"Well," faltered De Lancey, "I'll—she—"

"You know your promise!" reminded Bud.

"Yes; I know. But—oh, Bud, if you knew how loyal I've been to you—if you knew what offers I've resisted—the mine stands in my name, you know."

"Well?"

"Well, Aragon came around to me last week and said if I'd give him a half interest in it he'd—well, never mind—it was a great temptation. But did I fall for it? Not on your life! I know you, Bud, and I know you're honest—you'd stay by me to the last ditch, and I'll do the same by you. But I'm in love, Bud, and that would make a man forget his promise if he wasn't true as steel."

"Yes," commented Hooker dryly. "I don't reckon I can count on you much from now on. Here, take a look at this and see what you make of it." He drew the piece of ore that he had taken from Aragon from his pocket and held it up in the moonlight. "Well, feel of it, then," he said. "Shucks, you ought to know that piece of rock, Phil—it's the first one we found in our mine!"

"No!" exclaimed De Lancey, starting back. "Why—where'd you get it?"

"Never mind where I got it!" answered Hooker.

"The question is: What did you do with it?"

"Well, I might as well come through with it," confessed Phil, the last of his assurance gone. "I gave it to Gracia!"

"And I took it away from Aragon," continued Bud, "while he was digging some more chunks out of our mine. So that is your idea of being true as steel, is it? You've done noble by me and Kruger, haven't you? Yes, you've been a good pardner, I don't think!"

"Well, don't throw me down, Bud!" pleaded Phil. "There's some mistake somewhere. Her father must have found it and taken it away! I'd stake my life on it that Gracia would never betray me!"

"Well, think it over for a while," suggested Bud, edging his words with sarcasm. "I'm going up to the hotel!"

"No; come back!" cried De Lancey, clamoring at the bars. "Come on back, Bud! Here!" he said, thrusting his hand out through the heavy irons. "I'll give you my word for it—I won't see her again until we get our title! Will that satisfy you? Then give me your hand, pardner—I'm sorry I did you wrong!"

"It ain't me," replied Hooker soberly, as he took the trembling hand; "it's Kruger. But if you'll keep your word, Phil, maybe we can win out yet. I'm going up to find the *comisario*."

A brief interview with that smiling individual

and the case of Phil De Lancey was laid bare. He had been engaged in a desperate rivalry with Manuel del Rey for the hand of Gracia Aragon, and his present incarceration was not only for singing ragtime beneath the Aragon windows, but for trying to whip the captain of the *rurales* when the latter tried to place him under arrest.

And De Lancey was the prisoner not of the *comisario*, but of the captain of the *rurales*. Sore at heart, Bud rode up through the Mexican quarters to the *cuartel* of the *rurales*, but the captain was inexorable.

"No, *señor*," he said, waving an eloquent finger before his nose, "I cannot release your friend. No, *señor*."

"But what is he charged with," persisted Bud, "and when is his trial? You can't keep him shut up without a trial."

At this the captain of the *rurales* lifted his eyebrows and one closely waxed *mustachio* and smiled mysteriously.

"*Y como no*?" he inquired. "And why not? Is he not a Mexican citizen?"

"Well, perhaps he is," thundered Bud, suddenly rising to his full height, "but I am not! I am an American, Señor Capitan, and there are other Americans! If you hold my friend without a trial I will come and tear your jail down—and the *comisario* will not stop me, either!"

"Ah!" observed the dandy little captain

156

shrugging his *mustachio* once more and blinking, and while Hooker raged back and forth he looked him over appraisingly.

"One moment!" he said at last, raising a quieting hand. "These are perilous times, *señor*, in which all the defenders of Fortuna should stand together. I do not wish to have a difference with the Americans when Bernardo Bravo and his men are marching to take our town. No, I value the friendship of the valiant Americans very highly—so I will let your friend go. But first he must promise me one thing—not to trouble the Señor Aragon by making further love to his daughter!"

"Very well!" replied Bud. "He has already promised that to me; so come on and let him out."

"To you?" repeated Manuel del Rey with a faint smile. "Then, perhaps—"

"Perhaps nothing!" broke in Hooker shortly. "Come on!"

He led the way impatiently while the captain, his saber clanking, strode out and rode beside him. He was not a big man, this swashing captain of the rural police, but he was master, nevertheless, of a great district, from Fortuna to the line, with a reputation for quick work in the pursuance of his duty as well as in the primrose ways of love.

In the insurrections and raidings of the previous summer he had given the *coup de grâce* with his

157

revolver to more than one embryo bandit, and in his love-affairs he had shown that he could be equally summary.

The elegant Feliz Luna, who for a time had lingered near the charming Gracia, had finally found himself up against a pair of pistols with the option of either fighting Captain del Rey or returning to his parents. The young man concluded to beat a retreat. For a like offense Philip De Lancey had been unceremoniously thrown into jail; and now the *capitan* turned his attention to Bud Hooker, whose mind he had not yet fathomed.

"Excuse me, *señor*," he said, after a brief silence, "but your words left me in doubt—whether to regard you as a friend or a rival."

"What?" demanded Bud, whose knowledge of Spanish did not extend to the elegancies.

"You said," explained the captain politely, "that your friend had promised you he would not trouble the lady further. Does that mean that you are interested in her yourself, or merely that you perceive the hopelessness of his suit and wish to protect him from a greater evil that may well befall him? For look you, *señor*, the girl is mine, and no man can come between us!"

"Huh!" snorted Bud, who caught the last all right. Then he laughed shortly and shrugged his shoulders. "I don't know what you're talking

158

about," he said gruffly, "but he will stay away, all right."

"*Muy bien*," responded Del Rey carelessly and, dismounting at the jail, he threw open the door and stood aside for his rival to come out.

"*Muchas gracias, Señor Capitan*," saluted Bud, as the door clanged to behind his pardner. But Phil still bristled with anger and defiance, and the captain perceived that there would be no thanks from him.

"It is nothing," he replied, bowing politely, and something in the way he said it made De Lancey choke with rage. But there by the *cárcel* door was not the place for picking quarrels. They went to the hotel, where Don Juan, all apologies for his apparent neglect—which he excused on the ground that De Lancey had been held *incomunicado*—placated them as best he could and hurried on to the news.

"My gracious, Don Felipe," he cried, "you don't know how sorry I was to see you in jail, but the captain's orders were that no one should go near you—and in Mexico we obey the *rurales*, you know. Otherwise we are placed against a wall and shot.

"But have you heard the news from down below? Ah, what terrible times they are having there—ranches raided, women stolen, rich men held for ransom! Yes, it is worse than ever!

159

Already I am receiving telegrams to prepare rooms for the refugees, and the people are coming in crowds.

"Our friend, the Señor Luna, and his son Feliz have been taken by Bernardo Bravo! Only by an enormous ransom was he able to save his wife and daughters, and his friends must now pay for him.

"At the ranch of the rich Spaniard, Alvarez, there has been a great battle in which the red-flaggers were defeated with losses. Now Bernardo Bravo swears he will avenge his men, and Alvarez has armed his Yaqui workmen.

"He is a brave man, this Colonel Alvarez, and his Yaquis are all warriors from the hills; but Bernardo has gathered all the *insurrectos* in the country together—Campos, Rojas, the brothers Escaboza—and they may crush him with their numbers. But now there is other news—that they are marching upon Fortuna and El Tigre, to seize the mines and mills and hold the rich American companies up for ransom.

"No, *señores*, you must not return to your camp. Remain here, and you shall still have your room, though Spanish gentlemen sleep on the floors. No, allow me, Don Felipe! I wish to show you how highly I value your friendship! Only because we cannot disobey the *rurales* did I suffer you to lie in jail; but now you shall be my guest, you shall—"

"Nope," answered Bud; "we're safer out at the mine."

He glanced at De Lancey, in whose mind rosy visions were beginning to gather, and he, too, declined—with a sigh.

"Make it a bed for the night," he said. "I've got to get out of this town before I tangle with Del Rey again and find myself back in jail. And now lead me to it—I'm perishing for a bath and a sleep!"

They retired early and got up early—for Bud was haunted by fears. But as they passed through Old Fortuna the worst happened to him—they met Gracia, mounted on a prancing horse and followed by a *rural* guard, and she smote him to the heart with a smile.

It was not a smile for Phil, gone astray and wounding by chance; it was a dazzling, admiring smile for Bud alone, and he sat straighter in his saddle. But Phil uttered a groan and struck his horse with the quirt.

"She cut me!" he moaned.

"Aw, forget it!" growled Bud, and they rode on their way in silence.

161

XVI

At their camp by the Eagle Tail mine, even though they held it still and were heirs to half its gold, the two pardners were glum and sorrowful. The treacheries which Bud had forgiven in a moment of exaltation came back to him now as he brooded; and he eyed his friend askance, as if wondering what he would do next.

He recalled all the circumstances of their quest—the meeting with Kruger, Phil's insistence on the adventure, the oath of loyalty which they had sworn; and then the gradual breaking down of their brotherly devotion until now they were strangers at heart. Phil sat by himself, keeping his thoughts to himself, and he stood aloof while he waited for the worst to happen.

From the first day of their undertaking Hooker had felt that it was unlucky, and now he knew that the end was coming. His friend was lost to him, lost alike to a sense of loyalty and honor; he gloomed by himself and thought only of Gracia Aragon.

The oath which Phil himself had forced upon Bud was broken and forgotten; but Bud, by a sterner standard, felt bound to keep his part. One thing alone could make him break it— his word to Henry Kruger. The Eagle Tail mine he held in trust, and half of it was Kruger's.

"Phil," he said at last, when his mind was weary of the ceaseless grind of thoughts, "I believe that mineral agent is holding back our papers. I believe old Aragon has passed him a hundred or so and they're in cahoots to rob us. But I'll tell you what I'll do—you give me a power of attorney to receive those papers for you, and I'll go in and talk Dutch to the whole outfit."

"What do you want to do that for?" demanded De Lancey querulously. "Why can't you wait a while? Those papers have to go to Moctezuma and Hermosillo and all over the City of Mexico and back, and it takes time. What do you want to make trouble for?"

"Well, I'll tell you, Phil," answered Bud honestly. "I've got a hunch if we don't grab them papers soon we won't get 'em at all. Here these rebels are working closer all the time, and Aragon is crowding us. I want to get title and turn it over to Kruger, before we lose out somewhere."

"What's the matter with me going in and talking to the agent?" suggested Phil. Then, as he saw his pardner's face, he paused and laughed bitterly.

"You don't trust me anymore, do you, Bud?" he said.

"Well, it ain't that so much," evaded Hooker; "but I sure don't trust that Manuel del Rey. The

163

first time you go into town he's going to pinch you, and I know it."

"I'm going to go in all the same," declared De Lancey, "and if the little squirt tries to stop me—"

"Aw, Phil," entreated Bud, "be reasonable, can't ye? You got no call to go up against that little feller. He's a bad actor, I can see that, and I believe he'd kill you if he got the chance. But wait a little while—maybe he'll get took off in the fights this summer!"

"No, he's too cursed mean for that!" muttered De Lancey, but he seemed to take some comfort in the thought.

As for Bud, he loafed around for a while, cleaning up camp, making smoke for the absent Yaqui, and looking over the deserted mine, but something in the changed atmosphere made him restless and uneasy.

"I wonder where that dogged Indian went to?" he said for the hundredth time, as the deep shadows gathered in the valley. "By Joe, Phil, if Amigo comes back I'm going to go ahead on that mine! I want to keep him around here, and we might as well get out some ore, if it's only for a grub-stake. Come on—what do you say? We'll open her up—there's nothing to hide now. Well, I'll do it myself, then—this setting around is getting on my nerves."

His far-seeing eyes, trained from his boyhood

to search the hills for cattle, scanned the tops of the ridges as he spoke; and while he sat and pondered they noted every rock.

Then at last he rose up slowly and gazed at a certain spot. He waved his arm, beckoning the distant point of blackness to come in, and soon from around a point in the cañon the Yaqui appeared, bearing a heavy Mauser rifle on his arm.

Across his broad breast hung the same familiar cartridge-belt, two more encircled his hips, and he walked with his head held high, like the warrior that he was.

Evidently his flight had led to the place where his arms had been hid, for he wore the regulation knife bayonet at his hip and around his hat was the red ribbon of his people, but Bud was too polite to ask him about his journey. Since his coming the Yaqui had always maintained a certain mystery, and now, though his eyes were big with portent and he smiled at the jests about his gun, he simply waved his hand to the south and east and murmured:

"*Muchos revoltosos!*"

"*Seguro!*" answered Bud jokingly. "But have you killed any?"

"Not yet!" returned the Indian, and he did not smile at that.

"I wonder what that Indian is waiting around here for?" remarked Phil in English. "He must have his eye on somebody."

"Yeah, I bet," agreed Bud, regarding his savage friend with a speculative interest. "Most of them Yaqui soldiers was farm-hands in this country before they rounded them up. I reckon he's looking for the man that had him deported.

"Tired, Amigo?" he inquired in Spanish, and Ignacio gravely acknowledged that he was, a little.

"Then drink plenty coffee," went on Hooker. "Eat lots—to-morrow we go to work in the mine."

"To-morrow?" repeated the Indian, as if considering his other engagements. "Good!" He nodded a smiling assent.

After a month and more of idleness Bud and Amigo performed prodigies of labor in the cut, rolling down boulders, lifting them up on the tram, and clearing away the face of the cliff. Their tram was ramshackle, their track the abandoned rails from older workings, and their tools little more than their hands, but by noon the last broken fragments were heaved aside and the shattered ledge revealed.

A low cry of wonder escaped the Yaqui as he gazed at the rich vein of ore, and as he saw the grim smile on Bud's rugged countenance he showed his white teeth in sympathy.

"*Que bueno!*" he murmured. "How good!" gathering the precious fragments in his handkerchief.

At the camp they crushed the picked ore in a

166

mortar and panned it in the creek, and for the moment De Lancey dropped his air of preoccupancy as he stared at the streak of pure gold. Like a yellow film it lay along the edge of the last fine tailings, and when skillful washing had left it bare, it gleamed like a jewel in the pan.

"By Jove, Bud!" he cried, "that's the real stuff—and it goes a dollar to the pan easy!"

"Sure thing!" assented Bud. "Let's pound a lot of it and wash it as we go—then we'll have some getaway money when things break loose here!"

"I'll go you!" answered Phil, and Bud's heart warmed toward him as he watched him pound up a piece of ore and go to swirling the dirt in the pan.

But alas for the fond hopes he cherished! Even as he washed out the gold Phil's mind wandered far away, back to the hotel where Gracia Aragon sat watching by the window.

Her hair was the color of gold, spun fine and refined again; yes, it was worth more than this golden dross that he caught in the bottom of his pan. And what was gold if he could not have her?

He paused in his labor and a dreamy smile parted his lips—then he broke into a song:

"Sweet honey-bee, be sweet to me,
My heart is free, but here's the key;
Lock up the garden gate; honey, you
   know I'll wait,
Under the rambler rose tree-ee."

Once more he returned to his work, humming now the dulcet strains of "The Merry Widow," and when Bud came back from the cut it was to hear a coon song:

" 'Cos I want yer, ma honey, yes, I want
   yer, want yer, want yer;
'Cos I want yer, ma honey, yes, I do!"

So he labored and sang, until finally the labor ceased, and then the song. He went about other things, and other thoughts, not so cheerful, filled his mind.

Bud returned sadly to the company of the Yaqui and gave it up. Perhaps his pardner had been right when, riding out of Agua Negra, he had enlarged upon the dangers of Old Mexico, "the land of *mañana* and broken promises." Certainly his speech had been prophetic in regard to dark-eyed women; for, even as he had said, nothing seemed to please them better than to come between man and man.

It was a madness, he felt sure—the spell of the hot country, where the women look out from behind barred windows and men sing beneath their balconies at midnight. Already it had cost him his pardner—would it conquer *his* will as well and make him forget his trust?

In his impotence the idea of some perverse fate—some malign influence over which he had no control—was strong with Hooker; yet when the blow fell he was not prepared for it. It was the third day of their mining and, with Amigo, he had been driving into the face of the cliff.

Already their round of holes was drilled, the fuses cut, the charges set, and as he retreated before the blast he noticed absently that Cruz Mendez was in camp. The shots followed one after another, and he counted them to make sure there was no miss-fire—then he looked around and discovered that Phil was gone.

"Where is Don Felipe?" he inquired of Mendez, and that low-browed brother of the burro bowed fawningly before he replied.

"He has gone to Fortuna," he said, wiping his face with the bath-towel which he wore about his neck.

"And what for?" demanded Bud imperatively.

"I don't know, *señor*," writhed Mendez. "I brought him a letter."

"From whom?"

"I don't know—it was given to me by Juana, the servant of the Señorita Aragon."

"Ah!" breathed Bud, and pretended not to be surprised.

"Well, let 'im go!" he said to himself, and went back into the mine. It was what he had expected in a way, and his code bade him keep his hands off. But the next morning, when the evil was either avoided or done, he thrust his rifle into its sling and started for the town. At the jail he halted and gazed in through the windows— then he rode up to the hotel and asked for Phil.

"What? Have you not heard?" clamored Don Juan. "Ah, it is most unfortunate—I would not have had it happen for the world!"

"What?" inquired Bud succinctly.

"Why, the quarrel—the encounter with Capitan del Rey! I did my best, I assure you, to prevent it, for the town has been put under martial law and the captain is in full charge. They quarreled over the favor of a lady, and now your friend is in jail."

"I didn't see him when I come by," observed Hooker.

"Ah, no—not in the *cárcel*—in the *cuartel*, the guard-house of the *rurales*!"

"Much obliged!" nodded Bud, and rode on through the town. The street of the Mexican quarter was filled with strange people hurrying to and fro; long pack-trains loaded with trunks and curious bundles came swinging up from below; and a pair of *rurales*, looking fierce under their huge sombreros stood guard by the *cuartel* door.

"Where is the *capitan*?" demanded Hooker. After requesting him to hang his pistol-belt on his saddle-horn, a sergeant showed him in to the chief.

Manuel del Rey was very busy with papers and orders, but as the American appeared in the doorway he rose and greeted him with a bow.

"Ah, good morning, *señor*," he said, with one swift glance to read his mood. "You are in search of your friend—no?"

"*Sí, señor*," answered Hooker, but with none of the animosity which the captain had expected. "Where is he?"

"I regret very much," began the officer, speaking with military formality, "but it is my duty to inform you that the Señor De Lancey has left Fortuna. Last night he did me the honor to enlist in my company of *rurales*—he is now on his way to the north to assist in guarding the railroad."

"What?" shouted Bud, hardly able to believe his ears. But when the captain repeated it he no longer doubted his Spanish.

"But why?" he cried. "Why did he join the *rurales*?"

"Ah, *señor*," shrugged Del Rey, "was he not a Mexican citizen? Very well, then; he could be summoned for military service. But the circumstances were these: Your friend came yesterday to this town, where I am at present military commander, and made an unprovoked assault upon my person. For this, according to law, he should have been shot at sunrise. But, not wishing to occasion unpleasantness with the

171

Americans now residing here, I offered him the alternative of military service. He is now enlisted as a *rural* for a term of five years."

"Five years!" exclaimed Hooker; and then, instead of starting the expected rough-house— upon which the *rural* guards were prepared to jump on his back—he simply threw down his hat and cursed—not anyone in particular, but everything in general; and at the end of it he turned once more upon the watchful captain.

"*Dispenseme, señor*," he said, "this is the truth, is it?"

"*Sí, señor*," returned Captain del Rey. "But before leaving with his detachment your friend wrote this letter, which he requested me to deliver to you."

He offered with a flourish a sealed envelope, from which Bud extracted a short note.

DEAR BUD:

When you get this I shall be far away. I must have been mad, but it is too late now. Rather than be executed I have enlisted as a *rural*. But I shall try to be brave for her sake. Take care of her, Bud—for me!

PHIL.

Bud read it through again and meditated ponderously. Then he folded it up and thrust it into his pocket.

"*Muchas gracias, Señor Capitan,*" he said, saluting and turning upon his heel; and while all the Mexicans marveled at the inscrutable ways of *Americanos*, he mounted and rode away.

XVII

There was a world of Mexicans in the plaza when Hooker rode down through the town. Never, it seemed to him, had he seen so many or liked them less.

To the handful of Americans who remained to man the mill and mine, they were easily a hundred to one; and though their eyes were wide with fear of the imminent rebels, they had an evil way of staring at him which he did not relish.

Even at the hotel, where the Spanish-Mexican aristocracy was massed ten deep, he sensed the same feeling of veiled hostility and wondered vaguely what it might portend. If Philip De Lancey, for making love to a girl, was drafted into the army, what would happen to him if these people should ever break loose? And did they have the courage to do their worst?

He lingered around the door for a while, hoping to meet Don Juan or some American who would tell him the news; then, disgusted with everything, he flung away and left them to themselves. Fortuna was not a white man's country—he could see that without a diagram—but at the same time he intended to hold his mine until he could hear from Phil.

Let the tides of insurrection come and go, let

the red-flaggers take the town and the Federals take it back again—at the end he would still be found at the Eagle Tail, unless Phil received his title to the mine.

As for Aragon, whose fine Italian hand he perceived behind the sudden taking off of Phil, let him make what trades he would with the *rurales* and Manuel del Rey, even to the giving of his daughter's hand; but if, taking advantage of the unsettled times, he dared to try to steal their mine, then there would be war to the knife.

It is a fine, comforting thing to be single-minded and of one purpose. All the rest of life is simplified and ordered then, and a man knows when to raise his hand and when to hold it back.

In his letter Phil had said nothing about their mine, but he was a Mexican citizen still, and the mine was in his name. But he was his pardner and free to hold it in his stead; and that he determined to do—not only hold it, but work it for a stake. Then, when the title was passed and all made certain, they could turn it over to Kruger and quit the accursed country.

As for the girl, Bud decided that she could take care of herself without any assistance from him, and dismissed her from his mind.

Back at the mine he found Amigo guarding camp from the hilltop, and after telling him the gist of his troubles, the two of them went to work. Every day, while one of them dug out the ore, the other crushed and washed it and watched as he horned out the gold. Their rifles they kept beside them and pistols in their belts; and every time a Mexican dropped into camp, as one did now and then in the general unrest, he felt the silent menace of arms in readiness and continued on his way.

For a week they labored on together, grim, watchful, expectant—then, at the break of day, they heard a distant rattle of arms, like the tearing of a cloth, and knew that the battle was on.

The great whistle at Fortuna opened with its full, bass roar, and Amigo snatched up his gun and went loping down the cañon, drawn irresistibly by the sound of conflict. Bud lingered, climbing higher and higher to get a view of the country. But his young blood clamored for action too, and soon he was mounted and gone.

The fighting was not at the American town, but down the valley by Old Fortuna, and as Hooker galloped on toward the sound of the firing he noticed that it was on the move. Already the cowardly rebels were retreating—the volunteers from Fortuna were hurrying to get closer to them, the *rurales* were riding to flank them; and when Bud jumped his horse up the last hill and looked down into the broad, cultivated valley he saw the dust of their flight.

Down the fenced trail that led to the lower country the mounted *insurrectos* were spurring

176

in a rout; across the newly plowed fields of Aragon the men on foot were making a short cut for the hills; and all about them, like leaping grasshoppers, sprang up puffs of dust.

Now they plunged into the willow brush along the river, where it swung in against the ridge; and as their pursuers broke into the open they halted and returned the fire. The bullets struck up the dust like hailstones in front of the oncoming irregulars, a man or two in the lead went down, and they faltered. Then, as frantically as the rebels, they turned and ran for cover.

While defenders and invaders shot back and forth across the broad field, Bud put spurs to his horse and rode closer, and when he came out on another hilltop he was just in time to see the *rurales* come pelting in from the west, and take the *revoltosos* on the flank. There was a great deal of long-distance firing then, while the rebels slowly retreated, and finally, with a last defiant volley, the defenders turned back from their pursuit and marched triumphantly to Old Fortuna.

There, amid numerous *vivas*, Don Cipriano rolled out a cask of *mescal* and, after a fiery speech, invited the victors to help themselves. So they fell to drinking and carousing, and the one defender who had been wounded was bandaged and made much of, while a great crowd from the upper town looked on in awe and admiration.

At last Manuel del Rey and his *rurales* returned

177

from harassing the enemy and, with several wounded prisoners in their midst, the valor-drunk Mexicans formed a riotous procession and went marching back to town. Every horse and mule was carrying double, guns were being dropped, broad hats knocked off, and ever, as they marched, they shouted:

"*Viva Madero! Viva Mejico! Muerte á los revoltosos!*"

It was an edifying spectacle to an American, and with the rest Bud tagged along to the plaza, where they had speeches and cheers galore and more *mescal* at the company's *cantina*. But in the midst of it, while he sat laughing on his horse by the hotel, Bud felt a gravel strike his broad hat from above and, looking furtively up, he beheld Gracia Aragon smiling down at him from the balcony.

She beckoned him with a swift movement and gazed out over the assemblage again, and after a few moments of deliberation Hooker tied his horse and wandered into the hotel.

A tingle of excitement went over him as he tramped up to the ladies' parlor, for he had never met Gracia face to face. But he disguised his qualms by assuming a masklike grimness of countenance and, when the glorious Gracia glided out of her room to meet him, he only blinked and stood pat.

A long experience as a poker-player was all that

saved him from betrayal, for there was something in her very presence which made his heart leap and pound. But he only gazed at her somberly, without even so much as raising his hat.

Back in Texas, in his social world, it was considered almost unmanly thus to salute the ladies. So he stood there, his big sombrero pulled down over his mop of light hair, gazing at her without a blink.

Perhaps it was not altogether so friendly a scrutiny of her charming features as Gracia expected, for he remembered what she had done to his pardner; but if she sensed such a rare thing as disapproval from a young man, she was too excited to show it. Her lips trembled, and she looked back furtively, meanwhile drawing him into an alcove by the slightest twitch of his sleeve.

"Don't talk too loud," she whispered. "My mother is listening from the room—but for the love of God, tell me, where is Phil?"

"I don't know," answered Bud, trying to lower his big voice to a boudoir softness; "he joined the *rurales* and was ordered north—that's all I know."

"Yes, yes, to be sure; but haven't you heard from him?"

She seemed to be all impatience to snatch his news and fly with it, but Bud was in no such hurry. And so far was he from being a carpet knight that he immediately raised his voice to its normal bass. It was all right for Phil and his kind to talk by signs and whispers, but that was not his style.

"Not since he went away," he said. "He left me a little note, then, saying—"

"Saying what?" she demanded breathlessly.

"Well, saying that he had enlisted to keep from being executed, and—that's about all!"

"And not a word about me?"

"Yes," admitted Bud; "he said he'd try to put up with it—on account of you—and—"

"What?" she entreated, taking him beseechingly by the coat.

"Well," stammered Hooker, shifting his feet and looking away, "he told me to kinder take care of you—while he was gone."

"Ah!" she breathed, still standing close to him, "and will you do it?"

"I reckon so," said Bud, "if we have any trouble."

"But I'm in trouble now!" she cried. "I'm watched—I can't get away—and I'm afraid!"

"Afraid of what?" he demanded.

"Of him," she answered, her voice breaking— "of Manuel del Rey!"

"Well," replied Hooker bluntly, "I've got nothing to do with that—I can't interfere in your love-affairs—but if the's war and they try to take the town, you can count on me."

"Oh, thank you," she said, bowing satirically. "And do you expect a war?"

"Not with that bunch of *hombres*!" returned Bud, waving a disparaging hand toward the noise of the shouting. At this she broke down and laughed. Evidently she was not so fearful of discovery after all.

"You forget, sir," she said, "that I am a Mexican!"

Then, as he failed to show any signs of contrition, she changed her mood again.

"But wait!" she ran on, her eyes flashing. "Perhaps we are not so eager to defend our government when we have a new one every year. But if the men who are gathering in Chihuahua invade our country, you will find that as Sonorans those men will fight to the death.

"You laugh because you do not understand. But why should we Sonorans fight side by side with the Federals and *rurales*? Are they not the soldiers of Diaz, who have simply changed to another master? That Manuel del Rey was last year hunting down Maderistas in the hills; now he is fighting for Madero! And to-morrow? Who can say?"

She shrugged her shoulders scornfully, and Hooker perceived that she was in earnest in her dislike of the dashing captain, but prudence warned him to say nothing if he would escape being drawn into the quarrel.

"No," she went on, after an expectant pause, "let the *rurales* pursue these bandits—they are hired for that purpose! But if Orozco and Salazar join this *ladrón*, Bernardo Bravo, and seek to capture our towns, then, Señor Americano, you will see real war and men fighting to the death! Ah, you laugh again—you are a Texan and judge us Sonorans by the cowardly Chihuahuans—but it is the truth. And I, for one," she added naïvely, "would be almost glad to have war. Do you know why? To see if you would really defend me!"

She smiled, looking frankly into his eyes, and Bud blushed to the roots of his hair, but once again he held his peace.

"What, *señor*," she bantered; "you do not speak? Surely, then, your friend De Lancey was wrong when he said you would save me! For look, Mr. Hooker, I am promised to marry dear Phil; but how can I manage that when Manuel del Rey is watching me? It is impossible, is it not?"

"Seems so," muttered Bud, and in the back of his head he began to think quickly. Here was the fountainhead of his misfortunes, and if she had her way she would lay all his plans in ruins—and even then not marry Phil. In fact, from the light way she spoke, he sensed that she did not intend to marry him. Her grudge was against Manuel del Rey who drove away all her lovers.

"Well," he ventured, "there's no rush, I reckon—Phil's enlisted for five years."

"Ha!" she cried contemptuously. "And do you think he will serve? No! At a word from me he will flee to the border and I shall join him in the United States!"

"What?" demanded Bud. "Phil desert?"

In a moment he saw what such a move would mean to him—to Kruger and the Eagle Tail—and he woke suddenly from his calm.

"Here now," he said, scowling as he saw that she was laughing at him, "you've made me and Phil enough trouble. You let that boy alone, savvy?"

He stooped toward her as he spoke, fixing her with masterful eyes that had tamed many a bad horse and man, and she shrank away instinctively. Then she glanced at him shyly and edged over toward the open door.

"I will do what I please, Mr. Hooker," she returned, balancing on the verge of flight.

"All right," Bud came back; "but don't you call me in on it. You've made a fool out of Phil—I suppose you'd like to get me, too. Then your father would grab our mine."

"What do you mean?" she challenged, turning back upon him.

"I mean this," responded Hooker warmly: "Phil holds the title to our mine. If he deserts he loses his Mexican citizenship and his claim is no good. But you don't need to think that your father will get the mine then, because he'll have to whip me first!"

"O-ho!" she sneered. "So that is what you are thinking of? You are a true Gringo, Mr. Hooker—always thinking about the money!"

"Yes," returned Bud; "and even at that I believe your old man will best me!"

She laughed again, with sudden capriciousness, and stood tapping the floor with her foot.

"Ah, I see," she said at length, gazing at him reproachfully; "you think I am working for my father. You think I got poor Phil into all this trouble in order to cheat him of his mine. But let me tell you, Señor Gringo," she cried with sudden fire, "that I did not! I have nothing to do with my father and his schemes. But if you do not trust me—"

She turned dramatically to go, but when Hooker made no effort to stay her she returned once more to the attack.

"No," she said, "it was because he was an American—because he was brave—that I put my faith in Phil. These Mexican men are cowards—they are afraid to stand up and fight! But Philip dared to make love to me—he dared to sing to me at night—and when Manuel del Rey tried to stop him he stood up and made a fight!

"Ah, that is what I admire—a man who is brave. And let me tell you, Señor Hooker, I shall always love your friend! If I could run away I would marry him to-morrow; but this cur, Manuel del Rey, stands in the way. Even my own father is

184

against me. But I don't care—I don't care what happens—only do not think that I am not your friend!"

She paused now and glanced at him shyly, and as her eloquent eyes met his own Bud felt suddenly that she was sincere. The gnawing and corrosive doubts that had eaten at his heart fell away, and he saw her now in her true beauty, with no uneasy thoughts of treachery to poison his honest love.

"I believe you, lady," he said, "and I'm glad to know you," he added, taking off his hat and bowing awkwardly. "Anything I can do for you, don't hesitate to ask for it—only I can't go against my pardners on this mine."

He bowed again and retreated toward the door, but she followed him impulsively.

"Shake hands," she said, holding out both her own, "and will you help me?"

"Sure!" answered Bud, and as her soft fingers closed on his he took them gently, for fear that he might crush them and never know.

XVIII

A month of weary waiting followed that day of days in Fortuna, and still there was no word from Phil. Bernardo Bravo and his rebel raiders passed through the mountains to the east, and news came of heavy fighting in Chihuahua. Don Cipriano Aragon moved his family back to his hacienda and Gracia became only a dream.

Then, one day, as Hooker and the Yaqui were industriously pounding out gold, a messenger came out from town with a telegram in his hand.

> Am in Gadsden. No chance to hold mine.
> Kruger says quit.—P.

"No, I'll be 'sarned if I do!" muttered Bud. Then he sat down to think.

"Amigo," he said to the Yaqui, "are you a Mexican citizen? Can you get title to mine?"

"Me a Mexican?" repeated Amigo, tapping himself proudly on the chest. "No, *señor*! *Seguro que no*!"

"All right then," observed Bud bitterly, "here goes nothing—nowhere! I'll turn Mexican myself!"

He passed the messenger on the way to town, took out his first papers as a citizen, picked up the mineral agent's expert on the way back, and located the Eagle Tail in his own name. Before riding back to camp he wired to Kruger:

Have turned Mex and relocated claim.

HOOKER.

It was his last card, and he did not expect to win by it. Fate had been against him from the first, and he could see his finish, but his nature drove him to fight on. All that Aragon had to do now was to have *him* summoned for military service, and Del Rey would do the rest.

Then he could take over the mine. A mere formality—or so it seemed—but between Aragon and his mine stood the Texas blood. Hooker had been crowded to the wall, and he was mad enough to fight.

The news of De Lancey's desertion followed quickly after his flight—it came over the Federal wires in a report to Manuel del Rey—but by the time it got to Aragon that gentleman was too late. They rode into camp the next day—Aragon and the captain of the *rurales*—and at the first glimpse of that hated uniform Amigo was off like a buck. Bud went out sullenly to meet them, his black mood showing in his lowering eyes, and he halted them by the savagery of his cursing.

"You cock-eyed old reprobate," he snarled, advancing threateningly upon the paling Aragon, "this makes three times you've come into my camp and brought your gun with you! Now take it off!" he yelled, dropping suddenly into Spanish. "Take that gun off—do you understand?"

So violent and unexpected was his assault that it threw Aragon into a panic, and even Manuel del Rey softened his manner as he inquired into the cause.

"Never mind," answered Bud, smiling crustily as Aragon laid aside his arms; "I know that *hombre* well! Now what can I do for you, *capitan*?"

"Be so kind as to take your hand from your belt," replied Del Rey with a smile that was intended to placate. "Ah, thank you—excuse my nerves—now I can tell you the news. I regret to inform you, *señor*, that your friend, De Lancey, has deserted from my command, taking his arms and equipment with him. In case he is captured he will be shot as a deserter."

"Your news is old, *capitan*," rejoined Hooker. "I knew it two days ago. And you can tell Mr. Aragon that it is no use for him to try to get this mine—I became a Mexican citizen yesterday and located it myself."

"So we learned," responded the captain suavely. "It was part of my errand today to ask if you would not enlist in my company of *rurales*."

"*Muchas gracias, capitan*," answered Hooker with heavy irony. "I do not care to!"

"But your friend—" protested Manuel del Rey with an insinuating smile.

"My friend was in jail," put in Bud; "he was to be shot at sunrise. But *mira, amigo*, I am *not* in jail, and, furthermore, I do not intend to be."

"That is very creditable to you," laughed Del Rey; "but even then you are entitled to enlist. The country is full of turbulent fellows who have to be caught or killed. Come now, you understand my errand—why make it hard for me?"

"No, *señor*," returned Bud grimly, "I know nothing of your errand. But this I do know. I have done nothing for which I can be arrested, and if any man tries to make me join the army—" he hooked his thumb into his belt and regarded the captain fixedly.

"Ah, very well," said Del Rey, jerking his waxed *mustachios*, "I will not press the matter. But I understand from one of my men, *señor*, that you are harboring a dangerous criminal here— the same man, perhaps, whom I saw running up the cañon?"

He smiled meaningly at this, but Bud was swift to defend his Yaqui.

"No, *señor*," he replied, "I have no such criminal. I have a Mexican working for me who is one of the best miners in Sonora, and that is all I know about him."

"A Mexican?" repeated Del Rey, arching his eyebrows. "Excuse me, sir, but it is my business to know every man in this district, and he is no Mexican, but a Yaqui. Moreover, he is a fugitive and an outlaw, and if he had not been enlisted with the Federals I should have arrested him when he passed through Fortuna. So I warn you, sir, not to hide him, or you will be liable to the law."

"I'm not hiding him," protested Hooker scornfully. "I'm just hiring him as a miner, and any time you want him you can come and get him. He's up in the rocks there somewhere now."

"So!" exclaimed the captain, glancing uneasily at the hillside. "I did not think—but many thanks, *señor*, another time will do as well."

He reined his horse away as he spoke and, with a jerk of the head to Aragon, rode rapidly down the cañon. Aragon lingered to retrieve his fallen gun-belt and then, seeming to think better of his desire to speak, he made a single vindictive gesture and set spurs to his champing horse.

It was merely a fling of the hand, as spontaneous as a sigh or a frown, but in it Hooker read the last exasperation of the Spaniard and his declaration of war to the knife. He bared his strong teeth in reply and hissed out a blighting curse, and then Aragon was gone.

That evening, as the darkness came on and the cañon became hushed and still, Bud built a big fire and stood before it, his rugged form silhouetted against the flames. And soon, as quiet as a fox, the Yaqui appeared from the gloom.

"Did he come for me," he asked, advancing warily into the firelight, "that *capitan*?"

"Yes," answered Bud, "and for me, too. But you must have known him before, Amigo—he seems to be afraid of you."

A smile of satisfaction passed over the swarthy face of the Indian at this, and then the lines became grim again. His eyes glowed with the light of some great purpose, and for the first time since he had been with Bud he drew aside the veil from his past.

"Yes," he said, nodding significantly, "the *rural* is afraid. He knows I have come to kill him."

He squatted by the fire and poured out a cup of coffee, still brooding over his thoughts—then, with a swift gesture, he laid open his shirt and pointed to a scar along the ribs.

"He shot me there," he said.

"And so you have come to kill him?"

"Yes," answered Amigo; "but not now. Tomorrow I go to my people—I must take them my money first."

"Have you got a wife?" asked Hooker, forgetting for once his accustomed reserve.

"No," grumbled Amigo, shaking his head sadly, "no wife."

"Oh, you take your money to your father and mother."

"No. No father—no mother—*nadie!*"

He threw up his open hands to signify that all were gone, and Hooker said no more. For three months and more he had worked alongside this giant, silent Yaqui and only once had he sensed his past. That was when Amigo had torn his shirt in lifting, and across the rippling muscles of his back there had shown the long white wale of a whip.

It was the mark of his former slavery when, with the rest of his people, he had been deported to the henequen-fields of Yucatan and flogged by the overseer's lash—and Amigo was ashamed of it. But now that he was about to go, Bud made bold to ask him one more question, to set his mind at rest.

"Perhaps this captain killed your people?"

"No, *señor*," answered Amigo quietly; "they died."

He spoke the words simply, but there was something in his voice that brought up images of the past—of peaceful Yaquis, seized at every ranch in Sonora on a certain night; of long marches overland, prodded on by *rurales* and guards; of the crowded prison-ships from which the most anguished hurled themselves into the sea; and then the awful years of slavery in the poisoned tropics, until only the hardiest were left.

Amigo had seen it all, as the scars on his broad back proved—but he withdrew now into silence

192

and left his thoughts unsaid. As he sat there by the fire, one long, black hand held out to keep the gleam from his eyes, he made a noble figure, but the Yaqui songs which he had crooned on other nights were forgotten, and he held himself tense and still. Then at last he rose and gazed at Bud.

"You pay me my money," he said. "I go now."

"Sure," answered Bud, and after he had weighed out the equivalent in gold on his scales he flipped in some more for luck and gave him a sack to hold it.

"What you buy with all that," he inquired with a friendly grin; "grub?"

"No, *señor*," answered Amigo, knotting the precious gold in a handkerchief; "cartridges!"

"What for?" queried Bud, and then it was Amigo who smiled.

"To kill Mexicans with!" he replied, and in those words Hooker read the secret of his thrift.

While his wild brethren fought in the hills or prepared for the battles to come, it was his part to earn the money that should keep them in ammunition. It was for that, in fact, that Porfirio Diaz had seized all the peaceful Yaquis in a night and shipped them to Yucatan—for he saw that while they were working the wild Yaquis would never lack.

All the time that Amigo had been doing two men's work and saving on the price of a shirt he had held that cheerful dream in his mind—to kill more Mexicans!

Yet, despite the savagery in him, Hooker had come to like the Yaqui, and he liked him still. With the *rurales* on his trail it was better that he should go, but Bud wanted him to return. So, knowing the simple honesty of Indians, he brought out his own spare pistol and placed it in Amigo's hands. Often he had seen him gazing at it longingly, for it was lighter than his heavy Mauser and better for the journey.

"Here," he said, "I will lend you my pistol—and you can give it to me when you come back."

"Sure!" answered the Indian, hanging it on his hip. "*Adios*!"

They shook hands then, and the Yaqui disappeared in the darkness. In the morning, when a squad of *rurales* closed in on the camp, they found nothing but his great tracks in the dust.

XIX

It was June and the wind-storms which had swept in from the southeast died away. No more, as in the months that had passed, did the dust-pillar rise from the dump of the Fortuna mill and go swirling up the cañon.

A great calm and heat settled over the harassed land, and above the far blue wall of the Sierras the first thunder-caps of the rainy season rose up till they obscured the sky. Then, with a rush of conflicting winds, a leaden silence, and a crash of flickering light, the storm burst in tropic fury and was gone as quickly as it had come.

So, while the rich landowners of the hot country sat idle and watched it grow, another storm gathered behind the distant Sierras; and, as empty rumors lulled them to a false security, suddenly from the north came the news of dashing raids, of railroads cut, troops routed, and the whole border occupied by swarming rebels.

In a day the southern country was isolated and cut off from escape and, while the hordes of Chihuahua *insurrectos* laid siege to Agua Negra, the belated Spanish *haciendados* came scuttling once more to Fortuna. There, at least, was an American town where the courage of the Anglo-Saxon would protect their women in extremity.

And, if worst came to worst, it was better to pay ransom to red-flag generals than to fall victims to bandits and looters.

As the bass roar of the great whistle reverberated over the hills Bud Hooker left his lonely camp almost gladly, and with his hard-won gold-dust safe beneath his belt, went galloping into town.

Not for three weeks—not since he received the wire from Phil and located the Eagle Tail mine—had he dared to leave his claim. *Rurales*, outlaws, and Mexican patriots had dropped in from day to day and eaten up most of his food, but none of them had caught him napping, and he had no intention that they should.

A conspiracy had sprung up to get rid of him, to harry him out of the country, and behind it was Aragon. But now, with the big whistle blowing, Aragon would have other concerns.

He had his wife and daughter, the beautiful Gracia, to hurry to the town, and perhaps the thought of being caught and held for ransom would deter him from stealing mines. So reasoned Bud, and, dragging a reluctant pack-animal behind him, he came riding in for supplies.

At the store he bought flour and coffee and the other things which he needed most. As he was passing by the hotel Don Juan de Dios halted him for a moment, rushing out and thrusting a bundle of letters into his hands and hurrying back into the house, as if fearful of being detected in such an act of friendship.

Long before he had lost his pardner Bud had decided that Don Juan was a trimmer, a man who tried to be all things to all people—as a good hotel-keeper should—but now he altered his opinion a little, for the letters were from Phil. He read them over in the crowded plaza, into which the first refugees were just beginning to pour, and frowned as he skimmed through the last.

Of Gracia and vain protestations of devotion there was enough and to spare, but nothing about the mine. Only in the first one, written on the very day he had deserted, did he so much as attempt an excuse for so precipitately abandoning their claim and his Mexican citizenship. Phil wrote:

> My mail was being sent through head-quarters and looked over by Del Rey, so I knew I would never receive the papers, even if they came. I hope you don't feel hard about it, pardner. Kruger says to come out right away. I would have stayed with it, but it wasn't any use. And now, Bud, I want to ask you something. When you come out, bring Gracia with you. Don't leave her at the mercy of Del Rey. I would come myself if it wasn't sure death. Be quick about it, Bud; I count on you.

The other letters were all like that, but nothing about the mine. And yet it was the mine that Bud was fighting for—that they had fought for from the first. The railroad was torn up now, and a flight with Gracia was hopeless, but it was just as well, for he never would abandon the Eagle Tail.

In two months, or three, when the rebels were whipped off, his papers might come. Then he could pay his taxes and transfer his title and consider the stealing of Gracia. But since he had seen her and touched her hand something held him back—a grudging reluctance—and he was glad that his duty lay elsewhere. If she was his girl now he would come down and get her anyway.

But she was not his girl and, gazing back grimly at the seething plaza and the hotel that hid her from sight, he rode somberly down the road. After all, there was nothing to get excited about—every *revoltoso* in the country was lined up around Agua Negra and, with four hundred soldiers to oppose them and artillery to shell their advance, it would be many a long day before they took that town.

Twice already Agua Negra had fallen before such attacks, but now it was protected by rifle-pits and machine guns set high on mud roofs. And then there were the Yaquis, still faithful to Madero. They alone could hold the town, if they made up their minds to fight. So reasoned

Hooker, mulling over the news that he had heard. But he watched the ridges warily, for the weather was good for raiders.

A day passed, and then another, and the big whistle blew only for the shifts; the loneliness of the hills oppressed him as he gazed out at the quivering heat. And then, like a toad after a shower, Amigo came paddling into camp on the heels of a thunderstorm, his sandals hung on his hip and his big feet squelching through the mud.

Across his shoulders he wore a gay serape, woven by some patient woman of his tribe; and in the belt beside Bud's pistol he carried a heavy knife, blacksmithed from a ten-inch file by some Yaqui hillman. All in all, he was a fine barbarian, but he looked good to the lonely Bud.

"*Ola*, Amigo!" he hailed, stepping out from the adobe house where he had moved to avoid the rains; and Amigo answered with his honest smile which carried no hint of savagery or deceit.

Try as he would, Bud could not bring himself to think of his Yaqui as dangerous; and even when he balanced the Indian's murderous bowie-knife in his hands he regarded it with a grin. It was a heavy weapon, broad across the back, keen on one edge, and drawn to a point that was both sharp and strong. The haft was wrapped with rawhide to hold the clutch of the hand.

"What do you do with this?" queried Hooker. "Chop wood? Skin deer?"

199

"Yes, chop wood!" answered Amigo, but he replaced it carefully in his belt.

He looked the adobe house over thoughtfully, listened long to the news of the border and of the *rurales'* raid on their camp, and retired to the rocks for the night. Even Bud never knew where he slept—somewhere up on the hillside— in caves or clefts in the rocks—and not even the most pressing invitation could make him share the house for a night. To Amigo, as to an animal, a house was a trap; and he knew that the times were treacherous.

So indeed they were, as Hooker was to learn to his sorrow, and but for the Yaqui and his murderous knife he might easily have learned it too late.

It was evening, after a rainless day, and Bud was cooking by the open fire, when suddenly Amigo vanished and four men rode in from above. They were armed with rifles, as befitted the times, but gave no signs of ruffianly bravado, and after a few words Bud invited them to get down and eat.

"*Muchas gracias, señor*," said the leader, dismounting and laying his rifle against a log, "we are not hungry."

"Then have some coffee," invited Hooker, who made it a point to feed everyone who stopped, regardless of their merit; and once more the Mexican declined. At this Bud looked at him

200

sharply, for his refusal did not augur well, and it struck him the man's face was familiar. He was tall for a Mexican and heavily built, but with a rather sinister cast of countenance.

"Where have I seen you before?" asked Bud, after trying in vain to place him. "In Fortuna?"

"No, *señor*," answered the Mexican politely. "I have never been in that city. Is it far?"

"Ten miles by the trail," responded Hooker, by no means reassured, and under pretext of inviting them to eat, he took a look at the other men. If they had not stopped to eat, what then was their errand while the sun was sinking so low? And why this sullen refusal of the coffee which every Mexican drinks?

Bud stepped into the house, as if on some errand, and watched them unseen from the interior. Seeing them exchange glances then, he leaned his rifle just inside the door and went about his cooking.

It was one of the chances he took, living out in the brush, but he had come to know this low-browed type of semi-bandit all too well and had small respect for their courage. In case of trouble Amigo was close by in the rocks somewhere, probably with his gun in his hand—but with a little patience and circumspection the unwelcome visitors would doubtless move on.

So he thought, but instead they lingered, and when supper was cooked he decided to go to a

201

show-down—and if they again refused to eat he would send them on their way.

"*Ven amigos*," he said, spreading out the tin plates for them, "come and eat!"

The three low-brows glanced at their leader, who had done what little talking there was so far, and, seized with a sudden animation, he immediately rose to his feet.

"Many thanks, *señor*," he said with a cringing and specious politeness. "We have come far and the trail is long, so we will eat. The times are hard for poor men now—this traitor, Madero, has made us all hungry. It is by him that we poor working men are driven to insurrection—but we know that the Americans are our friends. Yes, *señor*, I will take some of your beans, and thank you."

He filled a plate as he spoke and lifted a biscuit from the oven, continuing with his false patter while the others fell to in silence.

"Perhaps you have heard, *señor*," he went on, "the saying which is in the land:

"*Mucho trabajo,*
Poco dinero;
No hay frijoles,
Viva Madero!*

---

* Much work, Little money; No beans, Long live Madero!

"That, in truth, is no jest to the Mexican people. This man has betrayed us all; he has ruined the country and set brother against brother. And now, while we starve because the mines are shut down, he gathers his family about him in the city and lives fat on the money he has stolen."

He ran on in this style, after the fashion of the *revoltosos*, and by the very commonplace of his fulminations Bud was thrown completely off his guard. That was the way they all talked, these worthless bandit-beggars—that and telling how they loved the *Americanos*—and then, if they got a chance, they would stick a knife in your back.

He listened to the big man with a polite toleration, being careful not to turn his back, and ate a few bites as he waited, but though it was coming dusk the Mexicans were in no hurry to depart. Perhaps they hoped to stop for the night and get him in his sleep. Still they lingered on, the leader sitting on a log and continuing his harangue.

Then, in the middle of a sentence, and while Bud was bending over the fire, the Mexican stopped short and leaned to one side. A tense silence fell, and Hooker was waked from his trance by the warning click of a gun-lock. Suddenly his mind came back to his guests, and he ducked like a flash, but even as he went down he heard the hammer *clack!*

The gun had snapped!

Instantly Hooker's hand leaped to his pistol and he fired from the hip pointblank at the would-be murderer. With a yell to the others, one of the Mexicans sprang on him from behind and tried to bear him down. They struggled for a moment while Bud shot blindly with his pistol and went down fighting.

Bud was a giant compared to the stunted Mexicans, and he threw them about like dogs that hang onto a bear. With a man in each hand he rose to his feet, crushing them down beneath him; then, in despair of shaking off his rider, he staggered a few steps and hurled himself over backward into the fire.

A yell of agony followed their fall and, as the live coals bit through the Mexican's thin shirt, he fought like a cat to get free. Rocks, pots, and kettles were kicked in every direction, and when Hooker leaped to his feet the Mexican scrambled up and rushed madly for the creek.

But, though Bud was free, the battle had turned against him, for in the brief interval of his fight the other two Mexicans had run for their guns. The instant he rose they covered him. Their chief, who by some miracle had escaped Bud's shot, gave a shout for them to halt. Cheated of his victim at the first, he was claiming the right to kill.

As Hooker stood blinded by the smoke and ashes the fellow took deliberate aim—and once more his rifle snapped. Then, as the other Mexicans stood agape, surprised at the failure of the shot, the cannonlike whang of a Mauser rent the air and the leader crumpled down in a heap.

An instant later a shrill yell rose from up the cañon and, as the two Mexicans started and stared, Amigo came dashing in upon them, a spitting pistol in one hand and his terrible "wood-chopping" knife brandished high in the other.

In the dusk his eyes and teeth gleamed white, his black hair seemed to bristle with fury, and the glint of his long knife made a light as he vaulted over the last rock and went plunging on their track. For, at the first glance at this huge, pursuing figure the two Mexicans had turned and bolted like rabbits, and now, as the Yaqui whirled in after them, Bud could hear them squealing and scrambling as he hunted them down among the rocks.

It was grim work, too; even for his stomach, but Hooker let the Indian follow his nature. When Amigo came back from his hunting there was no need to ask questions. His eyes shone so terribly that Hooker said nothing, but set about cleaning up camp.

After he had washed the ashes from his eyes, and when the fury had vanished from Amigo's face, they went as by common consent and gazed at the body of the chief of the desperados. Even in death his face seemed strangely familiar; but as Hooker stood gazing at him the Yaqui picked up his gun.

"Look!" he said, and pointed to a bullet-splash where, as the Mexican held the gun across his breast, Bud's pistol-shot had flattened harmlessly against the lock. It was that which had saved the Mexican chief from instant death, and the jar of the shot had doubtless broken the rifle and saved Bud, in turn, from the second shot.

All this was in the Yaqui's eye as he carefully tested the action; but, when he threw down the lever, a cartridge rose up from the magazine and glided smoothly into the breech. With a rifle full of cartridges the ignorant Mexican had been snapping on an empty chamber, not knowing enough to jack up a shell!

For a moment Amigo stared at the gun and the man, and his mouth drew down with contempt.

"Ha! *Pendejo*!" he grunted, and kicked the corpse with his foot.

But if the Mexican had been a fool, he had paid the price, for the second time he snapped his gun Amigo had shot him through and through.

XX

In a country where witnesses to a crime are imprisoned along with the principals and kept more or less indefinitely in jail, a man thinks twice before he reports to the police.

With four dead Mexicans to the Yaqui's account, and Del Rey in charge of the district, Hooker followed his second thought—he said nothing, and took his chances on being arrested for murder. Until far into the night Amigo busied himself along the hillside, and when the sun rose not a sign remained to tell the story of the fight.

Men, horses, saddles, and guns—all had disappeared. And, after packing a little food in a sack, Amigo disappeared also, with a grim smile in promise of return.

The sun rose round and hot, the same as usual; the south wind came up and blew into a bellying mass of clouds, which lashed back with the accustomed rain; and when all the earth was washed clean and fresh the last trace of the struggle was gone. Only by the burns on his hands was Hooker aware of the fight and of the treachery which had reared its head against him like a snake which has been warmed and fed.

Nowhere but in Mexico, where the low *pelado* classes have made such deeds a subtlety, could the man be found to dissimulate like that false assassin-in-chief. To pause suddenly in a protracted speech, swing over and pick up a gun, and halt his victim for the shooting by the preparatory click of the lock—that indeed called for a brand of cunning rarely found in the United States.

There was one thing about the affair that vaguely haunted Hooker—why was it that a man so cunning as that had failed to load his gun? Twice, and with everything in his favor, he had raised his rifle to fire; and both times it had snapped in his hands. Certainly he must have been inept at arms—or accustomed to single-shot guns.

The reputed magic of the swift-firing rifles evidently had been his undoing, but where had he got his new gun? And who was he, anyway? With those two baffling questions Bud wrestled as he sat beside his door, and at evening his answer came.

The sun was swinging low and he was collecting wood down the gulch for a fire when, with a sudden thud of hoofs, a horseman rounded the point and came abruptly to a halt. It was Aragon, and he was spying on the camp.

For a full minute he scanned the house, tent, and mine with a look so snaky and sinister that Bud could read his heart like a book. Here was the man who had sent the assassins, and he had come to view their work!

Very slowly Bud's hand crept toward his six-shooter, but, slight as was the motion, Aragon caught it and sat frozen in his place. Then, with an inarticulate cry, he fell flat on his horse's neck and went spurring out of sight.

The answer to Bud's questions was very easy now. The Mexican who had led the attempt on his life was one of Aragon's bad men, one of the four gunmen whom Hooker had looked over so carefully when they came to drive him from the mine, and Aragon had fitted him out with new arms to make the result more sure. But with that question answered there came up another and another until, in a sudden clarity of vision, Bud saw through the hellish plot and beheld himself the master.

As man to man, Aragon would not dare to face him now, for he knew that he merited death. By his sly approach, by the look in his eyes and the dismay of his frenzied retreat, he had acknowledged more surely than by words his guilty knowledge of the raid. Coming to a camp where he expected to find all dead and still, he had found himself face to face with the very man he had sought to kill. How, then, had the American escaped destruction, and what had occurred to his men?

Perhaps, in his ignorance, Aragon was raging at his hirelings because they had shirked their task; perhaps, not knowing that they were dead, he was waiting in a fever of impatience for them to accomplish the deed. However it was, Bud saw that he held the high card, and he was not slow to act.

In the morning he saddled up Copper Bottom, who had been confined to the corral for weeks, and went galloping into town. There he lingered about the hotel until he saw his man and started boldly toward him. Surprise, alarm, and pitiful fear chased themselves across Aragon's face as he stood, but Bud walked proudly by.

"Good morning, *señor*!" was all Bud said, but the look in his eyes was eloquent of a grim hereafter.

And instead of hurrying back to guard his precious mine Hooker loitered carelessly about town. His mine was safe now—and he was safe. Aragon dared not raise a hand. So he sat himself down on the broad veranda and listened with boyish interest to Don Juan's account of the war.

"What, have you not heard of the battle?" cried portly Don Juan, delighted to have a fresh listener. "Agua Negra has been taken and retaken, and the railroad will soon be repaired. My gracious! have you been out in the hills that long? Why, it was two weeks ago that the rebels captured the town by a *coup*, and eight days later the Federals took it back.

"Ah, there has been a real war, Mr. Bud!

You who have laughed at the courage of the Mexicans, what do you think of Bernardo Bravo and his men? They captured the last up train from Fortuna; loaded all the men into the ore-cars and empty coaches; and, while the Federals were still in their barracks, the train ran clear into the station and took the town by storm.

"And eight days later, at sundown, the Federals took it back. Ah, there was awful slaughter averted, *señor*! But for the fact that the fuse went out the two hundred Yaqui Indians who led the charge would have been blown into eternity.

"Yes, so great was the charge of dynamite that the rebels had laid in their mine that not a house in Agua Negra would have been left standing if the fuse had done its work. Two tons of dynamite! Think of that, my friend!

"But these rebels were as ignorant of its power as they were of laying a train. The Yaquis walked into the town at sundown and found it deserted— every man, woman, and child had fled to Gadsden and the rebels had fled to the west.

"But listen, here was the way it happened— actually, and not as common report has it, for the country is all in an uproar and the real facts were never known. When Bernardo Bravo captured the town of Agua Negra the people acclaimed him a hero.

"He sent word to the junta at El Paso and set up a new form of government. All was enthusiasm, and several Americans joined his ranks to operate the machine guns and cannon. As for the Federals, they occupied the country to the east and attempted a few sallies, but as they had nothing but their rifles, the artillery drove them back.

"Then, as the battle ceased, the rebels began to celebrate their victory. They broke into the closed *cantinas*, disobeying their officers and beginning the loot of the town, and while half of their number were drunk the Federals, being informed of their condition, suddenly advanced upon them, with the Yaquis far in the lead.

"They did not shoot, those Yaquis; but, dragging their guns behind them, they crept up through the bushes and dug pits quite close to the lines. Then, when the rebels discovered them and manned their guns, the Yaquis shot down the gunners.

"Growing bolder, they crept farther to the front—the rebels became disorganized, their men became mutinous—and at last, when they saw they would surely be taken, the leaders buried two tons of dynamite in the trenches by the bull-ring and set a time-fuse, to explode when the Yaquis arrived.

"The word spread through the town like wildfire—all the people, all the soldiers fled every which way to escape—and then, when the worst was expected to happen, the dynamite failed to explode and the Yaquis rushed the trenches at sundown."

"Did those Yaquis know about the dynamite?" inquired Bud.

"Know?" repeated Don Juan, waving the thought away. "Not a word! Their commanders kept it from them, even after they discovered the mine. And now the Indians are making boasts; they are drunk with the thought of their valor and claim that the rebels fled from them alone.

"The roadmaster came into town this morning on a velocipede and said that the Yaquis are insufferable, thinking that it was their renown as fighters and not the news of the dynamite that drove all the soldiers from town.

"However, Agua Negra is once more in the hands of the government; the track is clear and most of the bridges repaired; so why quarrel with the Yaquis? While they are, of course, nothing but Indians, they serve their purpose in battle."

"Well, I guess yes!" responded Bud warmly. "Serve their purpose, eh? Where were these Mexican soldiers and them Spanish officers when the Yaquis were taking the town? And that was just like a dog-goned Mexican—setting that time-fuse and then not having it go off. More'n likely the poor yap that fired it was so scairt he couldn't hold a match—probably never lit it, jest dropped the match and run. They're a bum bunch, if you want to know what I think. I'd rather have a Yaqui than a hundred of 'em!"

"A hundred of whom?" inquired a cool voice behind him, and looking up Hooker saw the beautiful Gracia gazing out at him through the screen door.

"A hundred Mexicans!" he repeated, and Gracia murmured "Oh!" and was gone.

"Miss Aragon is very loyal to her country," observed Don Juan, but Hooker only grunted.

Somehow, since those four Mexicans had come to his camp, he had soured on everything south of the line; and even the charming Gracia could not make him take back his words. If she had intended the remark as a challenge—a subtle invitation to follow her and defend his faith—she failed for once of her purpose, for if there was any particular man in Mexico that Bud hated more than another it was her false-hearted father.

Hooker had, in fact, thought more seriously of making her a half-orphan than of winning her goodwill, and he lingered about the hotel, not to make love to the daughter, but to strike terror to Aragon.

The company being good, and a train being expected soon, Bud stayed over another day. In the morning, when he came down for breakfast, he found that Aragon had fled before him. With his wife Juan, daughter, and retinue, he had moved suddenly back to his home. Hooker grinned when Don told him the news.

214

"Well, why not?" he asked, chuckling maliciously. "Here it's the middle of the rainy season and the war going on all summer and nary a rebel in sight. Where's that big fight you was telling about—the battle of Fortuna? You've made a regular fortune out of these refugees, Brachamonte, but I fail to see the enemy."

"Ah, you may laugh," shrugged the hotel-keeper, "but wait! The time will come. The rebels are lost now—someday, when you least expect it, they will come upon us and then, believe me, my guests will be glad they are here. What is a few weeks' bill compared to being held for ransom? Look at that rich Señor Luna who was here for a time in the spring. Against my advice he hurried home and now he is paying the price. Ten thousand pesos it cost to save his wife and family, and for himself and son his friends advanced ten thousand more. I make no evil prophecies, but it would be better for our friend if he stayed on at my poor hotel."

"Whose friend?" inquired Bud bluffly, but Don Juan struck him upon the back with elephantine playfulness and hurried off to his duties.

As for Hooker, he tarried in town until he got his mail and a copy of the Sunday paper and then, well satisfied that the times were quiet and wars a thing of the past, he ambled back to the Eagle Tail and settled down for a rest.

Flat on his back by the doorway, he lay on his

215

bed and smoked, reading his way through the lurid supplement and watching the trail with one eye. Since the fight with Aragon's Mexicans all his apprehensions had left him. He had written briefly to Phil and Kruger, and now he was holding the fort.

It had been a close shave, but he had escaped the cowardly assassins and had Aragon in his power—not by any force of law, but by the force of fear and the gnawing weakness of Aragon's own evil conscience.

Aragon was afraid of what he had done, but it was the suspense which rendered him so pitiable. On a day he had sent four armed Mexicans to kill this Texan—not one had returned and the Texan regarded him sneeringly. This it was that broke the Spaniard's will, for he knew not what to think. But as for Bud, he lay on his back by the doorway and laughed at the funny page.

As he sprawled there at his reading, Amigo came in from the hills, and he, too, was content to relax. Gravely scanning the colored sheet, his dark face lighted up.

It was all very peaceful and pleasant, but it was not destined to last.

XXI

On the morning after they had laughed at the comic paper and decided that all the world was fair, Hooker and Amigo were squatting by the fire and eating a man's-size breakfast.

The creek, swollen by yesterday's torrential rain, had settled to a rivulet. The wind had not risen and the sun was just over the hill when, with a rush and a scramble, Amigo threw down his cup and was off in a flash for the rocks.

A moment later two men rode down the cañon, and then two more, and two more. It was a column of men, all armed with rifles, and they cast envious eyes at Copper Bottom as they halted before the camp. As for Bud, he saluted gravely, for he knew them for what they were.

These were the lost forces of Bernardo Bravo and Salazar, Rojas, and the other bandit chiefs, and they marched, as he well knew, upon Fortuna. They marched quietly, and the great whistle had not blown.

It would make a rich prize, Fortuna, if they could take it by surprise! The ransom for the Spanish *haciendados* alone would amount to thousands of dollars, and the mine-owners could afford to pay anything in order to save their works.

A box of dynamite under the giant concentrator and the money would be produced at once and yet the scoundrels halted at a one-man camp to steal a single horse!

A flicker of scorn passed over Hooker's face as the leader came dashing up, but the Texan greeted him with a slow smile.

"*Buenos dias*, general!" he said. "You have many men."

"Enough!" observed the "general" hurriedly. "But some in the rear are on foot. As I suppose you are in sympathy with our great cause, I will ask you for that horse. Of course, I will give you a receipt."

He fetched out a blank-book as he spoke and motioned to a ragged beggar at his heels. Bud checked the man's rush with a look.

"One moment!" he said, and as the soldier turned back his general glanced up sharply.

"What is it?" he asked.

"Only this, Señor General," answered Bud. "You are welcome to anything I have—food, blankets, money—but I cannot give you that horse."

"But, *señor*," protested the general, regarding him with arrogant pig eyes that glinted wickedly, "this poor soldier's feet are sore. Surely you would not make him walk. Only name your price and I will give you a receipt for him, but my man must have the horse."

There was a pause and men began to dismount and move in closer. At a word from their commander any one of them would draw and kill him, as Hooker very well knew, but his love for Copper Bottom made him obdurate.

"If the man is lame," he said, "I will give him another horse—but he cannot have this sorrel."

He stepped quickly over to the corral and turned with his back to the gate, while the commander spat out orders in Spanish and armed men came running.

"*Señor*," he said, advancing bruskly upon the defiant Hooker, "I must trouble you for that pistol."

"No, *señor*!" answered the cowboy, keeping his hand upon his gun, "not to you nor no man—and I'll never give it up to a Mexican!"

"*Carái!*" exclaimed the officer impatiently, "you are an *Americano*—no?"

"Not only that," rumbled Bud, drawing himself up in his pride, "I am a *Tejano* also, and if any man touches that horse I'll kill him!"

His voice trembled with anger, but his hand was steady and the Mexicans did not deceive themselves.

"Ha, *uno Tejano*!" murmured the men who stood about, and one or two who had started to climb the fence thought better of it and dropped back to the ground.

Bud knew the fate of several men who had

219

proclaimed themselves Americans to the *insurrectos*—boastfully done, it was said to be the quickest way there was of drawing a Mexican bullet. But to be a Texan was different—somehow the very name suggested trouble to their minds and an Alamo fight to the death. Hooker saw that he had made an impression, and he was not slow to follow it up.

"If you need a horse," he said to the general, "let your man go up that arroyo and he will find one hobbled on the flat. Then give me your receipt for two hundred dollars gold and I will contribute a saddle."

It was a reasonable concession, under the circumstances, and, best of all, it saved the general's face. The hideous frown with which he had regarded the American changed suddenly to a look of pompous pride. He jerked an imperious head at his ragged retainer and drew forth his receipt-book with a flourish.

While he waited for the horse to appear he turned upon his snooping men and drove them to their mounts with curses. Evidently it was no sinecure to command in the army of the liberation, and the veiled mutterings of his followers showed that they were little better than tigers in leash.

Mounted upon horses, mules, and even burros, armed with every conceivable weapon from a musket to standard repeating rifles, they were a tatterdemalion army, more fit for "treason, strategems, and spoils" than the sterner duties of war.

Bud looked them over closely, well satisfied to have his back against a wall, and when the low-browed retainer came hurrying back with the horse he quickly took the worthless receipt and watched them on their way. Then, as the last camp-follower disappeared, he ran for his saddle and rifle and within a minute he was mounted and away.

There were rebels below him—very likely there were more to come—the only safe place for Copper Bottom was over the hills at Fortuna. Without stopping for path or trail he headed straight northwest over the ridges, riding as the cowboys do when they rake the range for cattle. Hardly had he topped the first high crest when he came in sight of Amigo, loaded down with his cartridge-belts and carrying his heavy Mauser.

In a long, shambling trot the Yaqui was drifting along the hillside with the free grace of a wild creature, and when Hooker pulled down his horse to keep pace with him he laughed and motioned him on. Taking the lead, he loped on over hogback and *barranca*, picking out the best trail by instinct and setting such a pace that Bud was hard-pressed to keep up with him.

He had heard it said that in the Yaqui country no white man, no matter how well he was mounted, could outdistance the Indians on foot, and now he knew it was true. But why this killing haste on the part of Amigo? He had neither friends nor kin in town; why, then, should he run so fast to warn them of the enemy?

They racked on, up one hill and down another, while the *insurrectos* followed the cañon that swung to the south, and finally, in a last scramble, they mounted a rocky ridge and looked down upon Old Fortuna.

Already the hard-driven peons were out in the fields at work and smoke was rising from the *mescal* still. Aragon was busy, but his labors would be worse than wasted if the red-flaggers took him prisoner. As Bud breathed his horse he hesitated whether to ride back and warn him or press on and notify Fortuna; but even for that brief spell the Yaqui could not wait.

"*Adios,*" he said, coming close and holding out his black hand; "I go this way!" And he pointed along the ridge.

"But why?" said Bud, still at a loss to account for his haste. Then, seeing the reticence in the Indian's eyes, he thrust out his hand in return.

"*Adios, amigo mio!*" he replied, and with a quick grip the Yaqui was gone.

With that same deceptive speed he shambled through the bushes, still lugging the heavy rifle and making for higher ground. Bud knew he had some purpose—he even had a sneaking idea that it was to take pot-shots at Captain del Rey—but six months in Mexico had made him careless, and he half hoped the Yaqui would win.

The *capitan* had it coming to him for his brutality, but with Aragon it was different—Aragon had a wife and daughter—and, with the memory of Gracia in his mind, Bud sent his horse plunging down the ridge to warn them before it was too late.

There were some brush fences to be jumped, but Copper Bottom took them flying, and as they cut into the river trail he made the mud-puddles splash. Across the fields to the south Bud could see the peons running for cover—the *insurrectos* must be in sight beyond the hills.

He was going south, they were moving west, but it was five miles north again to the town. Speed was what was needed and Copper Bottom gave his best. They dashed into Fortuna like a whirlwind, and Hooker raised his voice in a high yell.

"*Insurrectos!*" he shouted. "*Ladrones*! *Pr-onto á* Fortuna!"

There was a hush, a moment's silence, and then heads appeared from every window and women ran screaming with the news. Aragon came rushing from the store and confronted him angrily; then, reading conviction in his tones, he called for horses and ran frantically into the house.

A shrill screech came from the hillside, where a serving-woman had scampered to view the valley, and, as she pointed her finger and screamed, mothers laid hold of their little ones and started up the valley on foot.

Still the men ran about in the horse-pen and Aragon adjured his womenfolk in the house. Burning with impatience, Bud spurred his way to the corral where they were fumbling with reata and rigging and dropped a rope on the first horse he saw. Then he snatched a side-saddle from a trembling peon and slapped it on the brute's back. Grabbing up the bridle, he led the horse back to the house and bridled it while he shouted for haste.

Still the women tarried, and the sound of galloping came from the south. Then, as all seemed lost, the Mexicans came bumping out from the stable with the family coach, Aragon and his wife leaped in, and Gracia, neatly attired in a riding-skirt, came tripping down the steps.

Even in such times as these she seemed to realize her first duty to herself, and Hooker had to gaze for a moment before he helped her up. She offered her foot and vaulted lightly into the saddle; the coach went pounding on ahead; and as the servants scattered before her she galloped off at the side of Bud.

Behind them the rumble of distant hoofs rose up like the roaring of waters, and the shrieks of fleeing women echoed from the roadside, but once safely in the cañon their lead was never lessened and, with coach-horses galloping and postilions lashing from both sides, the whole cavalcade swept into the plaza while the town of Fortuna went mad.

Already the great whistle was blowing hoarsely, its deep reverberations making the air tremble as if with fear. Americans were running back and forth, distributing arms and rushing their women to cover; Don Juan, his chin quivering with excitement, was imploring all comers to be calm; and the Aragons, coming flying up to the door, added the last touch to the panic.

They with their own eyes had seen the rebels; they were riding in from the south! Other men, equally excited, swore they were coming from the north, and a disorderly body of Sonoran miners, armed as if by magic with guns which had long lain hidden, banked themselves about the store and office and clamored for more and more cartridges. Then a rip of gun-fire echoed from across the cañon, and the miners made a rush to the attack.

The whistle, which had obscured all sound as a cloud obscures the light, stopped suddenly in its roar, and the crowd at the hotel became calm. The superintendent, a wiry, gray-haired little man with decision in every movement, came running from his fortlike house on the hill and ordered all the women to take shelter there and take their children with them.

So, while the rifles rattled and stray bullets began to knock mud from the walls, they went straggling up the hill, rich and poor, patrician and peon, while the air was rent by the wails of the half-Indian Mexican women who held themselves as good as captured by the *revoltosos*, concerning whose scruples they entertained no illusions.

The women of the aristocracy bore themselves with more reserve, as befitting their birth and station, and the Americans who gathered about them with their protecting rifles pretended that all would be well; but in the mind of everyone was that same terror which found expression in the peon wail and, while scattered rebels and newly armed miners exchanged volleys on both sides of the town, the non-combatant Americans sought out every woman and rushed her up to the big house. There, if worst came to worst, they could make a last stand, or save them by a ransom.

So, from the old woman who kept the candy stand in the plaza to the wives of the miners and the cherished womenfolk of the landowners, they were all crowded inside the broad halls of the big house; and seventy-odd Americans, armed with company rifles, paced nervously along the broad verandas or punched loopholes in the adobe walls that enclosed the summer-garden behind.

Along with the rest went Hooker and Gracia, and, though her mother beckoned and her father frowned sternly, the willful daughter of the Aragons did not offer to leave him as they scampered up the hill. In fact, she rode close beside him, spurring when he spurred and, finally, when the shower of stray bullets had passed, she led on around the house.

"Won't you help me take my horse inside the walls?" she asked. Bud followed after her, circling the fortress whose blank adobe walls gave shelter to the screaming women, and she smiled upon him with the most engaging confidence.

"I know you will have to go soon," she said, "and I suppose I've got to be shut in with those creatures, but we must be sure to save our horses. Some bullets might hit them, you know, and then we could not run away!

"You remember your promise!" she reminded, as Bud gazed at her in astonishment. "Ah, yes, I knew you did—otherwise you would not have picked such a good horse for me. This roan is my father's best riding-horse. You must put yours inside the wall with him, and when the time is right we will get them and ride for the line."

"What?" cried Hooker incredulously, "with the

country full of rebels? They're liable to take the town in half an hour!"

"No, indeed they will not!" responded Gracia with spirit. "You do not understand the spirit of us Sonorans! Can't you see how the firing has slackened? The miners have driven your rebels back already, and they will do more— they will follow them up and kill them! Then, when the rebels are in flight and Del Rey and his *rurales* are away, that will be a good time for us to slip off and make our dash for the line!"

"Nothing doing!" announced Hooker, as he dismounted at the corral. "You don't know what you're talking about! But I will leave my horse here," he added. "I sure don't want *him* to get hurt."

"But you promised!" protested Gracia weakly.

"Promised nothing!" retorted Bud ungraciously. "I promised to take care of you, didn't I? Well, what's the use of talking, then? You better stay right here, where you're safe. Come on, let's go to the house!"

"No!" cried Gracia, her dark eyes turning misty with imminent tears. "Oh, Mr. Hooker!" she burst out, "didn't I keep them all waiting while I put on this riding-skirt? I thought you had come to take me away! What do I care to be safe? I want to be free! I want to run away—and go across the line to dear Phil!" she faltered. Then she looked up at him sharply and her voice took on an accusing tone.

"Aha!" she said, as if making some expected discovery, "so *that* is it! I thought perhaps you were *afraid!*"

"What?" demanded Bud, put suddenly upon the defensive.

"I might have known it," soliloquized Gracia with conviction. "You are jealous of dear Phil!"

"Who? Me?" cried Hooker, smiling down at her grimly. "Well, let it go at that," he said, as she regarded him with an arch smile. "I'd certainly be a fool to take all those chances for nothing. Let him steal his own girl—that's what I say!"

"Now that, Mr. Hooker," burst out Gracia in a passion, "is very unkind—and rude! Am I a woman of the town, to be stolen by one man or another? Am I—"

"That's what you would be," put in Bud, with brutal directness, "if these rebels got hold of you. No, ma'am, I wouldn't take you out of this town for a hundred thousand dollars. You don't know what you're talking about, that's all! Wait till the fighting is over—Gee! Did you hear that? Come on, let's get into the house!"

He ducked suddenly as a bullet went *spang* against the corrugated iron roof above them and, seizing her by the hand, he half dragged her through a side door and into the summer-garden.

Here a sudden outcry of women's voices

229

assailed their ears like a rush of wind and they beheld peon mothers running to and fro with their screaming children clasped to their breasts or dragging at their skirts. A few helpless men were trying to keep them quiet, but as the bullets began to thud against the adobe walls the garden became a bedlam.

Gracia stood and surveyed the scene for a moment, ignoring the hulking Bud with disdainful eyes. Then she snatched her hand indignantly away and ran to pick up a child. That was all, but Hooker knew what she thought of him.

He passed through the house, hoping to discover where she had gone, but all he heard was her commanding voice as she silenced the wailing women, and, feeling somehow very much out of place, he stepped forth into the open.

After all, for a man of his build, the open was best. Let the white-handed boys stay with the ladies—they understood their ways.

XXII

The superintendent's house stood on a low bench above the town, looking out over all the valley, but protected by a high hill behind, upon the summit of which was placed a mammoth black water-tank.

In its architecture the *casa grande* was an exact replica of a hot-country *hacienda*, a flat-roofed, one storied square of adobe bricks, whitewashed to keep off the sun and presenting on three sides nothing but the dead walls of house and garden, with dense trees planted near for shade. Along the front was a long arcade, the *corredor*, graced by a series of massive arches which let in the light and air. Inside were low chambers and long passages; and, behind, the *patio* and garden of orange and fig trees.

Built for a sumptuous dwelling, it became in a moment a fort and, with men on the high hill by the tank, it was practically impregnable to direct assault.

As Hooker stepped out onto the covered porch with his saddle-gun in his hand he became simply one more of a band of excited Americans, all armed and ready to defend the house to the last. Some were pacing back and forth in the *corredor*, others were hurrying up from the

Mexican quarters with a last belated handful of women, but the major portion were out on the open bench, either gazing north and south at the scenes of the distant firing or engaging in a curio-mad scramble for any spent bullet that struck.

The fighting, such as there was, was mostly up the cañon, where a large party of Sonoran miners had rushed in pursuit of the rebels. The firing down the cañon in the direction of Old Fortuna had died away to nothing, and for the moment it seemed as if the futile charge and retreat were the beginning and the end of the battle.

A party of rebels had penetrated clear into the town, but it was apparently more by accident than intention, and they had been quick to beat a retreat. As for the main command of the *insurrectos*, they were reported at Chular, six miles up the railroad, where they had surrounded and taken a small mining camp and captured a train at the summit.

The column to the south—the one which Hooker had encountered—had taken to the high hills west of the town, and, along the sky-line of the buttelike summits, they could now be seen in scattered bands making their way to the north.

The defenders of Fortuna consisted of a rag-tag garrison of twenty Federals and the hot-headed, charging miners. But apparently that was a combination hard to beat, for, while the Federals entrenched themselves behind the black tank on the hill and prepared to protect the town, the Sonorans in shouting masses drove everything before them and marched on to attack Chular.

But in this they made a mistake, for the rebel scouts, seeing the great body of defenders pressing on up the narrow cañon, rode back and informed the tricky Bernardo Bravo. He would be a poor general indeed who could not see the opening that was offered and, while the valiant Sonorans pursued the rebel cavalry up the pass, Bernardo Bravo sent the half of his thousand men to cut off their retreat from behind.

Along the broad top of the mountain above they came scampering by tens and twenties, closing in with a vastly superior force upon the now defenseless town. In the depths of the cañon below the miners were still chasing the elusive cavalry, their firing becoming faint as they clambered on toward the summit and the rebel headquarters at Chular.

They had, in fact, been handled like children, and the Americans joined in contemptuous curses of their mistaken bravery as they beheld in what straits it had left them.

Forbidden by the superintendent to participate in the combat, yet having in their care the women of the camp, they were compelled to stand passively aside while rebels by the hundred came charging down the ridges. Only in the last resort, and when all diplomacy and Federal defense had failed, would they be allowed to so much as cock a rifle. And yet—well, twenty determined Americans might easily turn back this charge.

Taking advantage of his Mexican citizenship, Hooker was already on the run for the trenches when the superintendent stopped him with a look.

"Let the Mexicans fight it out," he said. "They might resent it if you took sides, and that would make it bad for us. Just wait a while—you never can tell what will happen. Perhaps the *rurales* and Federals will stand them off."

"What, that little bunch?" demanded Bud, pointing scornfully at the handful of defenders who were cowering behind their rock-piles. "Why, half of them *pelónes* don't know what a gun was made for, and the *rurales*—"

"Well, the rebels are the same," suggested the superintendent pacifically. "Let them fight it out—we need every American we can get, so just forget about being a Mexican."

"All right," agreed Bud, as he yielded reluctantly to reason. "It ain't because I'm a Mexican citizen—I just want to stop that rush."

He walked back to the house, juggling his useless gun and keeping his eye on the distant ridges. And then, in a chorus of defiant yells, the men in the Federal trenches began to shoot.

In an air-line the distance was something over a mile, but at the first scattering volley the rebels halted and fired a volley in return. With a vicious *spang* a few stray bullets smashed against the reverberating steel tank, but no one was hurt, and the defenders, drunk with valor, began to shoot and yell like mad.

The bullets of the rebels, fired at random, struck up dust-jets in every direction, and from the lower part of the town came the shouting of the non-combatant Mexicans as they ran here and there for shelter. But by the trenches, and in the rear of the black tank, the great crowd of onlookers persisted, ducking as each successive bullet hit the tank and shouting encouragement as the defenders emptied their rifles and reloaded with clip after clip.

The rifles rattled a continuous volley; spent bullets leaped like locusts across the flat; men ran to and fro, now crouching behind the tank, now stepping boldly into the open; and the defiant shouts of the defenders almost drowned the wails of the women. Except for one thing it was a battle—there was nobody hurt.

For the first half-hour the Americans stayed prudently under cover, busying themselves at the suggestion of a few American women in providing a first-aid hospital on the sheltered porch. Then, as no wounded came to fill it and the rebels delayed their charge, one man after another climbed up to the trenches, ostensibly to bring down the injured.

As soldiers and bystanders reported no one hit, and the bullets flew harmlessly past, their solicitude turned rapidly to disgust and then to scorn. Strange as it may seem, they were disappointed at the results, and their remarks were derogatory as they commented on the bravery of *pelónes* and Mexicans in general.

From a dread of imminent attack, of charging rebels and retreating defenders, and a fight to the death by the house, they came suddenly to a desire for blood and battle, for dead men and the cries of the wounded; and all fear of the *insurrectos* left them.

"Come away, boys," grunted the burly road-master, who up to then had led in the work; "we wasted our time on that hospital—there'll be no wounded. Let's take ourselves back to the house and have a quiet smoke."

"Right you are, Ed," agreed the master mechanic, as he turned upon his heel in disgust. "This ain't war—them Mexicans think they're working for a moving-picture show!"

"I bet you I can go up on that ridge," announced Hooker, "and clean out the whole bunch with my six-shooter before you could bat your eye."

But the superintendent was not so sure.

"Never mind, boys," he said. "We're worth a lot of ransom money to those rebels and they won't give up so quick. And look at this now— my miners coming back! Those are the boys that will fight! Wait till Chico and Ramon Mendoza get after them!"

He pointed as he spoke to a straggling band of Sonorans, led by the much-vaunted Mendoza brothers, as they hurried to save the town, and a cheer went up from the trenches as the Federals beheld reenforcements. But a change had come over the fire-eating miners, and they brought other rebels in their wake.

As they trudged wearily into town and sought shelter among the houses a great body of men appeared on the opposite ridge, firing down at them as they retreated. The battle rapidly turned into a long-distance shooting contest, with the rebels on the ridges and the defenders in the valley, and finally, as the day wore on and a thunderstorm came up, it died out altogether and the rebels turned back to their camp.

Except for one lone Federal who had shot himself by accident there was not a single defender hurt, and if the enemy had suffered losses it was only by some such chance. But when the Sonoran patriots, holding up their empty belts, came clamoring for ammunition, the men by the big house took in the real catastrophe of the battle.

Seventeen thousand rounds of the precious thirty-thirties had been delivered to the excited miners and now, except for what few the Americans had saved, there was not a cartridge in camp. Very soberly the superintendent assured the leaders that he had no more. They pointed at the full belts of the American guard and demanded them as their right; and when the Americans refused to yield they flew into a rage and threatened.

All in all, it was a pitiful exhibition of hot-headedness and imbecility, and only the firmness of the superintendent prevented a real spilling of blood. The Mexicans retired in a huff and broke into the *cantina*, and as the night came on the valley reechoed to their drunken shoutings.

Such was war as the Sonorans conceived it. When Hooker, standing his guard in the *corredor*, encountered Gracia Aragon on her evening walk, he could scarcely conceal a grin.

"What are you laughing at, Señor Hooker?" she demanded with asperity. "Is it so pleasant, with a houseful of frightened women and screaming children, that you should make fun of our plight?"

"No, indeed," apologized Bud; "nothing like that. Sure must be bad in there—I stay outside myself. But I reckon it'll soon be over with. The Mexicans here in town have shot off all their ammunition and I reckon the rebels have done the same. Like as not they'll all be gone to-morrow, and then you can go back home."

"Oh, thank you for thinking about me!" she returned with a scornful curl of the lip. "But if all men were as open as you, Mr. Hooker, we women would never need to ask a question. This morning you told me I did not know what I was talking about—now I presume you are thinking what cowards the Mexicans are!

"Oh, I know! You need not deny it! You are nothing but a great big—*Tejano*! Yes, I was going to say 'brute,' but you are a friend of dear Phil's, and so I will hold my tongue. If it wasn't for that, I'd—" She paused, leaving him to guess.

"Oh, I do wish he were here!" she breathed, leaning wearily against the white pillar of an arch and gazing down through the long arcade.

"It was so close in there," she continued, "I could not stand it a minute longer. These Indian women, you know—they weep and moan all the time. And the children—I am so sorry for them. I cannot go now, because they need me; but to-morrow—if Phil were here—I would leave and ride for the line.

"Have you seen Del Rey to-day? No? Then all the better—he must be policing the town. It is only of him I am afraid. These rebels are nothing—I agree with you! No! I am not angry with you at all now! But to-morrow, just at dusk, when all is still as it is at this time; then, if Phil were here, I would mount my brave horse and ride out by the western pass."

She ended rather inconclusively, letting her voice trail off wistfully as she waited for him to speak, but something within moved Hooker to hold his peace, and he looked out over the town without commenting on her plans. It was evident to him that she was determined to enlist his sympathy and involve him in her wild plot, and each time the conversation veered in that direction he took refuge in a stubborn silence.

"What are you thinking, Mr. Hooker?" she asked at last, as he gazed into the dusk. "Sometimes I scold you and sometimes I try to please you, but I never know what you think! I did not mean that when I said I could read your thoughts—you are so different from poor, dear Phil!"

"M-m-m," mumbled Bud, shifting his feet, and his face turned a little grim.

"Aha!" she cried with ill-concealed satisfaction, "you do not like me to call him that, do you? 'Poor, dear Phil,'—like that! But do you know why I do it? It is to punish you for never coming near me—when I signed to you—when I waited for you—long ago! Ah, you were so cruel! I wanted to know you—you were a cowboy, and I thought you were brave enough to defend me—but you always rode right by. Yes, that was it—but Phil was different! He came when I sent for him; he sang songs to me at night; he took my part against Manuel del Rey; and now—"

"Yes!" commented Bud bruskly, with his mind

on "dear Phil's" finish, and she turned to peer into his face.

"So that is it!" she said. "You do not trust me. You think that I am not your friend—that I will serve you as he was served. Is that what you are thinking?"

"Something like that," admitted Hooker, leaning lazily against the mud wall. "Only I reckon I don't think just the way you do."

"Why? How do I think?" she demanded eagerly.

"Well, you think awful fast," answered Hooker slowly. "And you don't always think the same, seems like. I'm kind of quiet myself, and I don't like—well, I wouldn't say that, but you don't always mean what you say."

"Oh!" breathed Gracia, and then, after a pause, she came nearer and leaned against the low wall beside him.

"If I would speak from my heart," she asked, "if I would talk plain, as you Americans do, would you like me better then? Would you talk to me instead of standing silent? Listen, Bud—for that is your name—I want you to be my friend the way you were a friend to Phil. I know what you did for him, and how you bore with his love-madness—and that was my fault, too. But partly it was also your fault, for you made me angry by not coming.

"Yes, I will be honest now—it was you that I

wanted to know at first, but you would not come, and now I am promised to Phil. He was brave when you were careful, and my heart went out to him. You know how it is with us Mexicans—we do not love by reason. We love like children—suddenly—from the heart! And now all I wish in life is to run away to Phil. But every time I speak of it you shut your jaws or tell me I am a fool."

"Ump-um," protested Bud, turning stubborn again. "I tell you you don't know what you're talking about. These rebels don't amount to nothing around the town, but on a trail they're awful. They shoot from behind rocks and all that, and a woman ain't no ways safe. You must know what they're like—these old women don't think about nothing else—so what's the use of talking? And besides," he added grimly, "I've had some trouble with your old man and don't want to have any more."

"What trouble have you had?" she demanded promptly, but Hooker would not answer in words. He only shrugged his shoulders and turned away, crumpling his hat in his hand.

"But no!" she cried as she sensed the meaning of his concealment, "you must tell me! I want to know. Was it over your mine? Then you must not blame me, for he never has told me a word!"

"No?" inquired Bud, rousing suddenly at the memory of his wrongs. "Then maybe you will tell me how he got *this*"—he fetched a worn piece of ore from his pocket—"when my pardner gave it to *you!* It was right there I lost my pardner—and he was a good kid, too—and all because of that rock. Here, take a look at it—I took that away from your father!"

"Then he stole it from me!" flashed back Gracia as she gazed at the specimen. "Oh, have you thought all the time that I betrayed Phil? But didn't I tell you—didn't I tell you at the hotel, when you promised to be my friend? Ah, I see that you are a hard man, Mr. Hooker—quick to suspect, slow to forget—and yet I told you before! But listen, and I will tell you again. I remember well when dear Phil showed me this rock—he was so happy because he had found the gold. And just to make it lucky he let me hold it while we were talking through a hole in the wall. Then my father saw me and started to come near—I could not hand it back without betraying Phil—and in the night, when I was asleep, someone took it from under my pillow. That is the truth, and I will ask you to believe me; and if you have other things against me you must say what they are and see if I cannot explain.

"No!" she ran on, her voice vibrant with the memory of past quarrels. "I have nothing to do with my father! He does not love me, but tries to make me marry first one man and then another. But I am an American girl now, at heart—I do not want to sell myself; I want to marry for love! Can you understand that? Yes? No? Then why do you look away? Have you something that you hold against me? Ah, you shake your head—but you will not speak to me! When I was at school in Los Angeles I saw the cowboys in the West show, and they were different—they were not afraid of any danger, but they would talk, too. I have always wanted to know you, but you will not let me—I thought you were brave—like those cowboys."

She paused to make him speak, but Hooker was tongue-tied. There was something about the way she talked that pulled him over, that made him want to do what she said, and yet some secret, hidden voice was always crying: "Beware!" He was convinced now that she had never been a party to treachery; no, nor even wished him ill.

She was very beautiful, too, in the twilight, and when she drew nearer he moved away, for he was afraid she would sway him from his purpose. But now she was waiting for some answer—some word from him, though the question had never been asked. And yet he knew what it was.

She wanted him to steal away with her in the evening and ride for the border—and Phil. That was what she always wanted, no matter what she said, and now she was calling him a coward.

"Sure them bronco-riders are brave," he said in vague defense; "but there's a difference between being brave and foolish. And a man might be brave for himself and yet be afraid for other people."

"How do you mean?" she asked.

"Well," he said, "I might be willing to go out and fight a thousand of them *insurrectos* with one hand, and at the same time be afraid to take you along. Or I might—"

"Oh, then you *will* go, won't you?" she cried, clasping him by the hand. "You will, won't you? I'm not afraid!"

"No," answered Bud, drawing his hand away, "that's just what I won't do! And I'll tell you why. That country up there is full of rebels— the lowest kind there are. It just takes one shot to lay me out or cripple one of our horses. Then I'd have to make a fight for it—but what would happen to you?"

"I'd fight, too!" spoke up Gracia resolutely. "I'm not afraid."

"No," grumbled Bud, "you don't know them rebels. You've been shut up in a house all the time—if you'd been through what I have in the last six months you'd understand what I mean."

"If Phil were here, *he'd* take me!" countered Gracia, and then Bud lost his head.

"Yes," he burst out, "that's jest what's the matter with the crazy fool! That's jest why he's up across the line now a hollering for me to save his girl! He's brave, is he? Well, why don't he come down, then, and save you himself? Because he's afraid to! He's afraid of getting shot or going up against Manuel del Rey. By grab! it makes me tired the way you people talk! If he'd done what I told him to in the first place he wouldn't have got into this jack-pot!"

"Oh, my!" exclaimed Gracia, aghast. "Why, what is the matter with you? And what did you tell him to do?"

"I told him to mind his own business," answered Hooker bluntly.

"And what did he say?"

"He said he'd try anything—once!"

Bud spat out the phrase vindictively, for his blood was up and his heart was full of bitterness.

"Oh, dear!" faltered Gracia. "And so you do not think that Phil is brave?"

"He's brave to start things," sneered Bud, "but not to carry 'em through!"

For a moment Gracia huddled up against a pillar, her hand against her face, as if to ward off a blow. Then she lowered it slowly and moved reluctantly away.

"I must go now," she said, and Bud did not offer to stay her, for he saw what his unkindness had done.

"I am sorry!" she added pitifully, but he did not answer. There was nothing that he could say now.

In a moment of resentment, driven to exasperation by her taunts, he had forgotten his pledge to his pardner and come between him and his girl. That which he thought wild horses could not draw from him had flashed out in a fit of anger—and the damage was beyond amendment, for what he had said was the truth.

XXIII

There are two things, according to the saying, which cannot be recalled—the sped arrow and the spoken word. Whether spoken in anger or in jest our winged thoughts will not come back to us and, where there is no balm for the wound we have caused, there is nothing to do but let it heal.

Bud Hooker was a man of few words, and slow to speak ill of any one, but some unfamiliar devil had loosened his tongue and he had told the worst about Phil. Certainly if a man were the bravest of the brave, certainly if he loved his girl more than life itself—he would not be content to hide above the line and pour out his soul on note-paper. But to tell it to the girl—that was an unpardonable sin!

Still, now that the damage was done, there was no use of vain repining, and after cursing himself whole-heartedly Bud turned in for the night. Other days were coming; there were favors he might do; and perhaps, as the yesterdays went by, Gracia would forgive him for his plain speaking. Even to-morrow, if the rebels came back for more, he might square himself in action and prove that he was not a coward. A coward!

It had been a long time since any one had used that word to him, but after the way he had knifed "dear Phil" he had to admit he was it. But "dear Phil"! It was that which had set him off.

If she knew how many other girls—but Bud put a sudden quietus on that particular line of thought. As long as the world stood and Gracia was in his sight he swore never to speak ill of De Lancey again, and then he went to sleep.

The men who guarded the *casa grande* slept uneasily on the porch, lying down like dogs on empty sugar-sacks that the women might not lack bedding inside. Even at that they were better off, for the house was close and feverish, with the crying of babies and the babbling of dreamers, and mothers moving to and fro.

It was a hectic night, but Bud slept it out, and at dawn, after the custom of his kind, he arose and stamped on his boots. The moist coolness of the morning brought the odor of wet greasewood and tropic blossoms to his nostrils as he stepped out to speak with the guards, and as he stood there waiting for the full daylight the master mechanic joined him.

He was a full-bodied, round-headed little man with determined views on life, and he began the day, as usual, with his private opinion of Mexicans. They were the same uncomplimentary remarks to which he had given voice on the day before, for the rebels had captured one of his engines and he knew it would come to some harm.

"A fine bunch of *hombres*, yes," he ended, "and may the devil fly away with them! They took No. 9 at the summit yesterday and I've been listening ever since. Her pans are all burned out and we've been feeding her bran like a cow to keep her from leaking steam. If some ignorant Mex gets hold of her you'll hear a big noise—and that'll be the last of No. 9—her boiler will burst like a wet bag.

"If I was running this road there'd be no more bran—not since what I saw over at Aguas Calientes on the Central. One of those bum, renegade engine-drivers had burned out No. 743, but the rebels had ditched four of our best and we had to send her out. Day after day the boys had been feeding her bran until she smelled like a distillery. The mash was oozing out of her as Ben Tyrrell pulled up to the station, and a friend of his that had come down from the north took one sniff and swung up into the cab.

"Ben came down at the word he whispered—for they'd two of 'em blowed up in the north—and they sent out another man. Hadn't got up the hill when the engine exploded and blew the poor devil to hell! I asked Tyrrell what his friend had told him, but he kept it to himself until he could get his time. It's the fumes, boy—they blow up like brandy—and old No. 9 is sour!

"She'll likely blow up, too. But how can we fix her with these ignorant Mexican mechanics?

You should have been over at Aguas the day they fired the Americans.

"'No more *Americanos*!' says Madero. 'Let 'em all out and hire Mexicans! The national railroads of Mexico must not be in the hands of foreigners.'

"So they fired us all in a day and put a Mexican wood-passer up in the cab of old No. 313. He started to pull a string of empties down the track, threw on the air by mistake, and stopped her on a dead-center. Pulled out the throttle and she wouldn't go, so he gave it up and quit.

"Called in the master mechanic then—a Mexican. He tinkered with her for an hour, right there on the track, until she went dead on their hands. Then they ran down a switch-engine and took back the cars and called on the roadmaster—a Mex. He cracked the nut—built a shoo-fly around No. 313 and they left her right there on the main track. Two days later an American hobo came by and he set down and laughed at 'em. Then he throws off the brakes, gives No. 313 a boost past the center with a crowbar, and runs her to the roundhouse by gravity. When we left Aguas on a hand-car that hobo was running the road.

"Ignorantest *hombres* in the world—these Mexicans. Shooting a gun or running an engine, it's all the same—they've got nothing above the eyebrows."

"That's right," agreed Bud, who had been craning his neck; "but what's that noise up the track?"

The master mechanic listened, and when his ears, dulled by the clangor of the shops, caught the distant roar he turned and ran for the house.

"Git up, Ed!" he called to the roadmaster. "They're sending a wild car down the cañon— and she may be loaded with dynamite!"

"Dynamite or not," mumbled the grizzled roadmaster, as he roused up from his couch, "there's a derailer I put in up at kilometer seventy the first thing yesterday morning. That'll send her into the ditch!"

Nevertheless he listened intently, cocking his head to guess by the sound when it came to kilometer seventy.

"Now she strikes it!" he announced, as the rumble turned into a roar; but the roar grew louder, there was a clash as the trucks struck a curve, and then a great metal ore-car swung round the point, rode up high as it hit the reverse and, speeding by as if shot from a catapult, swept through the yard, smashed into a freight-car, and leaped, car and all, into the creek.

"They've sneaked my derailer!" said the roadmaster, starting on a run for the shops. "Who'll go with me to put in another one? Or we'll loosen a rail on the curve—that'll call for no more than a claw-bar and a wrench!"

"I'll go!" volunteered Bud and the man who stood guard, and as startled sleepers roused up on every side and ran toward the scene of the wreck they dashed down the hill together and threw a hand-car on the track.

Then, with what tools they could get together, and a spare derailer on the front, they pumped madly up the cañon, holding their breaths at every curve for fear of what they might see. If there was one runaway car there was another, for the rebels were beginning an attack.

Already on the ridges above them they could hear the crack of rifles, and a jet or two of dust made it evident that they were the mark. But with three strong men at the handles they made the hand-car jump. The low hills fled behind them. They rounded a point and the open track lay before them, with something—

"Jump!" shouted the roadmaster, and as they tumbled down the bank they heard a crash behind them and their hand-car was knocked into kindling-wood.

"Now up to the track!" the roadmaster panted, as the destroyer swept on down the line. "Find some tools—we'll take out a rail!"

With frantic eagerness he toiled up the fill and attacked a fish-plate, and Bud and the young guard searched the hillside for tools to help with the work. They fell to with sledge and claw-bar, tapping off nuts, jerking out spikes, and heaving to loosen the rail—and then once more that swift-moving something loomed up suddenly on the track.

"Up the hill!" commanded the roadmaster, and as they scrambled into a gulch a wild locomotive, belching smoke and steam like a fire-engine, went rushing past them, struck the loose rail, and leaped into the creek-bed. A moment later, as it crashed its way down to the water, there was an explosion that shook the hills. They crouched behind the cut bank, and the trees above them bowed suddenly to the slash of an iron hail.

"Dynamite!" cried the roadmaster, grinning triumphantly as he looked up after the shock; and when the fall of fragments had ceased, and they had fled as if by instinct from the place, they struck hands on their narrow escape. But back at the big house, with everybody giving thanks for their delivery from the powder-train, the master mechanic raised a single voice of protest.

" 'Twas not dynamite!" he yelled. "Powder-train be damned! It was No. 9! She was sour as a distillery! She blowed up, I tell ye—she blowed up when she hit the creek!"

And even after a shower of bullets from the ridge had driven them all to cover he still rushed to those who would listen and clamored that it was the bran.

But there was scant time to hold a post-mortem on No. 9, for on the summit of a near-by ridge, and overlooking the black tank, the rebels had thrown up a wall in the night, and from the security of this shelter they were industriously shooting up the town.

The smash of the first wild car had been their signal for attack, and as the explosion threw the defenders into confusion they made a rush to take the tank. Here, as on the day before, was stationed the Federal garrison, a scant twenty or thirty men in charge of a boy lieutenant.

Being practically out of ammunition, he did not stand on the order of his going, but as his *pelónes* pelted past the superintendent's house the reorganized miners, their belts stuffed with cartridges from their own private stock, came charging up from the town and rallied them in the rear.

In a solid, shouting mass they swept up the hill together, dropped down behind the defenses, and checked the astounded rebels with a volley. Then there was another long-range battle, with every sign of war but the dead, until at last, as the firing slackened from lack of cartridges, a white flag showed on the ridge above, and the leaders went out for a parley.

Properly speaking, Del Rey was in command of the town, but neither the Federals nor the miners would recognize his authority and the leadership went by default. While they waited to hear the rebel demands the Americans took advantage of the truce to bring up hot food from the hotel, where Don Juan de Dios stood heroically at his post. Let bullets come and go, Don Juan kept his cooks about him, and to those who had doubted his valor his coffee was answer enough.

"W'y, my gracious, Mr. Hooker!" he railed, as Bud refreshed himself between trips, "ain't you going to take any up to those women? Don't drink so much coffee now, but give it to the men who fight!"

"Ump-um," grunted Bud with a grin; "they got a skinful of *mescal* already! What they need is another car-load of ammunition to help 'em shoot their first rebel."

"I thought you said they wouldn't fight!" twitted Don Juan. "This is the battle of Fortuna that I was telling you about last week."

"Sure!" answered Bud. "And over there is the dead!"

He pointed to a riot of *mescal* bottles that marked the scene of the night's potations, and Don Juan gave him up as hopeless.

But, jest as he would, Bud saw that the situation was serious, for the foolhardy Sonorans had already emptied their cartridge-belts, and their guns were no better than clubs. Unless the rebels had been equally reckless with their ammunition they had the town at their mercy, and the first thing that they would demand would be the refugees in the big house.

The possession of the town; the arms of the defenders; food, clothing, and horses to ride— none of these would satisfy them. They would demand the rich Spanish landowners to be held for ransom, the women first of all. And of all those women huddled up in the *casa grande* not one would bring a bigger ransom than Gracia Aragon.

Bud pondered the outcome as the emissaries wrangled on the hillside, and then he went back to the corral to make sure that his horse was safe. Copper Bottom, too, might be held for ransom. But, knowing the rebels as he did, Hooker foresaw a different fate, and rather than see him become the mount of some rebel chieftain he had determined, if the town surrendered, to make a dash.

Riding by night and hiding in the hills by day, he could get to the border in two days. All he needed was a little jerked beef for the trip and he would be ready for anything.

So he hurried down to the hotel again and was just making a sack of food fast to his saddle when he heard a noise behind him and turned to face Aragon. For two days the once-haughty Don Cipriano had slunk about like a sick cat, but now he was headed for Gracia's big roan, and the look in his eyes betrayed his purpose.

"Where you going?" demanded Hooker in English, and at the gruff challenge the Spaniard stopped in his tracks. The old, hunted look came back into his eyes, he seemed to shrink before the stern gaze of the Texan, and, as the memory of his past misdeeds came over him, he turned as if to flee.

But there was a smile, an amused and tolerant smirk, about the American's mouth, and even for that look of understanding the harried *hacien-dado* seemed to thank him. He was broken now, thrown down from his pedestal of arrogance and conceit, and as Hooker did not offer to shoot him at sight he turned back to him like a lost dog that seeks but a kind word.

"Ah, *señor*," he whined, "your pardon! What?" as he sighted the sack of meat. "You are going, too? Ah, my friend"—his eyes lighted up suddenly at the thought—"let me ride with you! I will pay you—yes, anything—but if Bernardo Bravo takes me he will hang me! He has sworn it!"

"Well, you got it coming to you!" answered Hooker heartlessly.

"But I will pay you well!" pleaded Aragon. "I will pay you—" He paused as if to consider what would tempt him and then suddenly he raised his head.

"What is it you wish above everything?" he questioned eagerly. "Your title to the mine—no? *Bien*! Take me to the line—protect me from my enemies—and the papers are yours!"

"Have you got them with you?" inquired Hooker with businesslike directness.

"No, but I can get them!" cried Aragon, forgetful of everything but his desire to escape. "I can get them while you saddle my horse!"

"Where?" demanded Hooker craftily.

"From the *agente mineral*!" answered Aragon. "I have a great deal of influence with him, and—"

"*Bastante!*" exploded Bud in a voice which made Aragon jump. "Enough! If you can get them, *I* can! And we shall see, Señor Aragon, whether this pistol of mine will not give me some influence, too!"

"Then you will take them?" faltered Aragon as Hooker started to go. "You will take them and leave me for Bernardo Bravo to—"

"Listen, *señor!*" exclaimed Hooker, halting and advancing a threatening forefinger. "A man who can hire four men to do his dirty work needs no protection from me. You understand that—no? Then listen again. I am going to get those papers. If I hear a word from you I will send you to join your four men."

He touched his gun as he spoke and strode out into the open, where he beckoned the mineral agent from the crowd. A word in his ear and they went down the hill together, while Don Cipriano watched from above. Then, as they turned into the office, Aragon spat out a curse and went to seek Manuel del Rey.

XXIV

In a land of class privilege and official graft it is often only in times of anarchy that a poor man can get his rights. For eight months Hooker had battled against the petty intrigue of Aragon and the *agente mineral*, and then suddenly, when the times turned to war and fear gripped at their hearts, he rose up and claimed his own, holding out his brawny right hand and demanding the concession to his mine.

In a day the whirligig of fortune had turned, and it was the fighting man who dominated. He spoke quietly and made no threats, but the look in his eye was enough, and the *agente* gave him his papers.

With his concession inside his shirt and a belt of gold around his waist Bud stepped forth like a king, for there was nothing left in Mexico for him. Once on his horse and headed for the line and he could laugh at them all. In Gadsden he could show title to Kruger, he could give answer for his trust and look the world in the eye.

Yes, he was a man now—but his work was not quite done. Up at the big house, with the screeching women around her, was Gracia Aragon, and he owed her something for his rough words. To pay her for that he would stay.

Whatever she asked now he would grant it; and if worst came to worst he would take her with him and make good his promise to Phil. He had given his word and that was enough. Now he had only to wait.

The boy lieutenant, the brothers Mendoza, the superintendent, and Manuel del Rey, all were out on the hillside talking terms with Bernardo Bravo and his chiefs. With the rebels it was largely a bluff, since field-glasses had shown them to be short of cartridges; but they had over a thousand men massed along the ridges and, with courage, could easily take the town.

As for the Mendozas and their Sonoran miners, they were properly chagrined at their waste of ammunition and swore by Santa Guadalupe to fight it out with hand-grenades. Even as their leaders wrangled the Mexican powder-men were busily manufacturing bombs, and all the while the superintendent was glancing to the south, for swift couriers had been sent to Alvarez, the doughty Spanish *haciendado* of the hot country, to beg him to come to their relief.

Twice before Alvarez had met the rebels. The first time he spoke them well and they ran off all his horses. The second time he armed his Yaquis and Yaqui Mayo *rancheros* against them and drove them from his domain, inflicting a sanguinary punishment.

Since then he had been itching to engage

them in a pitched battle, and when the word reached him he would come. Two hundred and forty Yaquis, all armed with repeating rifles, would follow at his back, and even with his boasted thousands Bernardo Bravo could hardly withstand their valor. So, while the rebels parleyed, demanding a ransom of millions and threatening to destroy the town, the defenders argued and reasoned with them, hoping to kill the time until Alvarez should arrive.

In the open space in front of the house the refugees gathered in an anxious group, waiting for messengers from the front, and as Hooker walked among them he was aware of the malignant glances of Aragon. There were other glances as well, for he had won great favor with the ladies by ditching the powder-train, but none from Gracia or her mother.

From the beginning the Señora Aragon had treated him as a stranger, according to the code of her class, and Hooker had never attempted to intrude. But if Gracia still remembered that she was an American girl at heart, she forgot to show it to him. To all she was now the proud Spanish lady, thrown with the common people by the stress of circumstances, but far away from them in her thoughts.

The conference between the leaders dragged on and messengers came and went with the news— then, after hours of debate, it broke up suddenly in a row and the emissaries came back on the run. Even at that they narrowly escaped, for the rebels opened fire upon them from the ridges, and before they could get back to cover the dandy, Manuel del Rey, received a bullet-hole through the crown of his hat.

A grim smile flickered across Bud's face as he saw the damage it had wrought, for he knew that Amigo was in the hills—and a bullet shot down-hill goes high! Some trace of what was in his mind must have come to Del Rey as he halted in the shelter of the house, for he regarded the American sternly as Aragon spoke rapidly in his ear. But if they planned vengeance between them the times were not right, for a rattle of arms came from the lower town and the captain was up and away to marshal his men to the defense.

So far in the siege Del Rey had kept under cover, patrolling the streets and plaza and letting the volunteers fight, but now the war had shifted to his territory and his *rurales* were running like mad. For, matching treachery against deceit, the rebel leaders had sent men around to slip up near the town and at the first fusillade from the hillside they came charging up the creek.

Then it was that the ever-watchful *rurales* proved their worth. As the rebels appeared in the open they ran to the outlying houses and, fighting from the flat roofs, checked the advance until the miners could come to their aid.

But in the confusion another party of rebels had rushed down the gulch from the west, and while the fight was going on in the lower town they found lodgment in a big adobe house. And now for the first time there was fighting in earnest— the house-to-house fighting that is seen at its worst in Mexico. While women screamed in the *casa grande* and the Americans paced to and fro on the hill, the boom of a dynamite bomb marked the beginning of hand-to-hand.

With a fearlessness born of long familiarity with explosives the Sonoran miners advanced valiantly with their hand-grenades—baking-powder cans filled with dynamite and studded with fuminating caps. Digging fiercely through wall after wall they approached unperceived by the enemy and the first bomb flung from a roof filled the adobe with wounded and dead.

A dense pall of yellowish smoke rose high above the town and, as bomb after bomb was exploded and the yells of the miners grew louder with each success, the stunned invaders broke from cover and rushed helter-skelter up the gulch. Then there was a prodigious shouting from the Sonorans and more than one triumphant grenadier swung his can of giant powder by the sling and let it smash against the hill in a terrific detonation.

In the big house all was confusion. Soon the cheers of the defenders heralded victory and, in spite of all efforts to restrain them, the wives of the miners rushed into the open to gaze upon the triumph of their menfolk.

On the hilltops the ineffective rebel riflemen rose up from behind their stone wall to stare, until suddenly they, too, were seized with a panic and ran to and fro like ants. Then, around the curve below the concentrator, a tall man came dashing up on a pure white horse, and behind him, charging as he charged, came the swarthy Yaquis of Alvarez, their new rifles gleaming in the sun.

Up along the hillside and after the fugitives they ran with vengeful eagerness, racing one another for the higher ground and the first shot at the rebels. First Alvarez on his white horse would be ahead and then, as they encountered rocks, the Yaquis would surge to the front. It was a race and at the same time it was a rout, for, at the first glimpse of that oncoming body of warriors, the cowardly followers of Bernardo Bravo took to their heels and fled.

But over the rocks no Chihuahuan, no matter how scared, can hope to outdistance a Yaqui, and soon the *pop, pop* of rifles told the fate of the first luckless stragglers. For the Yaquis, after a hundred and sixty years of guerrilla warfare, never waste a shot; and as savage yells and the crash of a sudden volley drifted down from the rocky heights the men who had been besieged in

265

Fortuna knew that death was abroad in the hills.

Fainter and fainter came the shots as the pursuit led on to the north and, as Hooker strained his eyes to follow a huge form that intuition told him was Amigo, he was wakened suddenly from his preoccupation by the touch of some unseen hand. He was in the open with people all about him—Spanish refugees, Americans, triumphant miners and their wives—but that touch made him forget the battle above him and instantly think of Gracia.

He turned and hurried back to the corral where Copper Bottom was kept, and there he found her waiting, with her roan all saddled, and she challenged him with her eyes. The sun gleamed from a pistol that she held in her hand, and again from her golden hair, but he saw only her eyes, so brave and daring, and the challenge to mount and ride.

Only for a moment did he stand before her gaze, and then he caught up his saddle and spoke soothingly to his horse. They rode out of the corral together, closing the gates behind them and passing down a gulch to the rear. All the town lay silent below them as they turned toward the western pass.

Soldiers, miners, and refugees, men, women, and children, every soul in Fortuna was on the hill to see the last of the battle. It had been a crude affair, but bravely ended, and something in the dramatic suddenness of this victory had held all eyes to the close. Bud and Gracia passed out of town unnoticed, and as soon as they had rounded the point they spurred on till they gained the pass.

"I knew you would come!" said Gracia, smiling radiantly as they paused at the fork.

"Sure!" answered Hooker with his good-humored smile. "Count me in on anything— which way does this trail go; do you know?"

"It goes west twelve miles toward Arispe," replied Gracia confidently, "and then it comes into the main road that leads north to Nogales and Gadsden."

"What is there up here?" inquired Bud, pointing at a fainter trail that led off toward the north. "This country is new to me. Don't know, eh? Well, if we followed that trail we'd run into them rebels, anyway, so we might as well go to the west. Is your saddle all right? We'll hit it up then—I'd like to strike a road before dark."

They hurried on, following a well-marked trail that alternately climbed ridges and descended into arroyos, until finally it dropped down into a precipitous cañon where a swollen stream rushed and babbled and, while they still watched expectantly for the road, the evening quickly passed.

First the slanting rays of the sun struck fire from high yellow crags, then the fire faded and the sky glowed an opal-blue; then, through dark blues and purples the heavens turned to black above them and all the stars came out. Thousands of frogs made the cañon resound with their throaty songs and strange animals crashed through the brush at their approach, but still Hooker stayed in the saddle and Gracia followed on behind.

If she had thought in her dreams of an easier journey she made no comment now and, outside of stopping to cinch up her saddle, Bud seemed hardly to know she was there. The trail was not going to suit him—it edged off too far to the south—and yet, in the tropical darkness, he could not search out new ways to go.

At each fork he paused to light a match, and whichever way the mule-tracks went he went also, for pack-mules would take the main trail. For two hours and more they followed on down the stream and then Hooker stopped his horse.

"You might as well get down and rest a while," he said quietly. "This trail is no good—it's taking us south. We'll let our horses feed until the moon comes up and I'll try to work north by landmarks."

"Oh—are we lost?" gasped Gracia, dropping stiffly to the ground. "But of course we are," she added. "I've been thinking so for some time."

"Oh, that's all right," observed Hooker philo-sophically; "I don't mind being lost as long as I know where I'm at. We'll ride back until we get out of this dark cañon and then I'll lay a line due north."

They sat for a time in the darkness while their horses champed at the rich grass and then, unable to keep down her nerves, Gracia declared for a start. A vision of angry pursuers rose up in her mind—of Manuel del Rey and his keen-eyed *rurales*, hot upon their trail—and it would not let her rest.

Nor was the vision entirely the result of nervous imagination, for they had lost half the advantage of their start, as Hooker well knew, and if he made one more false move he would find himself called on to fight. As they rode back through the black cañon he asked himself for the hundredth time how it had all happened—why, at a single glance from her, he had gone against his better judgment and plunged himself into this tangle. And then, finally, what was he going to do about it?

Alone, he would have taken to the mountains with a fine disregard for trails, turning into whichever served his purpose best and following the lay of the land. Even with her in his care it would be best to do that yet, for there would be trailers on their track at sun-up, and it was either ride or fight.

Free at last from the pent-in cañon, they halted at the forks, while Bud looked out the land by moonlight. Dim and ghostly, the square-topped peaks and buttes rose all about him, huge and impassable except for the winding trails. He turned up a valley between two ridges, spurring his horse into a fast walk.

From one cow trail to another he picked out a way to the north, but the lay of the ground threw him to the east and there were no passes between the hills. The country was rocky, with long parallel ridges extending to the northeast, and when he saw where the way was taking him Bud called a halt till dawn.

By the very formation he was being gradually edged back toward Fortuna, and it would call for fresh horses and a rested Gracia to outstrip their pursuers by day. If the *rurales* traveled by landmarks, heading for the northern passes in an effort to outride and intercept him, they might easily cut him off at the start; but if they trailed him—and he devoutly hoped they would—then they would have a tangled skein to follow and he could lose them in the broken country to the north.

So thinking, he cut grass among the rocks, spreak down their saddle-blankets, and watched over the browsing horses while Gracia stretched out on the bed. After a day of excitement and a night of hard riding there is no call for a couch of down, and as the morning star appeared in the east she slept while Bud sat patiently by.

It was no new task to him, this watching and

waiting for the dawn. For weeks at a time, after a hard day's work at the branding, he had stood guard half the night. Sleep was a luxury to him, like water to a mountain-sheep—and so were all the other useless things that town-bred people required.

People like Gracia, people like Phil—they were different in all their ways. To ride, to fight, to find the way—there he was a better man than Phil; but to speak to a woman, to know her ways, and to enter into her life—there he was no man at all.

He sighed now as he saw the first flush of dawn and turned to where she slept, calm and beautiful, in the solemn light. How to waken her, even that was a question, but the time had come to start.

Already, from Fortuna, Del Rey and his man-killing *rurales* would be on the trail. He would come like the wind, that dashing little captain, and nothing but a bullet would stop him, for his honor was at stake. Nay, he had told Bud in so many words:

"She is mine, and no man shall come between us!"

It would be hard now if the *rurales* should prove too many for him—if a bullet should check him in their flight and she be left alone. But how to wake her! He tramped near as he led up the unwilling mounts; then, as time pressed, he spoke to her, and at last he knelt at her side.

271

"Say!" he called, and when that did not serve he laid his hand on her shoulder.

"Wake up!" he said, shaking her gently. "Wake up, it's almost day!"

Even as he spoke he went back to the phrase of the cow-camp—where men rise before it is light. But Gracia woke up wondering and stared about her strangely, unable to understand.

"Why—what is it?" she cried. Then, as he spoke again and backed away, she remembered him with a smile.

"Oh," she said, "is it time to get up? Where are we, anyway?"

"About ten miles from Fortuna," answered Hooker soberly. "Too close—we ought to be over that divide."

He pointed ahead to where the valley narrowed and passed between two hills, and Gracia sat up, binding back her hair that had fallen from its place.

"Yes, yes!" she said resolutely. "We must go on—but why do you look at me so strangely?"

"Don't know," mumbled Bud. "Didn't know I was. Say, let me get them saddle-blankets, will you?"

He went about his work with embarrassed swiftness, slapping on saddles and bridles, coiling up ropes, and offering her his hand to mount. When he looked at her again it was not strangely.

"Hope you can ride," he said. "We got to get over that pass before anybody else makes it—after that we can take a rest."

"As fast as you please," she answered steadily. "Don't think about me. But what will happen if—they get there first?"

She was looking at him now as he searched out the trail ahead, but he pretended not to hear. One man in that pass was as good as a hundred, and there were only two things he could do—shoot his way through, or turn back. He believed she would not want to turn back.

XXV

Though the times had turned to war, all nature that morning was at peace, and they rode through a valley of flowers like knight and lady in a pageant. The rich grass rose knee-deep along the hillsides, the desert trees were filigreed with the tenderest green and twined with morning-glories, and in open glades the poppies and sand-verbenas spread forth masses of blue and gold.

Already on the mesquit-trees the mocking-birds were singing, and bright flashes of tropical color showed where cardinal and yellow-throat passed. The dew was still untouched upon the grass, and yet they hurried on, for some premonition whispered to them of evil, and they thought only to gain the far pass.

To the west and north rose the high and impassable mountain which had barred their way in the night; across the valley the flat-topped Fortunas threw their bulwark against the dawn; and all behind was broken hills and gulches, any one of which might give up armed men. Far ahead, like a knife-gash between the ridges, lay the pass to the northern plains, and as their trail swung out into the open they put spurs to their horses and galloped.

Once through that gap, the upper country

would lie before them and they could pick and choose. Now they must depend upon speed and the chance that their way was not blocked.

Somewhere in those hills to the east Bernardo Bravo and his men were hidden. Or perhaps they were scattered, turned by their one defeat into roving bandits or vengeful partizans, laying waste the Sonoran ranches as they fought their way back to Chihuahua. There were a hundred evil chances that might befall the fugitives, and while Bud scanned the country ahead Gracia cast anxious glances behind.

"They are coming!" she cried at last, as a moving spot appeared in the rear. "Oh, there they are!"

"Good!" breathed Hooker, as he rose in his stirrups and looked.

"Why good?" she demanded curiously.

"The's only three of 'em," answered Bud. "I was afraid they might be in front," he explained, as she gazed at him with a puzzled smile.

"Yes," she said; "but what will you do if they catch us?"

"They won't catch us," replied Hooker confidently. "Not while I've got my rifle. Aha!" he exclaimed, still looking back, "now we know all about it—that sorrel is Manuel del Rey's!"

"And will you kill him?" challenged Gracia, rousing suddenly at the name. Hooker pretended not to hear. Instead, he cocked his eye up at

275

the eastern mountain, whence from time to time came muffled rifle-shots, and turned his horse to go. There was trouble over there to the east somewhere—Alvarez and his Yaquis, still harrying the retreating rebels—and some of it might come their way.

"Ah, how I hate that man!" raged Gracia, spurring her horse as she scowled back at the galloping Del Rey and his men who were riding onward rapidly.

"All right," observed Bud with a quizzical smile, "I'll have to kill him for you then!"

She gazed at him a moment with eyes that were big with questioning, but the expression on his rugged face baffled her.

"I would not forget it," she cried impulsively. "No, after all I have suffered, I think I could love the man who would meet him face to face! But why do you—ah!" she cried, with a sudden tragic bitterness. "You smile! You have no thought for me—you care nothing that I am afraid of him! Ah, *Dios*, for a man who is brave—to rid me of this devil!"

"Never mind!" returned Bud, his voice thick with rising anger. "If I kill him it won't be for *you!*"

He jumped Copper Bottom ahead to avoid her, for in that moment she had touched his pride. Yes, she had done more than that—she had destroyed a dream he had, a dream of a beautiful woman, always gentle, always noble, whom he had sworn to protect with his life. Did she think he was a *pelado* Mexican, a hot-country lover, to be inflamed by a glance and a smile? Then Phil could have her!

"Ah, Bud!" she appealed, spurring up beside him, "you did not understand! I know you are brave—and if he comes"—she struck her pistol fiercely—"I will kill him myself!"

"Never mind," answered Bud in a kinder voice. "I'll take care of you. Jest keep your horse in the trail," he added, as she rode on through the brush, "and I'll take care of Del Rey."

He beckoned her back with a jerk of the head and resumed his place in the lead. Here was no place to talk about men and motives. The mountain above was swarming with rebels, there were *rurales* spurring behind—yes, even now, far up on the eastern hillside, he could see armed men—and now one was running to intercept them!

Bud reached for his rifle, jacked up a cartridge, and sat crosswise in his saddle. He rode warily, watching the distant runner, until suddenly he pulled in his horse and threw up a welcoming hand. The man was Amigo—no other could come down a hillside so swiftly—and he was signaling him to wait.

"Who is that man?" asked Gracia, as she reined in at his side. "Do you know him?"

"Sure do!" responded Hooker jovially. "He's the best friend I got in Mexico!

"*Kai*, Amigo!" he hailed, as the Yaqui came quartering down the hill, and, apparently oblivious of the oncoming pursuers, he rode out of the trail to meet him. They struck hands and Amigo flashed his familiar smile, glancing shyly over the horse's back at the daughter of the Aragons.

"I knew horse," he explained, with a gentle caress for Copper Bottom. "My people—up there—kill Mexicans! Where you go?"

"North—to the line," answered Bud, pointing up the pass.

"*Muy malo*!" frowned the Yaqui, glancing once more at the woman behind. "*Muchos revoltosos*!"

"Where?" asked Bud.

"Everywhere!" replied Amigo with a comprehensive wave of the hand. "But no matter," he added simply. "I will go with you. Who are these horsemen behind?"

"*Rurales*!" responded Hooker, and the Yaqui's black eyes dilated.

"Yes," nodded Bud as he read the swift question in their glance. "He is there, too—Del Rey!"

"*Que bueno*!" exclaimed the Indian, fixing his eagle glance upon the riders. He showed his white teeth in a smile. In an instant he saw his opportunity, he saw his enemy riding into a trap, and turned his face to the pass.

"Come!" he said, laying hold of a *látigo* strap,

278

and as Hooker loped on up the steady incline he ran along at his stirrup. In his right hand he still carried the heavy Mauser, but his sandaled feet bore him forward with tireless strides, and only the heaving of his mighty chest told the story of the pace.

"Let me take your gun," suggested Hooker, as they set off on their race, but Amigo in his warrior's pride only shook his head and motioned him on and on. So at last they gained the rugged summit, where the granite ribs of the mountain crop up through the sands of the wash and the valley slopes away to the north. To the south was Del Rey, still riding after them, but Amigo beckoned Bud beyond the reef and looked out to the north.

"*Revoltosos*!" he exclaimed, pointing a sun-blackened hand at a distant ridge. "*Revoltosos*!" he said again, waving his hand to the east. "Here," waving toward the west, "no!"

"Do you know that country?" inquired Hooker, nodding at the great plain with its chains of parallel Sierras, but the Indian shook his head.

"No," he said; "but the best way is straight for that pass."

He pointed at a distant wedge cut down between the blue of two ridges, and scanned the eastern hills intently.

"Men!" he cried, suddenly indicating the skyline of the topmost ridge. "I think they are *revoltosos*," he added gravely. "They will soon cross your trail."

"No difference," answered Bud with a smile. "I am not afraid—not with you here, Amigo."

"No, but the woman!" suggested Amigo, who read no jest in his words. "It is better that you should ride on—and leave me here."

He smiled encouragingly, but a wild light was creeping into his eyes and Hooker knew what he meant. He desired to be left alone, to deal with Del Rey after the sure manner of the Yaquis. And yet, why not? Hooker gazed thoughtfully at the oncoming *rurales* and walked swiftly back to Gracia.

"This Indian is a friend of mine," he said, "and I can trust him. He says it will be better for us to ride on—and he will take care of the *rurales*."

"Take care?" questioned Gracia, turning pale at a peculiar matter-of-fact tone in his voice.

"Sure," said Hooker; "he says there are *revoltosos* ahead. It will be better for you, he says, to ride on."

"*Madre de Dios*!" breathed Gracia, clutching at her saddle; and then she nodded her head weakly.

"You better get down for a minute," suggested Hooker, helping her quickly to the ground. "Here, drink some water—you're kinder faint. I'll be right back—jest want to say good-by."

He strode over to where Amigo had posted himself behind a rock and laid a hand on his arm.

"*Adios*, Amigo!" he said, but the Yaqui only glanced at him strangely.

"Anything in my camp, you are welcome to it," added Hooker, but Amigo did not respond. His black eyes, far-seeing as a hawk's, were fixed intently before him, where Del Rey came galloping in the lead.

"You go now!" he said, speaking with an effort, and Hooker understood. There was no love, no hate, left in that mighty carcass—he was all warrior, all Yaqui, and he wanted Del Rey to himself.

"We'll be going," Hooker said to Gracia, returning swiftly, and his subdued tones made her start. She felt, as one feels at a funeral, the hovering wings of death, yet she vaulted into her saddle and left her thoughts unsaid.

They rode on down the valley, spurring yet holding back, and then with a roar that made them jump the heavy Mauser spoke out—one shot! And no more. There was a hush, a long wait, and Amigo rose slowly from behind his rock.

"God!" exclaimed Hooker, as he caught the pose, and his voice sounded a requiem for Manuel del Rey.

Then, as Gracia crossed herself and fell to sobbing, he leaned forward in his saddle and they galloped away.

XXVI

Though men may make a jest of it in books, it is a solemn thing to kill a man, even to be near when one is killed. If Gracia had slain Del Rey herself in a passion her hot blood might have buoyed her up, but now her whole nature was convulsed with the horror of it and she wilted like a flower.

An hour before she had burned with hatred of him, she had wished him dead and sought the man who would kill him. Now that his life had been snipped off between two heart-beats she remembered him with pity and muttered a prayer for his soul. For Hooker, for De Lancey, she had no thought, but only for the dashing young captain who had followed her to his death.

Of this Bud had no knowledge. He realized only that she was growing weaker, and that he must call a halt, and at last, when the walls of their pass had widened and they rode out into the open plain, he turned aside from the trail and drew rein by a clump of mesquit.

"Here, let me take you," he said, as she swayed uncertainly in the saddle. She slid down into his arms and he laid her gently in the shade.

"Poor girl," he muttered, "it's been too much for you. I'll get some water and pretty soon you can eat."

He unslung the canteen from his saddle-flap, gave her a drink, and left her to herself, glancing swiftly along the horizon as he tied out their mounts to graze. But for her faintness he would have pushed on farther, for he had seen men off to the east; but hunger and excitement had told upon her even more than the day-and-night ride.

For a woman, and sitting a side-saddle, she had done better than he had hoped; and yet—well, it was a long way to the border and he doubted if she could make it. She lay still in the shade of the mesquit, just as he had placed her, and when he brought the sack of food she did not raise her head.

"Better eat something," he suggested, spreading out some bread and dried beef. "Here's some oranges I got from Don Juan—I'll jest put them over here for you."

Gracia shuddered, sighing wearily. Then, as if his words had hurt her, she covered her face and wept.

"What did you tell that man?" she asked at last.

"W'y—what man?" inquired Hooker, astonished. "Ain't you going to eat?"

"No!" she cried, gazing out at him through her tears, "not until I know what you said. Did you tell that Indian to—to kill him?"

She broke down suddenly in a fit of sobbing, and Hooper wiped his brow.

"W'y, no!" he protested. "Sure not! What made you think that?"

"Why—you rode over and spoke to him—and he looked at me—and then—he—killed him!"

She gave way to a paroxysm of grief at this, and Bud looked around him, wondering. That she was weak and hungry he knew, but what was this she was saying?

"I reckon I don't understand what you're driving at," he said at last. "Wish you'd eat something—you'll feel better."

"No, I won't eat!" she declared, sitting up and frowning. "Mr. Hooker," she went on very miserably, "what did you mean this morning when you—laughed? I said I hated poor Manuel—and you said—well, what you did—and then you laughed! Did you think—oh, you couldn't have—that I really wanted him killed?"

"W'y, sure not!" cried Hooker heartily. "I knowed you was fooling! Didn't I laugh at you? Say, what kind of a feller do you think I am, anyway? D'ye think I'd get an Indian to do my killing?"

"Oh, then didn't you?" she cried, suddenly brightening up. "You know, you talk so rough sometimes—and I never do know what you mean! You said you guessed you'd have to kill him for me, you know, and—oh, it was too awful! I must be getting foolish, I'm so tired, but—what *did* you tell that Indian?"

Bud glanced at her sharply for a moment and then decided to humor her. Perhaps, if he could get her quieted, she would stop talking and begin to eat.

"He asked me who was after us," he said, "and I told him it was Del Rey."

"Yes, and what did he say then?"

"He didn't say nothing—jest lined out for the pass."

"And didn't you say you wanted—him—killed?"

"No!" burst out Bud, half angrily. "Haven't I told you once? I did not! That Indian had reasons of his now, believe me—he's got a scar along his ribs where Del Rey shot him with a six-shooter! And, furthermore," he added, as her face cleared at this explanation of the mystery, "you'd better try to take me at my word for the rest of this trip! Looks to me like you've been associating with these Mexicans too much!"

"Why, what do you mean?" she demanded curtly.

"I mean this," answered Hooker, "being as we're on the subject again. Ever since I've knowed you you've been talking about brave men and all that; and more'n once you've hinted that I wasn't brave because I wouldn't fight.

"I'd jest like to tell you, to put your mind at rest, that my father was a sergeant in the Texas Rangers and no hundred Mexicans was ever able to make him crawl. He served for ten years on the Texas border and never turned his back to no man—let alone a Mex. I was brought up by him to be peaceable and quiet, but don't you never think, because I run away from Manuel del Rey, that I was afraid to face him."

He paused and regarded her intently, and her eyes fell before his.

"You must excuse me," she said, looking wistfully away, "I did not—I did not understand. And so the poor Yaqui was only avenging an injury?" she went on, reaching out one slender hand toward the food. "Ah, I can understand it now—he looked so savage and fierce. But"—she paused again, set back by a sudden thought— "didn't you know he would kill him?"

"Yes, ma'am," answered Hooker quietly, "I did!"

"Then—then why didn't you—"

"That was between them two," he replied doggedly. "Del Rey shot him once when he was wounded and left him for dead. He must have killed some of his people, too; his wife mebbe, for all I know. He never would talk about it, but he come back to get his revenge. I don't shoot no man from cover myself, but that ain't it—it was between them two."

"And you?" she suggested. "If *you* had fought Del Rey?"

"I would have met him in the open," said Hooker.

"And yet—"

"I didn't want to," he ended bluntly. "Didn't want to fight him and didn't want to kill him. Had no call to. And then—well, there was you."

"Ah!" she breathed, and a flush mounted her pale cheeks. She smiled as she reached out once more for the food and Hooker resolved to do his best at gallantry, it seemed to make her so happy.

"So you were thinking of me," she challenged sweetly, "all the while? I thought perhaps I was a nuisance and in the way. I thought perhaps you did not like me because—well, because I'm a Mex, as you say."

"No, ma'am," denied Hooker, gazing upon her admiringly. "Nothing like that! When I say Mex I mean these low, *pelado* Mexicans—Don Juan tells me you're pure Spanish."

"With perhaps a little Yaqui," she suggested slyly.

"Well, mebbe he did say that, too," confessed Bud. "But it's jest as good as Spanish—they say all the big men in Sonora have got some Yaqui blood—Morral, that was vice-president; the Tornes brothers, governors—"

"And Aragon!" she added playfully, but at a look in his eyes she stopped. Bud could not look pleasant and think of Aragon.

"Ah, yes," she rattled on. "I know! *You* like the Yaquis better than the Spanish—I saw you shaking hands with that Indian. And what was it you called him—Amigo?"

"That's right," smiled Hooker; "him and me have been friends for months now out at the mine. I'd do anything for that feller."

"Oh, now you make me jealous," she pouted. "If I were only a Yaqui—and big and black—"

"Never mind," defended Bud. "He was a true friend, all right, and true friends, believe *me,* are scarce."

There was a shade of bitterness in his voice that did not escape her, and she was careful not to allude to Phil. His name, like the name of her father, always drove this shy man to silence, and she wanted to make him talk.

"Then you ought to be friends with *me,*" she chided, after a silence. "I have always wanted to be your friend—why will you never allow it? No, but really! Haven't I always shown it? I remember now the first time that I saw you—I was looking through my hole among the passion-flowers and you saw me with your keen eyes. Phil did not—but he was there. And you just looked at me once—and looked away. Why did you never respond when I came there to look for you? You would just ride by and look at me once, and even Phil never knew."

"No," agreed Bud, smiling quietly. "He was

crazy to see you, but he rode right by, looking at the windows and such."

"The first time I met him," mused Gracia, "I asked about you. Did he ever tell you?"

Bud hung his head and grinned sheepishly. It was not difficult to make out a case against him.

"Is it something I have done?" she asked at last. "Is that why you never liked me? Now, Mr. Hooker, please speak to me! And why do you always sit so far away—are you afraid of me? But look"—she moved closer to him—"here we are alone, and I am not afraid of you!"

"Of course not," answered Bud, looking across at her boldly. "Why should you be—you ain't afraid of nothing!"

"Is that a compliment?" she demanded eagerly. "Oh, then I'm so happy—it's the first you ever paid me! But *have* I been brave," she beamed, "so far? Have I been brave, like a man?"

"Sure have!" remarked Hooker impersonally, "but we ain't there yet. Only thing I don't like about you is you don't eat enough. Say, don't pick up them crumbs—let me pare off some more of this jerked beef for you. Can't nobody be brave when they're hungry, you know, and I want to bring you in safe."

"Why?" she inquired, as she accepted the handful of meat. "Is it on Phil's account?" she ventured, as he sat gazing stoically at the horses. "You were such friends, weren't you?" she went on innocently. "Oh, that is why I admire the Americans so much—they are so true to each other!"

"Yes," observed Hooker, rolling his eyes on her, "we're fine that way!"

"Well, I mean it!" she insisted, as she read the irony in his glance.

"Sure! So do I!" answered Hooker, and Gracia continued her meal in silence.

"My!" she said at last; "this meat is good! Tell me, how did you happen to have it on your saddle? We left so suddenly, you know!"

She gazed up at him demurely, curious to see how he would evade this evidence that he had prepared in advance for their ride. But once more, as he had always done, Hooker eluded the cunningly laid snare.

"I was figuring on pulling out myself," he replied ingenuously.

"What? And not take me?" she cried. "Oh, I thought—but dear me, what is the use?"

She sighed and drooped her head wearily.

"I am so tired!" she murmured despondently. "Shall we be going on soon?"

"Not unless somebody jumps us," returned Bud. "Here, let me make you a bed in the shade. There now"—as he spread out the saddle-blankets temptingly—"you lay down and get some sleep and I'll kinder keep a watch."

"Ah, you are so kind!" she breathed, as she

sank down on the bed. "Don't you know," she added, looking up at him with sleepy eyes that half concealed a smile, "I believe you like me, after all."

"Sure," confessed Bud, returning her smile as honestly; "don't you worry none about me—I like you fine."

He slipped away at this, grinning to himself, and sat down to watch the plain. All about him lay the waving grass land, tracked up by the hoofs of cattle that had vanished in the track of war. In the distance he could see the line of a fence and the ruins of a house. The trail which he had followed led on and on to the north. But all the landscape was vacant, except for his grazing horses. Above the mountains the midday thunder-caps were beginning to form; the air was very soft and warm, and—He woke up suddenly to find his head on his knees.

"Ump-um-m," he muttered, rising up and shaking himself resolutely, "this won't do—that sun is making me sleepy."

He paced back and forth, smoking fiercely at brown-paper cigarettes, and still the sleep came back. The thunder-clouds over the mountains rose higher and turned to black; they let down skirts and fringes and sudden stabs of lightning, while the wind sucked in from the south. And then, with a slash of rain, the shower was upon them.

At the first big drops Gracia stirred uneasily in her sleep. She started up as the storm burst over them; then, as Bud picked up the saddle-blankets and spread them over her, she drew him down beside her and they sat out the storm together. But it was more to them than a sharing of cover, a patient enduring of the elements, and the sweep of wind and rain. When they rose up there was a bond between them and they thrust and parried no more.

They were friends, there in the rush of falling water and the crash of lightning overhead. When the storm was over and the sun came out they smiled at each other contentedly without fear of what such smiles may mean.

XXVII

As the sun, after a passing storm, comes forth all the more gloriously, so the joy of their new-found friendship changed the world for Bud and Gracia. The rainbow that glowed against the retreating clouds held forth more than a promise of sunshine for them, and they conversed only of pleasant things as they rode on up the trail.

Twenty miles ahead lay the northern pass, and from there it was ten more to Gadsden, but they spoke neither of the pass nor of Gadsden nor of who would be awaiting them there. Their talk was like that of children, inconsequential and happy. They told of the times when they had seen each other, and what they had thought; of the days of their childhood, before they had met at Fortuna; of hopes and fears and thwarted ambitions and all the young dreams of life.

Bud told of his battle-scarred father and their ranch in Arizona; of his mother and horse-breaking brothers, and his wanderings through the West; Gracia of her mother, with nothing of her father, and how she had flirted in order to be sent to school where she could gaze upon the upstanding Americans. Only Bud thought of the trail and scanned the horizon for rebels, but he seemed more to seek her eyes than to watch for enemies and death.

They rode on until the sun sank low and strange tracks struck their trail from the east. Bud observed that the horses were shod, and more tracks of mounted men came in beyond. He turned sharply toward the west and followed a rocky ledge to the hills, without leaving a hoof-print to mark the way of their retreat.

By the signs the land ahead was full of bandits and *ladrones*, men to whom human life was nothing and a woman no more sacred than a brute. At the pass all trails converged, from the north and from the south. Not by any chance could a man pass over it in the daytime without meeting someone on the way, and if the base *revoltosos* once set eyes upon Gracia it would take more than a nod to restrain them.

So, in a sheltered ravine, they sought cover until it was dark, and while Gracia slept, the heavy-headed Bud watched the plain from the heights above.

When she awoke and found him nodding Gracia insisted upon taking his place. Now that she had been refreshed her dark eyes were bright and sparkling, but Bud could hardly see. The long watching by night and by day had left his eyes bloodshot and swollen, with lids that drooped in spite of him. If he did not sleep now he might doze in the saddle later, or ride blindly into some rebel camp; so he made her promise to call him and lay down to rest until dark.

The stars were all out when he awoke, startled by her hand on his hair, but she reassured him with a word and led him up the hill to their lookout. It was then that he understood her silence. In the brief hours during which he had slept the deserted country seemed suddenly to have come to life.

By daylight there had been nothing—nothing but dim figures in the distance and the tracks of horses and mules—to suggest the presence of men. But now as the velvet night settled down upon the land it brought out the glimmering specks of a hundred camp-fires to the east and to the north. But the fires to which Gracia pointed were set fairly in their trail, and they barred the way to Gadsden.

"Look!" she said. "I did not want to wake you, but the fires have sprung up everywhere. These last ones are right in the pass."

"When did you see them?" asked Hooker, his head still heavy with sleep. "Have they been there long?"

"No; only a few minutes," she answered. "At sundown I saw those over to the east—they are along the base of that big black mountain—but these flashed up just now; and see, there are more, and more!"

"Some outfit coming in from the north," said Bud. "They've crossed over the pass and camped at the first water this side."

"Who do you think they are?" asked Gracia in an awed voice. "*Insurrectos*?"

"Like as not," muttered Bud, gazing from encampment to encampment. "But whoever they are," he added, "they're no friends of ours. We've got to go around them."

"And if we can't?" suggested Gracia.

"I reckon we'll have to go through, then," answered Hooker grimly. "We don't want to get caught here in the morning."

"Ride right through their camp?" gasped Gracia.

"Let the sentries get to sleep," he went on, half to himself. "Then, just before the moon comes up, we'll try to edge around them, and if it comes to a showdown, we'll ride for it! Are you game?"

He turned to read the answer, and she drew herself up proudly.

"Try me!" she challenged, drawing nearer to him in the darkness. And so they stood, side by side, while their hands clasped in promise. Then, as the night grew darker and no new fires appeared, Hooker saddled up the well-fed horses and they picked their way down to the trail.

The first fires were far ahead, but they proceeded at a walk, their horses' feet falling silently upon the sodden ground. Not a word was spoken and they halted often to listen, for others, too, might be abroad. The distant fires were dying now, except a few, where men rose up to feed them.

The braying of burros came in from the flats to the right and as the fugitives drew near the first encampment they could hear the voices of the night guards as they rode about the horse herd. Then, as they waited impatiently, the watch-fires died down, the guards no longer sang their high falsetto, and even the burros were still.

It was approaching the hour of midnight, and as their horses twitched restively at the bits they gave them the rein and rode ahead at a venture.

At their left the last embers of the fires revealed the sleeping forms of men; to their right, somewhere in the darkness, were the night herd and the herders. They lay low on their horses' necks, not to cast a silhouette against the sky, and let Copper Bottom pick the trail.

With ears that pricked and swiveled, and delicate nostrils snuffing the Mexican taint, he plodded along through the greasewood, divining by some instinct his master's need of care. The camp was almost behind them, and Bud had straightened up in the saddle, when suddenly the watchful Copper Bottom jumped and a man rose up from the ground.

"Who goes there?" he mumbled, swaying sleepily above his gun, and Hooker reined his horse away before he gave him an answer.

"None of your business," he growled impatiently. "I am going to the pass." And as the sentry stared stupidly after him he rode on through the bushes, neither hurrying nor halting until he gained the trail.

"Good luck!" he observed to Gracia, when the camp was far behind. "He took me for an officer and never saw you at all."

"No, I flattened myself on my pony," answered Gracia with a laugh. "He thought you were leading a packhorse."

"Good," chuckled Hooker; "you did fine! Now don't say another word—because they'll notice a woman's voice—and if we don't run into some more of them we'll soon be climbing the pass."

The waning moon came out as they left the wide valley behind them, and then it disappeared again as they rode into the gloomy shadows of the cañon. For an hour or two they plodded slowly upward, passing through narrow defiles and into moonlit spaces, and still they did not mount the summit.

In the east the dawn began to break and they spurred on in almost a panic. The Mexican *paisanos* count themselves late if they do not take the trail at sun-up—what if they should meet some straggling party before they reached the pass?

Bud jumped Copper Bottom up a series of cat steps; Gracia's roan came scrambling behind; and then, just as the boxed walls ended and they gained a level spot, they suddenly found themselves in the midst of a camp of Mexicans— men, saddles, packs, and rifles, all scattered at their feet.

"*Buenos días!*" saluted Bud, as the blinking men rose up from their blankets. "Excuse me, *amigos*, I am in a hurry!"

"*A donde va? A donde va?*" challenged a bearded man as he sprang up from his brush shelter.

"To the pass, *señor*," answered Hooker, still politely, but motioning for Gracia to ride on ahead. "*Adios!*"

"Who is that man?" bellowed the bearded leader, turning furiously upon his followers. "Where is my sentinel? Stop him!"

But it was too late to stop him. Bud laid his quirt across the rump of the roan and spurred forward in a dash for cover. They whisked around the point of a hill as the first scattered shots rang out; and as a frightened sentinel jumped up in their path Bud rode him down. The man dropped his gun to escape the fury of the charge and in a mad clatter they flung themselves at a rock-slide and scrambled to the bench above. The path was rocky, but they pressed forward at a gallop until, as the sun came up, they beheld the summit of the pass.

"We win!" cried Bud, as he spurred up the last incline.

As he looked over the top he exploded in an oath and jerked Copper Bottom back on his haunches. The leader of a long line of horsemen was just coming up the other side, not fifty feet below him. Bud looked to each side—there was no escape—and then back at the frightened girl.

"Keep behind me," he commanded, "and don't shoot. I'm going to hold 'em up!"

He jumped his horse out to one side and landed squarely on the rim of the ridge. Gracia drew her horse in behind him and reached for the pistol in her holster; then both together they drew their guns and Bud threw down on the first man.

"Go on!" he ordered, motioning him forward with his head. "*Pr-r-ronto!*" He jerked out his rifle with his left hand and laid it across his lap.

"Hurry up now!" he raged, as the startled Mexican halted. "Go on and keep a-going, and the first man that makes a break I'll shoot him full of holes!"

He sat like a statue on his shining horse, his six-shooter balanced to shoot, and something in his very presence—the bulk of his body, the forward thrust of his head, and the burning hate of his eyes—quelled the spirits of the rebels. They were a ragtag army, mounted on horses and donkeys and mules and with arms of every known make.

The fiery glances of the American made them cringe as they had always cringed before their masters, and his curses turned their blood to water. He towered above them like a giant, pouring forth a torrent of oaths and beckoning them on their way, and the leader was the first to yield.

With hands half-raised and jaw on his breast he struck spurs to his frightened mule and went dashing over the ridge.

The others followed by twos and threes, some shrinking, some protesting, some gazing forth villainously from beneath their broad hats. As they looked back he whirled upon them and swore he would kill the first man that dared to turn his head.

After all, they were a generation of slaves, those low-browed, unthinking peons, and war had not made them brave. They passed on, the whole long line of bewildered soldiery, looking in vain for the men that were behind the American, staring blankly at the beautiful woman who sat so courageously by his side.

When the last had gone by Bud picked up his rifle and watched him around the point. Then he smiled grimly at Gracia, whose eyes were still round with wonder, and led the way down the trail.

XXVIII

The high pass and the *insurrectos* were behind them now and the rolling plains of Agua Negra were at their feet. To the northeast the smoke banners of the Gadsden smelters lay like ribbons across the sky, and the line was not far away.

Yet, as they came down from the mountains, Bud and Gracia fell silent and slackened their slashing pace. The time for parting was near, and partings are always sad.

Bud looked far out across the valley to where a train puffed in from the south, and the sight of it made him uneasy. He watched still as it lay at the station and, after a prolonged stare in the direction of Agua Negra, he reined sharply to the north.

"What is it?" asked Gracia, coming out of her reverie.

"Oh, nothing," answered Bud, slumping down in his saddle. "I see the railroad is open again—the' might be somebody up there looking for us."

"You mean—"

"Well, say a bunch of *rurales*."

He turned still farther to the north as he spoke and spurred his jaded horse on. Gracia kept her roan beside him, but he took no notice, except as he scanned the line with his bloodshot eyes.

He was a hard-looking man now, with a rough stubble of beard on his face and a sullen set to his jaw. As two horsemen rode out from distant Agua Negra he turned and glanced at Gracia.

"Seems like we been on the run ever since we left Fortuna," he said with a rueful smile. "Are you good for just one more?"

"What is it now?" she inquired, pulling herself together with an effort. "Are those two men coming out to meet us? Do you think they'd stop us?"

"That's about our luck," returned Hooker. "But when we dip out of sight in this swale here we'll turn north and hit for the line."

"All right," she agreed. "My horse is tired, but I'll do whatever you say, Bud."

She tried to catch his eyes at this, but he seemed lost in contemplation of the horsemen.

"Them's *rurales*," he said at last, "and heading straight for us—but we've come too far to get caught now. Come on!" he added bruskly, and went galloping up the swale.

For two miles they rode up the wash, their heads below the level of the plain, but as Bud emerged at the mouth of the gulch and looked warily over the cut bank he suddenly reached for his rifle and measured the distance to the line.

"They was too foxy for me," he muttered, as Gracia looked over at the approaching *rurales*.

"But I can stand 'em off," he added, "so you go ahead."

"No!" she cried, coming out in open rebellion. "Well, I won't leave you—that's all!" she declared, as he turned to command her. "Oh, come along, Bud!" She laid an impulsive hand on his arm and he thrust his gun back into the sling with a thud.

"All right!" he said. "Can't stop to talk about it. Go ahead—and flay the hide off of that roan!"

They were less than a mile from the line, but the *rurales* had foreseen their ruse in dropping into the gulch and had turned at the same time to intercept them. They were pushing their fresh horses to the utmost now across the open prairie, and as the roan lagged and faltered in his stride Bud could see that the race was lost.

"Head for that monument!" he called to Gracia, pointing toward one of the international markers as he faced their pursuers. "You'll make it—they won't shoot a woman!"

He reached for his gun as he spoke.

"No, no!" she cried. "Don't you stop! If you do I will! Come on!" she entreated, checking her horse to wait for him. "You ride behind me—they won't dare shoot at us then!"

Bud laughed shortly and wheeled in behind her, returning his gun to its sling.

"All right," he said, "we'll ride it out together then!"

He laid the quirt to the roan. In the whirl of racing bushes a white monument flashed up suddenly before them. The *rurales* were within pistol-shot and whipping like mad to head them. Another figure came flying along the line, a horseman, waving his hands and motioning. Then, riding side by side, they broke across the boundary with the baffled *rurales* yelling savagely at their heels.

"Keep a-going!" prompted Hooker, as Gracia leaned back to check her horse. "Down into the gulch there—them *rurales* are liable to shoot yet!"

The final dash brought them to cover, but as Bud leaped down and took Gracia in his arms the roan spread his feet, trembled, and dropped heavily to the ground.

"He'll be all right," soothed Bud, as Gracia still clung to his arm. Then, as he saw her gaze fixed beyond him, he turned and beheld Philip De Lancey.

It was the same Phil, the same man Bud had called pardner, and yet when Hooker saw him there he stiffened and his face grew hard.

"Well?" he said, slowly detaching Gracia's fingers and putting her hand away.

As Phil ran forward to greet them he stepped sullenly off to one side. What they said he did not know, for his mind was suddenly a blank; but when Phil rushed over and wrung his hand he came back to earth with a start.

"Bud!" cried De Lancey ecstatically, "how can I ever thank you enough? You brought her back to me, didn't you, old man? Thank God, you're safe—I've been watching for you with glasses ever since I heard you had started! I knew you would do it, pardner; you're the best friend a man ever had! But—say, come over here a minute—I want to speak to you."

He led Hooker off to one side, while Gracia watched them with jealous eyes, and lowered his voice as he spoke.

"It was awful good of you, Bud," he whispered, "but I'm afraid you've got in bad! The whole town is crazy about it. Old Aragon came up on the first train, and now they've wired that you killed Del Rey. By Jove, Bud! wasn't that pulling it a little strong? Captain of the *rurales*, you know—the whole Mexican government is behind him—and Aragon wants you for kidnapping!"

"What's that?" demanded Gracia, as she heard her own name spoken.

Bud looked at Phil, who for once was at a loss for words, and then he answered slowly.

"Your father is down at the station," he said, "looking for—you!"

"Well, he can't have me!" cried Gracia defiantly. "I'm across the line now! I'm free! I can do what I please!"

"But there's the immigration office," interposed

Phil pacifically. "You will have to go there—and your father has claimed you were kidnapped."

"Ha! Kidnapped!" laughed Gracia, who had suddenly recovered her spirits. "And by whom?"

"Well—by Bud here," answered De Lancey hesitatingly.

Gracia turned as he spoke and surveyed Hooker with a mocking smile. Then she laughed again.

"Never mind," she said, "I'll fix that. I'll tell them that I kidnapped *him!*"

"No, but seriously!" protested De Lancey, as Bud chuckled hoarsely. "You can't cross the line without being passed by the inspectors, and—well, your father is there to get you back."

"But I will not go!" flung back Gracia.

"Oh, my dear girl!" cried De Lancey, frowning in his perplexity, "you don't understand, and you make it awful hard for me. You know they're very strict now—so many low women coming across the line, for—well, the fact is, unless you are married you can't come in at all!"

"But I'm *in!*" protested Gracia, flushing hotly. "I'm—"

"They'll deport you," said De Lancey, stepping forward to give her support.

"I know it's hard, dear," he went on, as Bud moved hastily away, "but I've got it all arranged. Why should we wait? You came to marry me, didn't you? Well, you must do it now—right away! I've got the license and the priest all

307

waiting—come on before the *rurales* get back to town and report that you've crossed the line. We can ride around to the north and come in at the other side of town. Then we—"

"Oh, no, no!" cried Gracia, pushing him impulsively aside. "I am not ready now. And—"

She paused and glanced at Bud.

"Mr. Hooker," she began, walking gently toward him, "what will you do now?"

"I don't know," answered Hooker huskily.

"Will you come with us—will you—"

"No," said Bud, shaking his head slowly.

"Then I must say good-by?"

She waited, but he did not answer.

"You have been so good to me," she went on, "so brave, and—have I been brave, too?" she broke in pleadingly.

Hooker nodded his head, but he did not meet her eyes.

"Ah, yes," she sighed. "You have heard what Phil has said. I wish now that my mother were here, but—would you mind? Before I go I want to—give you a kiss!"

She reached out her hands impulsively and Hooker started back. His eyes, which had been downcast, blazed suddenly as he gazed at her, and then they flitted to Phil.

"No," he said, and his voice was lifeless and choked.

"You will not?" she asked, after a pause.

308

"No!" he said again, and she shrank away before his glance.

"Then good-by," she murmured, turning away like one in a dream, and Bud heard the crunch of her steps as she went toward the horses with Phil. Then, as the tears welled to his eyes, he heard a resounding slap and a rush of approaching feet.

"No!" came the voice of Gracia, vibrant with indignation. "I say *no!*" The spat of her hand rang out again and then, with a piteous sobbing, she came running back to Bud, halting with the stiffness of her long ride.

"I hate you!" she screamed, as Phil came after her. "Oh, I hate you! No, you shall *never* have the kiss! What! if Bud here has refused it, will I give a kiss to *you?* Ah, you poor, miserable creature!" she cried, wheeling upon him in a sudden fit of passion. "Where were *you* when I was in danger? Where were *you* when there was no one to save me? And did you think, then, to steal a kiss, when my heart was sore for Bud? Ah, coward! You are no fit pardner! No, I will never marry you— never! Well, go then! And hurry! Oh, how I hate you—to try to steal me from Bud!"

She turned and threw her arms about Hooker's neck and drew his rough face down to hers.

"You do love me, don't you, Bud?" she sobbed. "Oh, you are so good—so brave! And now will you take the kiss?"

"Try me!" said Bud.

Center Point Large Print
600 Brooks Road / PO Box 1
Thorndike, ME 04986-0001 USA

(207) 568-3717

US & Canada:
1 800 929-9108
www.centerpointlargeprint.com

3 1333 05292 6589